Applause for Grego
A Season in Lights

....

"*A Season in Lights* is an intimate, heartfelt ballad to creativity and the passion of the artist. Phillips' writing is lyrical as a love song and as uplifting as a dream. It is not only one of my new favorite books, but possibly one of the most important odes to New York City's artists and the fragility of life since *Rent*."

—Nicole Evelina
USA Today bestselling author of
The Guinevere's Tale Trilogy

"By drawing us into the glitz and glam of New York City's creative scene, and by examining the gritty reality beneath the shine, Phillips taps all the senses while reminding us that, no matter what happens in life, the show must go on—especially for those who dare to dream. Want a sensual but poignant romp behind the curtain? This book delivers."

—Julie Cantrell
New York Times and *USA TODAY*
bestselling author of *Perennials*

"Written by a true creative, *A Season in Lights* paints a moving picture of artists, dancers and musicians. Gregory Erich Phillips weaves together the heartaches and lucky breaks of two main characters, Tom and Cammie, and their friends and families. The vignettes culminate with the impact of coronavirus on NYC and ends with a surprisingly tender and uplifting finale."

—Carole Van Den Hende
award-winning author of *Goodbye, Orchid*

"Gregory Erich Phillips' *A Season in Lights* is a heartfelt and moving love letter to New York City and its artistic community."

—Geoffrey Owens actor and director

"A unique, well-crafted tale adds to the lore and lure of life as an artist braving the challenges of the big city. The pursuit of the performing arts and romance are set against the looming specter of today's COVID-19 pandemic and the 1980s AIDS crisis. The author offers profound insights into the unpleasant realities of chasing a dream and wraps with an exquisite, soul-stirring conclusion."

—Lafayette Summers pianist, composer and singer

"*A Season in Lights* taps into the core of the soul of the New York City theatre community family – from the stage managers to the musicians and dancers, to the actors whose every heartbeat is dedicated to the performance of their art. Having myself been involved in local theatre and experiencing this thrill, not only upon the stage, but in the hectic confines of the green room behind it, and, sadly, witnessing the devastating impact of the Covid epidemic on theatre, I bow to Phillips' perfectly captured portrayal of it. Break a leg, Gregory Phillips!"

—Joe Palmer author of *A Mariner's Tale*

"Music and dance thrum in this poignant story about aspiring artists struggling to survive as part of New York's subway class. Two would-be lovers at opposite ends of their dreams of making it on the big stage share a memorable but fleeting season filled with passion, love, friends, and family. Bursting with charm, this beautiful tale is chock-full of powerful subjects: depression, racism, HIV in the '80s, and the current Covid pandemic. It will touch your heart, make you want to dance, sing, and cry all at the same time."

—R. Scott Boyer
award-winning author of *Bobby Ether and the Jade Academy* and *Temple of Eternity*

A SEASON IN LIGHTS

A Novel in Three Acts

....

By

Gregory Erich Phillips

LUCID
HOUSE
PUBLISHING

LU(ID
HOUSE
PUBLISHING

Published in Atlanta, Georgia, United States of America by Lucid House Publishing, LLC www.LucidHousePublishing.com

Cover design/Design Director: Troy King/ Cover Photo: Kevin Garrett / Interior design: Amit Dey

A Season in Lights is a work of fiction. Names, places, characters, and incidents are a product of the author's imagination or used fictitiously. Any resemblance to actual persons, living or dead, events, or locales is entirely coincidental.

Library of Congress Cataloging-in-Publication Data:
Phillips, Gregory Erich, 1977—
A season in lights/a novel in three acts by Gregory Erich Phillips– / 1st edition /
Atlanta: Lucid House Publishing, [2021]

Library of Congress Control Number: 2021934446
ISBN: 978-1-950495-12-2

Broadway/Off -Broadway—Fiction 2. Theater 3. Coronavirus 4 Broadway dancer 5. New York City lockdown 6. Ballet 7. Pandemic 8. AIDS epidemic 9. Romance 10. Performing arts 11. Sibling rivalry 12. Interracial romance 13. Family drama 14. Racism

FIC069000
FIC019000
FIC048000

Lucid House Publishing books are available for special promotions and bulk purchase discounts. For details, contact info@LucidHousePublishing.com

Act I

Prologue

....

March 2020

he silence was deafening. The shouts, the honks, the clatter—all gone, but the hush was anything but peaceful. The Brooklyn streets had the tomb-like silence of a hive after its bees had fled.

Many things about New York City are frozen in time. I love that about this city. When we put on that show in the funky little off-Broadway theatre, it could have been any time, from the twenties till now. But even New York couldn't stay frozen in time forever. Once time thawed out, it caught up fast. This pandemic would leave scars that might never heal.

The city always rebounds from its tragedies. New Yorkers are resilient as hell. They rebuilt after 9/11, after the financial crisis, after Hurricane Sandy, and they would rebuild after this. But each time something was lost. Some *ones* were lost, too.

Usually it was us—the artists, the musicians, the dancers—who led the way, bringing the spirit of the city back. But this thing would hit us the hardest. Many of us would be the ones who were lost. I'm not sure I even counted as one of *us* anymore.

Less than a year ago, when the curtain fell after the opening night applause, I assumed the New York City I knew—and my place in it—could last forever.

●   ●   ●

Chapter One

. . . .

June 2019

"**H**urry up, Cammie... full cast photo."

"Okay. Zip me up?"

I hustled to put myself together in the corner I had claimed in front of the green room mirror. Percy rushed over to zip up the back of my post-show little black dress. I followed him out. My stage makeup and fake eyelashes would look garish in the house lights for the cast photo, but that was all part of the fun.

We gathered on the uneven wooden stage. Nine of us, all feeling like the biggest stars on Broadway.

Snap, snap. "Here, take one with mine."

I took back my phone and looked. We were a ragtag group indeed, but I smiled with joy. At least I didn't *look* like the oldest one in the group. It was my first cast photo since coming to New York City. I knew it would be the first of many.

I returned to my corner of the green room, and the temperature spiked in the tiny chamber as everyone else piled in. It should not have been possible to fit nine people, with all our costumes, shoes, props and supplies into that glorified closet, much less for us each to have our own little space in it. Such was the intricate dance of theatre we all knew so well. For each bit of action that the audience saw on stage, twice the action happened back here. It was a constant whirl of flying garments, sweaty bodies in varying degrees of nudity, powder, glitter, champagne corks and the fumes of hairspray. Oh, how I had missed it all.

I stuffed my dance paraphernalia into my gym bag and slid it under the counter. My costumes pressed against all the others on the teetering rack, waiting for us to do it all again tomorrow.

Percy gave me a sweaty hug.

"Honey, you were divine!"

"It's a great show," I said. "I'm so proud of you."

I slipped behind the heavy, purple curtain that smelled of the cigarette smoke that had been collecting there since the Twenties.

Was it actually a great show? I asked myself as I walked back across the stage.

The bright golden bulbs of the houselights illuminated the greenish interior walls and dark red carpet revealing their well-worn state. Without a proper backstage entrance for the cast—only a side door to the back alley—we had to troop out through the house. We were lucky the green room was actually behind the stage instead of in some other random corner of the building. As I made my way out, a few lingering guests at the bar complimented me on my performance.

I scampered up the five steps from the theatre door to street level. If you hadn't been looking for it, you could pass by a hundred times without knowing there was a theatre on this block.

I made up my mind: It was a *good* show… not a great show. In the right hands it could be successful. It gave the audience what they wanted: catchy songs, well-choreographed dances, an edgy, modern story, and one shocking glimpse of tit (not mine). But tonight's performance had been rough. There hadn't been money to rent the stage out for a proper dress rehearsal. The stage was too small for the cast ensemble. Even though we had marked out the same sized space in the studio to practice, when the number finally came, we had to contain our dancing instead of letting it flow… especially all five-foot-eleven of me.

The preparation had been hard on Percy, and I thought it showed in his performance. It was his show, so all the work fell to him—writer, composer, director and star. Such was the "off-Broadway" reality. He was even the benefactor, thus the tight budget. I knew his boyfriend Jonathan contributed, but a partner's money comes with no less stress than your own. I sure hoped Percy could get some rest before tomorrow night's show. Then, after a matinee on Sunday, our run, barely begun, would come to an end.

The June night simmered. I hadn't bothered to bring a jacket down with me from uptown, but I was perfectly comfortable in my sleeveless dress. I left my light brown hair in its updo. If I took it out in this humidity it would curl up to hell and beyond. I thought about walking across town. I was full of energy, but my feet ached from dancing on the hard oak floor. Ninth was a lot farther from Park Avenue than it sounded. I put my arm up for a cab.

Normally it irritated me when a cabbie drove through Times Square, always making the trip take twice as long as it needed to be. But tonight, I eagerly looked out at the neon glow and bustle of activity.

The lights! Their glow had lured me here. The stage lights made me feel alive again. They made me *want* to feel alive and that was not to be taken for granted. I got my first taste of it tonight, but this... *these* lights, the lights of Broadway were the ones I lusted for.

Mine became one of fifty or more yellow cabs fighting for a place on 42nd Street with unheeded honks and swears. Each time we stopped at red, a swarm of hundreds enveloped us: tourists, revelers, theatre goers... the upper crust and lowest rungs of New York's populace, shuffling together on those Midtown streets. The crowd parted at the green light, and my cab pressed on through the din. Gigantic lighted faces and pictures flashed across the rotating advertisements that illuminated entire sides of buildings. The changing colors played off the glass of my window. I basked in the light, as warm as if I were lying on the beach under a hot sun.

I had ached for this warmth since my parents first brought me from our home in Pennsylvania to see a Broadway show. I was twelve, with a few years of ballet under my belt. The trip itself was stressful. Andrea, only five then, was confused and scared by the spectacle. She cried and fussed the whole time... including at the show. We saw *Cats*. Of course, it was *Cats*! My mother complained that there was no story, But I was enthralled by the dancing, and would hardly stop singing about Magical Mister Mistoffelees for the next year. I even petitioned— unsuccessfully—to rename the family's black cat.

The next morning my mother stayed in the hotel with Andrea while my dad took me to the real treat of the trip... a kids' ballet class at Steps. I cherish so many wonderful memories of my dad taking me to ballet classes when he was between jobs, but that day was the most vivid memory of them all. From then on, I knew I needed to be here, one more orbit around the sun that was Times Square. I never thought it would take twenty years.

That trip turned me into a theatre kid. Throughout the rest of my youth, I would live to be dancing and on stage. My best memories were from the shows I was in. My first kiss at sixteen was on stage, and whether it was fake or not, I thought it was the most romantic thing that could be. I haven't changed much in the years since.

Why did I wait so long? Why waste all those years in ease and comfort when the demon never stopped clutching at my heels? Why, when this was here for me all along? The answer wasn't complicated. I had been too afraid to try. Somehow it was easier to wallow in depression than to shake up my life.

The fears were justified. It was tough being here. I never had any extra money, and after nine months, my first real show had been tonight. Each month I wondered if it would be the last month I could afford rent at my humble shared apartment in Washington Heights.

It was all so worth it.

I had nothing to lose anymore, no reason not to face my fears. I'd try anything to shock my heart back into joy. This was finally about me—about doing what I loved and stepping out from under the dark cloud that had hung over me for so long.

I directed the cabby west out of the beautiful chaos. He dropped me in front of a club in the upper 40s between Ninth and Tenth. I breathed my moment of thick heat between the blasts of air-conditioning from cab and club.

My eyes took a moment to adjust to the dim club, after the sparkle of the lights outside. A row of hanging Art Deco lamps reflected off the black marble bar on the left, leading me straight into the crowded room as I looked for a seat. I found my customary end stool. The girl behind the bar brought me a glass of Prosecco without me having to ask for it.

I could tell she was a performer by how she moved, probably a dancer like me. Looking at her taut shoulders and neck in her tank top, I guessed she was an aerialist or something like that. Many service industry folks in the city straddled the line between saying they were performers working a side job, or waiters and bartenders who were former performers. I wondered how this girl would answer if I asked her. I was a whisker away from taking up waitressing myself on off nights.

The crowd in the piano bar was a mix of regulars from the neighborhood, couples at the end of a Friday night date, and tourists seeking their idea of a classic night out in the city. These tourists made an effort to blend in, but they all failed. New Yorkers knew their own.

A jazz singer stood in front of a draped curtain on a small platform that made a good makeshift stage. He was a handsome young man with a silky voice. In another era he could have been the next Sinatra. A baby grand piano stood beside him on the parquet floor. Most of the patrons were drawn in by the charm of his face and voice. I didn't care about the singer, much as I enjoyed his rendition of *I've Got You Under My Skin*. I came to this place for the pianist.

The singers changed from night to night. Tom, at the piano, was the constant—unnoticed by most, but giving the performance its nuance. Even many of the regulars who perceived something different about the music here failed to credit the genius at the ivories. Without Tom and his gifts as a musician, this would have just been one more of a hundred places to hear an unknown jazz singer in the city. The intricate poignancy with which Tom played each of these ponderously familiar songs gave the singers and their listeners just enough freshness to enjoy them as if for the first time.

Despite the crowd and the lights in his eyes, Tom scanned the room and found me, He didn't smile or acknowledge my presence, but I saw that microsecond of recognition flicker across his face. His subtleties with me were as delicate as with his keyboard and just as effective.

Sipping my bubbles, I basked in the energy fueled by my post-show high. Percy's show was nowhere close to "the big time," but it was a start. I had now been in a real off-Broadway show. No one could ever take that away from me.

Before Percy cast me, I had labored away teaching jazz dance at a Upper West Side studio on 98th, hoping for a chance. I knew I was a good dancer, and I was more than serviceable as a singer and actress. But it had been almost impossible to even get an audition. I didn't have a reputation here to carry me, and I was too old to qualify as an up-and-comer worth taking a chance on.

Now I knew how it worked. It wasn't about how good you were, it was about who you knew. That was how I finally got a part. The studio manager where I taught was Percy's ex. Hearing of his old flame's trouble finding quality dancers for his show, he recommended me. Only after I got the part did I find out that I wasn't getting paid. No wonder Percy had trouble filling out the cast!

I was happy to dance *gratis...* for now. Better than not being in a show at all.

The musicians took their break. Tom came over and stood beside my barstool. He kissed my cheek and put his hand on my leg.

"For a man who wanted to play classical, your touch with jazz continues to amaze me," I said.

"Thanks, hon'." He smiled. The bartender handed Tom a bottled beer.

"How did your show go?"

"So fun!" I hopped on my seat. I'd been hoping he'd ask.

"I'm glad you're getting to do what you love."

I smiled. Tom understood.

"I'll never understand why you don't love playing jazz," I said after a moment. "You play so beautifully."

"I love jazz, too. It's fun to play. But something about classical piano music gets me right here." He reached up and tapped his heart, then put his hand back on my leg, where I wanted it. "I suppose I'm also stubborn. I didn't appreciate being shoehorned into a jazz career. Think about it... I was a young, black piano man in the Eighties. Nobody was calling me up to play Beethoven. So here I am. It's not a bad life."

"You should have played like a square to fool 'em."

He laughed. "I could never pass for a square, even when I play Beethoven."

I loved watching him laugh. His bright eyes conveyed his love for life, as well as his deep understanding for everything happening within his sphere. While a goatee made many men look stern, on Tom it balanced the natural shape of his lips. It was only in his beard that I saw any gray. His short-cropped hair was still completely black. I liked sitting on the barstool looking up at him as he stood (when standing I was a little taller than him), feeling his warm, confident hand on my skin.

Tom looked more handsome now than in the pictures I had seen from when he was younger. He had grown into his face through the years, even though his skin was now creased around his eyes. The most attractive thing about him was the way he carried himself—and in how he touched his surroundings with the same delicacy as he played the piano.

I hadn't taken the time to dwell on how much older Tom was than me. Partly because I felt so old myself—auditioning for parts next to girls half my age. Besides, why worry about age when we had no expectations for…whatever Tom and I were to each other?

When he returned to the piano, I got my phone out of my purse. I posted the cast picture to Instagram and Facebook and tagged everybody. I couldn't wait for my friends back home to see it and start commenting. A subtle brag about my first success—my little way of saying "See, I can make it in the big city."

When I moved here, the reactions of my friends and family were mixed. Although nearly everyone publicly encouraged me for following my dream, I perceived the tilted heads and raised eyebrows. People were supposed to do this at 23, not 33. I had a whole life behind me—a career and a marriage. Mom was the only one who said outright she thought I was being foolish. She had every right to say so. I also had every right to live my own life. If I failed here, I could always go back to the life that was expected of me.

Mom only knew part of the story. She thought I still had a lot to lose. She was wrong.

As always, as the clock hit 11:00 I looked around for any real Broadway performers drifting in for a nightcap after their shows. It happened once, back in April, when half the cast of *Wicked* came pouring in on their own post-show high. Several of them knew Tom and one even sang a song with him. This club was a few blocks too far from Broadway for that to happen regularly.

Most of the people left when the music ended at midnight. Tom came back to the bar and sat down beside me, nursing another beer. He energy matched mine.

We talked easily for the next two hours until the club emptied out. By then, my adrenaline from performing had dwindled, but I didn't want the night to end. I enjoyed his company. Every moment with him felt special and rare.

We walked hand-in-hand back to his apartment, two blocks up and one block over. The tree-lined street felt so peaceful compared to the whirl of activity a few avenues away. The glow of Times Square illuminated the night sky to the east like a neon milky way.

"Hell's Kitchen," said Tom. "I'm not sure the name suits the neighborhood anymore."

"What's changed the most, in the time you've lived here?"

"The people who walk up those stairs."

We took our own walk up three flights to the apartment where Tom had spent eighteen years. It was sparsely furnished, decorated with only a few timeless pieces. Its hardwood floors and high brick walls gave the place a cozy warmth. There was a tiny, unused kitchen off the living room. I wondered if Tom had ever tried to light his stove. I absentmindedly tried once, and it seemed like the pilot light had been off for eons. The oven was exclusively used for storage, always in short supply in New York City apartments.

I dropped my bag on the floor, kicked off my shoes, and reclined on his couch, my gangly legs draped over one end and my head resting on the other. The couch was against the wall at an angle with his upright piano. On the piano stand I saw a simple child's scale book, left open from one of his lessons earlier in the day. Tom sat on the piano bench and stroked my hair and gently massaged my temples with his long fingers.

"Play something for me." I tilted my head back until I could see his face.

"What would you like to hear?"

"Play what *you* want to play."

It was a complicated request, considering his life and his career.

He turned around on the bench, closing the lesson book. He thought for a moment, then lightly struck one note with his right index finger.

I closed my eyes, enjoying the anticipation that the note created. It was impossible yet to know what song he had chosen, what genre, what mood. A second note came while the first was still sustained. The second note moved, creating the first sense of rhythm, then the first note changed together with a third note from his left hand and I knew, after five notes, that it was Bach.

The simple invention never sustained more than two notes at the same time—one in the treble and one in the bass. The simplicity would make a beginner think he could play it. But the genius of Bach was in the apparent simplicity. It took a master like Tom to give the piece meaning.

I relaxed, swept away by the music, the fatigue from putting so much into my performance, and the Proseccos I had drunk. I didn't remember Tom finishing the piece. I must have dozed off. I just remembered him standing over me, smiling. I took his hand and followed him into the bedroom.

It was after 10:00 when I awoke. Tom stood shirtless with his back to me. I listened as he ordered breakfast for delivery. He spoke quietly, not aware I was awake. I smiled as he ordered exactly what I would have chosen for myself—scrambled eggs with some tortillas on the side... yes tortillas, he repeated, just like I always needed to.

I dearly loved this man. I loved him without illusions for what our romance had been and what it could be. All I knew was that Tom treated me with a beautiful care I never dared to think was possible through my five years of marriage. More importantly, he had opened up the New York City I wanted to believe in—full of grandeur, mystery and ugliness. The very thing that made it seem certain our love would not last—our twenty-year age difference—also freed me up to learn a way of life from him, to learn to be the girl I still dreamed I could be.

It would have been easy to say there was inevitability surrounding my romance with Tom. But I don't think that was true. I don't really believe in destiny or fate. You have to take your chances when they come. Still there *was* a magnetism between us from the beginning. Perhaps that magnetism made it inevitable that once we were in a room together, we had to fall in love.

I met him before I actually moved to the city. Well, perhaps *met* isn't the right word.

Once I became an adult, I tried to come visit New York City at least once a year. In college, and for several years after, I kept it up, always with one or several willing friends. We would drive or take the train, see a show, go to the clubs and pile as many girls as possible into one expensive midtown hotel room. Every trip, I made sure to take a class or two, just as I did on that first trip when I was twelve. If I came to the city with other dancers, they joined me, but usually I went alone.

Soon it became harder to find friends to accompany me. They got jobs, got married, had babies. Then *I* got married and began teaching dance full time at the local college. Before I knew it, three years had passed without a single trip to the city. When I finally came back, accompanied by my friends Julia and Kate, the trip had an air of married women reliving their pasts. I hated it.

Two *more* years before I made the trip solo. I was twenty-nine then, four years into a monotonous marriage. I had spent almost a full year in a fog of depression, at the mercy of my personal demon. I *needed* my dose of New York in a way no one else around me understood.

As usual, I attended an adult ballet class, this time at Lincoln Center. My main passion had become musicals, but on days like that I remembered how much I still loved ballet. The teachers of the adult classes always singled me out as one of the best dancers in the room. I had kept myself sharp, which isn't easy to do with all the pressures of adult life. There was some nostalgia for past dreams each time I came to Lincoln Center and walked past the three great theatres—homes to the Opera, Symphony and Ballet. As a girl, I had felt certain I would one day dance on those stages.

I never had fully learned my way around Lincoln Center. Tucked north of the Metropolitan Opera is a veritable labyrinth of smaller auditoriums, recital halls and rehearsal rooms, both above and below ground, eventually melding into the Julliard Conservatory and the School of American Ballet. It was in one of these halls where the adult ballet classes were held that year.

I didn't usually notice the pianists who accompanied ballet classes. They were nearly indistinguishable in their precision. There was no room for personal style in that job. The pianist was expected to be rhythmically precise, supporting the teacher without ever getting in the way. The good ones made themselves as unnoticeable as if they had been a CD.

I did notice the pianist that day, but not because of his music. He knew his job and played without emotion. I noticed him because he was classy and handsome. I learned later that he rarely accompanied ballet classes anymore, although he had done it frequently when he was younger. That day he'd filled in for a colleague with a last-minute conflict.

The class was invigorating, and I was hardly tired when it ended. I lingered an extra moment or two in the room and was the last girl to change out of her pointe shoes.

As I wandered out, I carelessly followed the way I thought I had come, not heeding all the twists and turns of the journey. Not even realizing I was lost, I turned a corner and emerged onto a stage. I still don't know which stage it was. It didn't matter. Gazing up at the hundreds of empty seats tiered out before me, my heart skipped a beat. Dozens of black stage lights hung above, ready to pour down their heat. The dust from the crevices of this forgotten theatre tickled my nose. I stood still and looked around, surprised at finding myself alone. Anyone who spends any time here knows there is nothing rarer than a moment alone in New York City.

I couldn't help myself. Changing back into my pointe shoes and leaving my bag at the side of the stage, I walked out into the middle, stood for a moment in third position, then pointed my left foot and rose in *relevé* with my right leg held in *attitude*.

But this being New York City, I should have known I was not entirely alone.

As my right foot came slowly back toward the floor, a note sounded, then another, a perfect fourth above, precisely as my foot touched back down. I should have been startled—caught dancing where I should not have been. But the gentle notes of the piano, wherever it was, compelled me to dance another step. After three more notes, I recognized the melody of Chopin's *Etude No. 3* in E Major, one of my very favorites. I turned in place, bent low, then fully extended my body back, dancing slowly at first, unsure if the dream would continue. Growing bolder, I began to use the floor and ran into a pair of *grand jeté* leaps.

I closed my eyes and felt like the auditorium was filled and the stage lights were hot and bright. My dream of performing a ballet at Lincoln Center was coming true. I improvised a dance that somehow felt perfectly choreographed. Whatever movement I made, the music flowed with me. The melody bent with *rubato*, the phrasing following where I took it. So different from the mechanical playing in class, steady as a metronome, now it was as if I played the piano myself with my feet. Afraid to break the spell, I didn't dare look upstage where the music emanated.

I danced vigorously through the development section of the piece, using all the energy I could muster, then repeated my early steps as the recapitulation brought back the melody. I slowed my movements as the music came toward its end, and the melody slowed with me. I folded my body down in *repose* on the stage floor as the last note sounded. It had only lasted a few minutes, but they were some of the best minutes of my life.

Looking up, the auditorium was empty. The stage lights were still cold.

I turned to see who had given me this gift. The elegant pianist from class stood up, smiling. His face appeared full of understanding and love. He bowed his head courteously, then walked away. He knew not to cheapen his gift by lingering. Exit, stage-right.

That day marked the first time I saw Tom. I could never forget him. But in a city of eight million people, I hardly dared hope to ever see him again.

Jolting me out of my memories, my phone buzzed with two text messages arriving in quick succession: one from Percy with *"URGENT!* changes to tonight's choreography"; the other from my mother, saying her train was almost at Penn Station.

Chapter Two

....

The Bronx – 1986

•••• irst he heard a hum, barely perceptible through the voic-
• es on the platform and the ruckus on the street above.
• Then a hint of light painted the walls far down the dark
•••• tunnel. Before the actual headlights of the train came
• into view, the tunnel merely changed from black to gray, as the
texture of the track and curved walls became clear. When the
train rounded its last corner, the headlights slashed sharply
through the darkness, illuminating the vibrant graffiti on the
tunnel walls. The hum became a clatter, then a roar.

The people on the platform shuffled, peering down the tunnel
to see whether it was the B or the D. He didn't back away from
the track, standing firm as the sharp wind swept through the
platform, just ahead of the speeding subway. The shrill treble of
the breaks drowned out all other noise as the lit windows rushed
by. The train ground to a screeching stop.

Tom picked up his big bag and slung it over his shoulder. It held
everything he owned. This D train would whisk him off to a new life.
After all the work and all the setbacks, he had his job in the city. It
wasn't a perfect job, but it would be the first step to greater things.
The doors opened to the press of people coming off. Tom shifted to
his right to let them through, then shoved his way on.

"Tom, hold up!"

Nothing was keeping Tom from getting on this train. He stepped through the doors before turning to see his brother racing down the stairs to the platform. *Really, Art, now?* Tom felt guilty for hoping his brother wouldn't make it in time.

Just as the doors started to close, Art thrust his saxophone case in. The doors lurched obstinately, pressing inward despite the obstruction of the hard-shell instrument case. Art grabbed at one of the doors, his own bag slipping off his shoulder to the elbow. Tom couldn't help himself and grabbed the other door, pushing it back just enough for his older brother to slip inside. The doors slammed shut and the train lurched off.

"What the hell are you doing?" Tom asked. "The last place I wanna see you is on a downtown train."

"C'mon man." Art grinned from ear to ear. That smile was his charm. Even Tom couldn't say no to it. "This is your big chance. You gotta take me with you. Give your brother a break too."

"If you get in trouble down there, they won't let you off the hook like they do up here. They'll lock you up and throw away the key. And I won't help you. I can't afford to get sucked in."

"All that's behind me. I just need a new start... same as you."

Tom sighed, placed his bag on the floor firmly between his feet. and grabbed an overhead strap to steady himself in the train car,

"You better not make me regret this."

As the express train neared the city, Tom stared at the dark, heavily graffitied walls of the tunnels as the subway sped by. Every few minutes the light of a local stop broke through, giving him a glimpse of other riders waiting on the platforms.

Art was right that he needed a fresh start. But it was one thing to have a chance to start over, and another to really do it. It would take a lot of work to make it as a musician in Manhattan. Would Art commit to that kind of work? How long before his older brother got seduced by easy and familiar habits:

little cons, petty thefts, a couple of hits to sell in the park, maybe one for himself to take the edge off. Maybe being across the Harlem river from their rough neighborhood would make these temptations more distant for Art. Maybe not.

They got off at the busy stop at Columbus Circle, on the edge of Central Park. The two scarcely noticed the familiar smell of car exhausts and refuse. What caught Tom's attention was the massive marble monument to Columbus. He'd seen it many times before, but today was different. He would be seeing it all the time on his way to his new gig at Lincoln Center.

"C'mon," Tom slung his bag onto his shoulder, as Art looked eagerly around. "Let's find the place. I don't have a lot of time." They started west on 59th Street, then south on Ninth Avenue.

Tom once again did the math of how much of his savings would go toward first and last month's rent, plus security on the one-bedroom apartment waiting for them on 51st. As long as he kept this new job, he should just be able to afford it. He had saved a little by taking the apartment on the ground floor, already planning to befriend a neighborhood cat to help with cockroaches and rats.

Reaching the block, he paused on the street, double checking the address, then making mental notes of his new street. Art waited silently beside him. The brick buildings made a picturesque neighborhood despite their poor states of repair. Some had stoops, others, like his, had their entrances just below street level. A row of honey locust trees, thick with spring foliage, lined the sidewalk.

He hopped down the steps and opened the door.

"It ain't much." Tom dropped his bag on the creaking wooden floorboards.

"It's a palace!"

"The bedroom's mine. If you wanna stay, you sleep out here."

"Fine by me."

"I got to change and get up to Lincoln Center. What you gonna do?"

"Take my axe to the park and earn some coin. I ain't gonna be no free loader." Art threw his bag in a corner, grabbed his saxophone case and left.

Tom fished in his bag for the sandwich and coke he had brought. He sat down on the floor with his back against the wall of the unfurnished apartment, glad for a moment alone. There would be time tomorrow morning to buy some cheap furniture and begin to make the place a home. For now, the bare floorboards suited him just fine. They were *his* floorboards in the damn city!

He sipped at his coke, surprised to find it still moderately cool. He could have stayed with his mother in The Bronx and take the train in every day. Plenty of folks did. His mother made it known that she wished he had chosen that and how much she hated to see her baby boy leave the nest at nineteen. But Tom hadn't wanted this to be just a new job. He wanted a complete change, a new direction, an opportunity that would lead to more. He needed to be out of the echo from the Grand Concourse.

Modeled on Paris' Champs-Élysées, there wasn't anything grand about the dilapidated stretch where he'd grown up. That block was like a small town inserted into the metropolis—with the good and bad that came from that. Everyone knew each other and watched out for each other. It was a true community.

But everyone also knew too much. You couldn't escape your past or your family. Your reputation formed at birth. Tom always knew people thought of him in context with his father and brother. He resented it.

His father left the family before landing himself in prison for selling drugs. Better that it happened in that order, at least. He returned briefly after his release, but quickly disappeared, never to be heard from again. Rumor had it he was in L.A. Tom didn't know or care.

His brother dropped out of school to run drugs for the project dealer. Art had been arrested several times for B&E and petty theft, but he was never busted for drugs. Everyone knew he was there the night his boss went down, but Art slipped away. Tom had always been the good kid, determined to craft a different life for himself. But these connections followed you. He glanced warily over at Art's bag in the corner.

He inherited good things from his family, too. His father had been a jazz pianist, his mother a locally celebrated jazz and gospel singer, and his brother played sax brilliantly. Tom originally learned piano from his dad and taught himself to read music. One year his school music teacher gave him a book of Mozart sonatas. By then his dad was in prison.

When he began playing the classical music at home his brother made fun of him endlessly, but Tom was hooked on the beauty of the music. He learned all the sonatas on the old family upright. His mother, skeptical at first, began to encourage him, even though she cautioned him not to put too much stock in a white art form. He began to use all his savings to buy sheet music: Bach, Beethoven, Shubert, Chopin, Liszt.

But there was little opportunity in the Bronx to play the music he loved. Nor could he escape his birthright as a jazz pianist. After all, Tom *could* play jazz piano as good as anyone. If there was work to be had playing with his brother, or accompanying his mother singing, he never said no. Even now, he expected he and Art could make a little extra cash playing together. Yet that was exactly the thing he'd hoped to avoid by moving down here.

The kind of jazz he played wasn't even so hot anymore. It was the music of his parents' generation. Hip-hop was the style of the day. Musicians his own age in the South Bronx were flocking to Afrika Bambaataa's Zulu Nation. But that wasn't the music for him.

Finished with his lunch, Tom changed his shirt. He had saved his favorite purple one for his first day on the gig, knowing he would sweat on the subway. As he walked north on Ninth Avenue toward Lincoln Center, he broke into a grin. He felt good and strode confidently, ready to take on this great city and the opportunities it offered him.

He arrived at the locked door to the ballet school twenty minutes before noon. After fifteen minutes the ballet master arrived.

"Hey, guy. You must be the new piano player." He chuckled. "You're *obviously* not here to dance."

Tom had not been around ballet before. But one look at the ballet master made the distinction clear. They were both fit, slender men. But the ballet master's physique had an unnatural precision to each bone and tendon of his body. He looked thinner than could be healthy. Even his face was gaunt. His graying blonde hair was cropped short. He moved and spoke with effeminate grace, marked by the exacting nature of his life's work.

"I'm Charles." He unlocked the door. "I presume they gave you the repertoire list for today's classes?"

"Yes sir, I have it all." Tom lifted the packet of sheet music under his arm. Most of these pieces he could play from memory.

"Good. Quick, before the students arrive, let me hear you play a bit."

Charles fell noiselessly to the floor and changed his shoes as Tom lifted the keyboard lid of the upright piano. He sat down and began to play a Chopin waltz. It was one of the more complex pieces that had appeared on today's list. The ballet master listened for only a few measures before standing and dramatically waving his hand for Tom to stop.

"Is this your first time playing for ballet?"

"Yeah."

"I thought so. You can obviously play, but you're not giving a concert. What we need is rhythm." He started snapping his fingers, walking toward the piano and speaking with the exact rhythm that he snapped. "Strict, precise rhythm. You are a metronome. What you just played was too beautiful for ballet classes, too much feeling."

Upon seeing my expression, he emitted a rollicking laugh. "You're going to hate it, guy, but play so we forget you're there."

Students began to rush into the room *en masse*, chattering, shedding outer layers of clothes and changing out their street shoes for ballet slippers. Bags, coats, and shoes formed an orderly line against the wall across from the mirror. At first Tom thought they were all girls, but as they lined up at the barre, he spotted two young men in the group, though their physiques were almost indistinguishable.

Charles nodded at Tom, who began to play the first piece on the list he had been given, the slow movement of a Schumann sonata, at a tempo faster than he would have chosen to play it. The piece was easy, but he felt nervous. The command to take the emotion out of music was difficult to process. The dancers started their barre exercise. Tom hoped he was meeting Charles' expectations.

"*Demi, grand plié,* down," called out the ballet master, though the dancers were clearly familiar with the routine. "Stretch, 4, 5, 6... Arms! Now *en bas. Tendu.* Repeat. *Demi plié.*"

For a moment Tom relaxed, playing the music as he knew it. Suddenly, Charles was at his side. He beat on the top of the piano with the side of his hand. "Steady," he snarled, before turning back to the dancers.

Tom's heart raced. He was playing as steady a rhythm as he knew how.

"That's it, ladies. *Tendu à la seconde. Port de bras*, right arm. Turn, aaaaand hold." He breathed, long and audibly in rhythm. "*Dégagé, piqué*, and side, and close."

Tom had stopped looking at the music on his page, relying on memory. He watched the ballet master as if he was a conductor. The subtle movements of his limbs and lips indicated the precise rhythm he wanted. Tom was a quick learner, but the ballet master had been right: He hated it. Playing without emotion went against every musical impulse that coursed through him.

As the class progressed, Tom felt he was doing better. Watching helped. But on the pieces he knew less well, he needed to follow the music and concentrate on the notes. Then his instincts crept into his playing. Approaching noiselessly, Charles would be back, banging the side of his hand on the top of the piano and scowling.

Tom concentrated harder. He'd had rough first days on jobs before. He was determined not to lose this opportunity. He forced the rhythm he saw from the ballet master into his own heartbeat, challenging himself to succeed.

The class ended and another began. Then after a half hour break, two more classes in immediate succession. In the third class, Charles only came and banged on the piano once. In the fourth class, not at all. Tom's hands were tired by the end of it, and his brain was thoroughly exhausted. It had been a grueling afternoon. According to the schedule, there was a two-hour break before he would play for two evening classes with a different instructor.

Charles leaned against the wall as the girls gathered their things. He called out a farewell to each of them by name as they left. Tom packed up his music. The evening classes would be in a different room.

"You did well today," Charles said after all the students had left.

Tom looked at him in surprise.

"I mean it. You got better with each class. I was hard on you, but you've got to learn how it's done. You're going to do fine." He dropped to the floor to change his shoes, with the same lightness that had impressed and startled Tom throughout the day.

"You probably come from a jazz background, don't you?" Charles asked.

Tom stiffened and tightened his lips as he stood by the piano. Charles saw it. A look of understanding passed over his face. There was a long pause in the room.

"I'd like to hear you play a piece you love," he said. "There are no dancers here anymore. I don't count. Play it the way you want."

Tom stood still for a moment. He had spent the afternoon terrified of this man for reasons he couldn't entirely understand. Now he didn't understand the look on the older man's face. Finally, he sat back down. He stubbornly wanted to go the complete opposite direction from the repertoire he had been assigned. He began to play Franz Liszt's *Liebestraum*. Charles closed his eyes as Tom gave it all the intensity and rhythmic variation the piece demanded. He listened to the whole thing in silence.

"That was beautiful," he said, several long moments after Tom had finished. "It really was. You're a classical musician through and through. You hate that people think you play jazz because you're black. I saw it on your face the moment I asked."

Tom nodded. The man didn't even know what he'd said. Jazz wasn't even black music anymore—hadn't been for a long time—but white people still thought it was.

"I'm sorry for assuming that. You're always going to face that. The classical world is pathetically white. You'll always be explaining yourself and making excuses for who you are." Charles paused. "For me, it's the opposite. I'm accepted as myself in the ballet world. It's one of the only places where I *am* accepted. It's even a bit *expected.* I mean from Tchaikovsky to Jerome Robbins, to *my* not-so-humble self. But away from here I pretend to be someone I'm not. I'm not courageous enough to really be myself anywhere other than here."

Tom looked at him in confusion. "What are you talking about?"

Charles laughed boisterously. "Are you *that* sheltered? I'm gay! Lord, can't you tell?"

It took Tom a moment to process this revelation. He felt silly for not knowing, but he *had* been sheltered. He could not think of one person he had known, who he *knew* was gay, let alone admitted it. In a room alone with Charles, Tom felt a sudden, unsettling discomfort. As soon as he recognized the feeling he felt ashamed of it, but it didn't go away.

Charles hopped to his feet.

"Let me buy you a cup of coffee. It's the least I can do after all the scares I gave you today. I'll give you all my pointers on how to survive this new world you've thrown yourself into."

Tom stood stiffly, unconscious of the message his body language conveyed. Charles laughed.

"Don't worry, guy. I know you're straight as Fifth Avenue." He walked to the piano and clapped Tom on the back. "You've

26

got a lot to learn if you want to make it in New York City in the Nineteen-fucking-Eighties!"

●   ●   ●

Tom didn't leave Lincoln Center until after nine o'clock. It felt strange walking back through the garishly-lit streets, toward a home that still felt like a foreign place. He wondered if there would be a time when this *would* feel like home. This was the third time today that he had passed these same Ninth Avenue buildings, but everything looked different at night.

In the cool of the night, the city was coming alive.

"They don't call it Hell's Kitchen for nothin'!" he said under his breath. Already, he sensed that the worst of the city's past and the best of its future shared those few crowded streets. Drag queens, prostitutes and petty thieves prowled 9th and 10th Avenues at night, ready to serve or exploit those drifting west from Midtown in search of a cheap thrill. The day-time markets and delis had drawn iron gates across their store fronts when the googly neon eyes came on above, announcing that the upstairs peep shows were open for business. Has-beens and wanna-bes competed for room on the stages of the seedy night clubs that dotted the Avenues. He counted himself among the latter, desperate to avoid becoming the former.

When he came to see apartments, the disrepair of many of the buildings shocked him. Many matched the dilapidated state of his neighborhood. He felt lucky his own apartment was in as good shape as it was. Now, by night, he understood why. Clearly, the landlords didn't trust their tenants enough to put in the expense of renovations—sometimes not even of basic repairs. No wonder long-term leases weren't required around here.

After one day on the job, he didn't know if he would make it. It was harder than he had expected. Playing piano had never felt like a *job* before today. His shoulders slouched, and his hands ached from the tension he'd held in them all day. Tomorrow he would rally his confidence again, but at the moment he lacked the energy to walk tall.

He found his apartment by number rather than by recognition. Inside, Art paced restlessly.

"C'mon, man, we gotta go right now."

"Whoa, what's up?" Tom set his music folio on the floor next to his bag.

"I met this cat today. He heard me playing in the park and liked my sound. Anyway, they've got a gig they need to fill and are holding auditions tonight."

"Why aren't you there?"

"They need two guys… a piano and another. Don't much care what kind of horn. Already got drums and bass. Come on, hurry. The studio's twelve blocks south a' here. They might be done by now but let's try."

Art had his sax case in hand, headed for the door. Tom paused for a moment and sighed. He was tired. Dog tired. All he wanted was a little rest. But this was New York City. There was never time to rest if you wanted to make it. It would be good to have another gig, to supplement the meager salary paid by the ballet school… if he could even keep that job. And maybe a steady stream of gigs would keep Art out of trouble.

Tom sighed heavily, then mustered all his energy and followed his brother out the door.

Chapter Three

•••••••••••••••••••••••

June 2019

"Three minutes!" Percy intoned into the green room.
"Thank you, three minutes," I responded
automatically.

I kept fussing with my makeup and costume even
though I had been ready for awhile. Everyone was ready except
Cleopatro, who was still nearly naked. His makeup alone had
taken twice as long as any of us girls.

The green room door opened again. Marcello, the stage tech,
popped in his head. "It's a full house! We even added a row of
folding chairs in back."

Percy beamed at him. Just twenty-four hours ago, in the
run-up to opening night, those two had fought bitterly over the
set-up of the VIP tables. Marcello won, and Percy had started
the show practically in tears, though we narrowly avoided a
full-fledged meltdown. Thank God! Now they were friends
again. The highs and lows of stage emotions.

I didn't come on till the second number, so I stood back
against the bulk of costumes that threatened to topple their
rack.

"Cammie, can you tighten my straps a bit?" Paula backed
toward me. The soft smell of powder rose from her shoulders.

I could barely get my finger behind her straps to adjust them, they were already so tight. But if Paula wanted to hike her boobs up to her chin, who was I to stop her? I gave her another half inch on both sides.

Paula was cute. She was the right girl for the lead; I wouldn't argue with that, even though I was a much better dancer and just as good a singer. It helped to be twenty-two with dimples and C-cups.

The three musicians went out first—Ellie on keyboard, Nick on guitar and Brian on drums. Percy, Paula and Heather stood ready to enter at Marcello's cue. Cleopatro (nearly dressed now), Darnel and I waited in the green room for our later entrances.

Three minutes became ten and the show began. As soon as I heard the opening notes, I left the green room to prepare for my entrance.

I had to approach the stage through the audience at the beginning of the second song, but there was no way around the stage from the green room. I slipped through the side door into the alley, carrying my dance shoes while wearing flip-flops. I wove through the dumpsters and crates as plates clattered in the bustling, neighborhood restaurants. Above, I heard the hum of several dozen air-conditioners laboring against the June heat, dripping little puddles along both sides of the alley. I scampered all the way around the block and through the front door of the theatre. Changing my shoes in the darkness, I left my sandals with Robert at the bar.

"Can I get a glass of water and a napkin?" I whispered.

Last night I had struggled at first on stage. Without a proper dress-rehearsal, I only had a chance to mark out a few steps before dancing for real. I had underestimated the slickness of the floor for dancing at full speed. Wetting the bottoms of my shoes would help.

Handing the napkin and glass back to Robert, I crept to the back wall to await my cue.

I knew where my mother was seated, but I made a concerted effort not to look in that direction. Glad as I was for her to be there, I couldn't let her affect my concentration after our strained afternoon together. My presence here in New York was only the latest of my many choices over the years that she found questionable. I shouldn't have cared anymore, but I did. I wanted her to be proud of me. I wanted her to understand why this was so important.

I wished my dad could have come. He would have loved seeing the show, but his diabetes made it tough for him to travel anymore.

Once the song started, I would have to pass close by all the guests. It was always best not to look toward people you knew. A teacher once told me to look at people's noses. It gave them the impression you were looking them in the eyes, while keeping you from getting distracted from your choreography. This advice was invaluable, especially in a small theatre like this.

The first song ended. Paula and Heather left the stage. Percy stood to the side. As the music resumed, the stage lights swept toward me. The whole theatre erupted with the colors of a circus—blood red, deep green, purple, pink, blue—rainbows of light tinkling off champagne flutes and diamond studs. The old stage lights sizzled as loud as the band.

I stood tall as eyes followed the lights onto me. I made my leggy entrance through the seats, feeling the heat of the lights. I carefully weaved through the VIP tables in front. This was why Percy had wanted the tables pushed closer together. He was trying to make it easier for me—bless him. But Marcello had been right. If these patrons were paying extra for prime seating, they deserved to be comfortable. I managed my way through just fine, smiling at as many noses as possible, and leaped dramatically onto the stage.

My solo dance was short. Percy stepped forward and we sang our duet. When he exited, Cleopatro and Darnel joined me on stage for our jazzy *pas de trois*.

Afterwards I barely had time to catch my breath in the green room before changing costumes and running back out for another scene.

It was a whirlwind until the Act One curtain fell. I could tell we were sharper tonight and hoped Percy felt it too.

We poured into the green room at intermission and stripped down as a champagne bottle popped. I peeled off my costume and put on my robe. My first costume in Act Two was bulky and hot. I would suffocate if I put it on too early.

Intermission was anything but relaxing. Percy wanted to change the choreography of the opening number of Act Two. Our original choreography had been compressed to fit the stage, but he was having his doubts. Suggesting a change had gotten us all throwing out ideas and this stressed him out even more. We dancers were over-thinking it. Ellie, our piano player, stepped up to be the voice of reason.

"I'm not a dancer," she said in a voice that had clearly been born and bred deep in Brooklyn. "But I think what you did last night worked out alright. The chances of changing it now and pulling it off in unison are low... if you ask me."

We all nodded. I hadn't gotten to know Ellie too well, but she was clearly the leader of the musicians and now I could see why. With her dark pants and vest, and the gray corduroy cap that she had worn throughout rehearsals she kept a low profile but exuded a quiet authority. Percy acquiesced, and we left the choreography as it was.

That number went just fine—beautifully in fact. But the second number of Act Two nearly fell apart.

Disagreement would flare up over whose fault it was. Ellie may have started playing too early. Paula may have forgotten she was supposed to sing on the first verse. I think it was Percy who missed his own cue... it happens, even on a song he composed himself. From backstage, Heather and I had no idea when to enter. Our cue was long since lost.

We looked at each other in dismay. Whatever we did, we had to enter together. The audience was probably still unaware that the music was off, but we both knew Percy—still singing valiantly on stage—was struggling. If we startled him by entering when he didn't expect us, it could be disastrous. On a normal stage, we could have seen him from behind the curtain, which would have given us some clue as to his expectations. But on this funky stage we could only rely on sound.

Percy regrouped just in time. Using the pause at the end of the verse he improvised. He spoke a line to get Paula and the band back in unison with him, and at the same time returned the song to the moment of our cue. For all his faults, he was still the theatre genius we had all come to love and respect. Heather and I entered, delighted to do so with confidence. Percy sang the closing of the song beautifully, and not a soul in the audience suspected how close it had come to unraveling.

Before I knew it, the finale had come. I danced stronger and more confidently than the night before, kicking my legs out in all their glory. Yes, the stage was far too small for the whole ensemble, but by strategically adjusting my angles I gave the choreography the flair it needed without kicking anyone. I was good at this stuff!

I knew I performed well ... in ways that were probably lost on everyone in this audience. I had contributed to the show coming off as intended. I could only hope some bigtime Broadway producer who happened to be in the audience might have appreciated me. But really, they would all have better things to do on a Saturday night in Manhattan.

The applause was longer and louder than it had been on opening night. We were all smiles as we bowed. The stage lights were hot on my face. I savored the feeling. This moment after a show was the best kind of feeling in the world, giving you chills and making you hot all over at the same time. It was almost like an orgasm—with my heart still thumping from the dance, my cheeks flushed from the heat of the lights, the pungent smell of sweat intoxicating. It felt so good it brought tears to my eyes in the brief moment before it passed.

The green room exploded again in garments, glitter and champagne corks. Arms, legs and boobs loosened from sweat-soaked fabric as hair shook free from a thousand pins. I took the glass that was handed to me but quickly changed and packed up my things. My mother waited. I would enjoy some time with these new friends tomorrow at the cast dinner following the closing matinee.

Heather caught my eye as I started out. She lifted her palm for a high five. I smiled and slapped her hand. She grasped it for an extra moment. I felt satisfied. *She* knew how much I had brought to the performance.

I paused again on the stage before walking across toward the audience. I savored each moment of my New York City theatre success, unsure how long it would last. Sure, this show was small… they didn't even pay me. But it was also a dream come true.

I saw my mother and walked down to her. I feared my post-show high would be cut short. All afternoon it seemed like she was burning to say something to me. I didn't expect it to be good. Would it just be how disappointed she was that I had given up a good career for this pipe dream, or that she had run into Alex and what a great guy he was and why did we get divorced again? Or was there real bad news from home? Maybe Dad's health.

"Did you like the show, Mom?"

"You danced very well. It was nice to hear you sing, too. I haven't heard you sing in a long time."

"Percy composed all the songs himself."

"I didn't understand the story. It was an odd show, I'll be honest. But you did well. It's what you wanted."

Would it kill her to say she enjoyed it?

I took one more sip of my champagne, then put down the glass.

My mom was built the complete opposite of me, although plenty remained to give us away as family. She was a good six inches shorter with a stocky build. I had seen in pictures that when she was a girl her hair had waves like mine, but for as long as I could remember it had been cropped short. The light brown had now mostly turned to gray.

I had certainly inherited her strength. Mine was channeled into my legs and my hard feet that had miraculously never been injured. Hers was channeled into the broad shoulders and firm arms that had worked construction in Lancaster for thirty-five years and showed no signs of slowing down. She had the energy of a woman who had always been the primary bread winner, with both daughters "finding" themselves as artists and her husband no longer able to work. After nine months apart, I noticed the deepening fatigue in her eyes. Maybe that was a first sign of her slowing down.

We walked to the door, pausing at the bar. Robert handed me my flip-flops with a wink.

"I'm starving," I said once we were outside. "Do you mind if we grab something?"

"At this hour?"

I laughed. "It's only 10:30. There's a taqueria on the corner."

Back in her hotel room I sat on one of the beds enjoying my tacos—one pork, two veggie—while she arranged her things in the room. She was only staying for the one night and I was staying with her, but I could tell she enjoyed being in a hotel.

The room was too small for two double beds, but this was New York, so the hotelier had made it work. When Mom pulled out the drawers of the dresser, they bumped up against the end of one of the beds. The blinds were pulled shut, since the window view was of another hotel room mere feet away, but through the cracks the lights of the city at night danced in their endless story.

I tried to push aside the omen of bad news I had imagined Mom bringing with her on this morning's train. That was the kind of thinking that could get me in trouble. How often had I failed to appreciate the good just because I feared how it might end? I wouldn't let myself get pulled down that rabbit-hole again. That was where my demon lived.

"When was the last time you talked to Andrea?" she asked as I polished off my last taco.

I honestly couldn't remember. I felt like I had talked to my sister fairly recently, but when I thought about it, it had probably been several months, if not longer. We commented on and "liked" each other's posts on Facebook and Instagram all the time, making me feel like I was up to speed on everything in her life. In reality I only saw the surface.

"I'm worried about her. I wish you'd come home. Something's not right with her, but whatever it is she won't tell me. She's clearly in a really bad place."

"Do you know what's going on?"

I knew how my little sister could be. Her emotions ran very high or very low. It had been that way since she was a child. I suppose we were similar that way, though it was always more obvious with her.

Mom took a deep breath.

"A week ago, she was on the front couch in her clothes when I got up for work. It was a Saturday, but I've been working a few of those lately. It must have been about five in the morning, and she was completely drunk. She doesn't even live at the house anymore, so I don't know why she was there."

"Muscle memory."

"I tried to rouse her. I didn't want your father to see her like that. All I could do was lean her against myself and pull her, practically sleep-walking, upstairs. She smelled awful. She was laughing at first, but by the time we got upstairs she was saying she wanted to die. She wasn't herself. It frightened me. We've turned your old room into a guest room, so that's where I put her. As soon as she fell back on the bed she was out again.

"That afternoon when I got home, she was gone, so I called her at her apartment. She seemed just like herself again. I asked her about it, and she said she didn't even remember what she did the previous night or how she got to the house. Said she didn't remember me bringing her upstairs. I don't know if that was true or if she just didn't want to talk about it. I was worried and told her so. I couldn't stop thinking about it, so I called her again that night. By then I could tell she was drinking again, and she yelled at me to mind my own business."

Classic Andrea. Crying for help as loud as she could, and then shouting about it when someone answered the call.

Whether it was a tantrum at the theatre show when she was five, or black-out drinking in front of our parents at twenty-six, it was basically the same. What made me so different? Pride, I suppose.

"Has she been painting at all?" I asked.

"Not that I know of. Whenever I ask, she says she doesn't want to talk about it. It's a shame. She was so talented. I had hoped going to that school would take her to the next level, but we all know how that turned out."

It all made perfect sense, and I felt like an idiot for failing to see it coming. Worse, I knew my blindness was due to being so focused on myself lately. From the time I decided I was coming to New York, it had been all about me. That was the only way I could have kept my resolve and kept my spirits up. Maybe my move here was a bit selfish, but didn't I deserve to take this chance—finally—while I still could?

I had been so proud, even jealous of Andrea when she left for Temple straight out of high school to study painting. It was the kind of chance I wished I had taken when I was that age. But it didn't go well. Andrea quickly soured on it, having hoped for a *different* chance that summer. She was too much of a free spirit to submit to the restraints of a University art program. After two years, she came home, broken down by the high expectations and competition, and burdened with student loan debt. She took three years to finish her accounting degree closer to home at Muhlenberg College. That had been two full years ago now.

While at Muhlenberg, Andrea had a far worse alcoholic adventure than what Mom recently saw. That one landed her in the hospital. She damn near drank herself to death that night, and Mom would never know about it, thanks to me. Was she headed that way again?

"I'll give her a call this week," I said.

Mom sighed… a sigh with meaning as clear as words.

"Please consider coming back home for a while. Andrea's always looked up to you. You'd be a better influence than her other friends in town."

That part I could certainly agree with. I had seen the pictures on Facebook of who she partied with. No wonder she was getting soaking drunk all the time. Only the worst of her high school friends had stayed in Lancaster. That was one reason I was so desperate not to go back.

"You know you owe it to her." Mom looked me pointedly in the eyes.

I swallowed a lump in my throat. Yes, I did know. In my guiltier moments I blamed all of Andrea's artistic failures on myself. It felt icky for Mom to bring it up now.

"Maybe with you around she would find some direction," she said. "I'd love to see her painting again. And it would do your father so much good to have you close, too."

Yes, I owed it to all of them. I had never been a good sister, or a good daughter, or a good wife. There went my heart, sinking into the familiar muck of guilt, inadequacy and regret.

"Think about it," Mom barreled on. "You could teach again. You must barely be scraping by now."

"I'm teaching here. I know you don't understand why I need to be here, but I'm just starting to make it. I can't give up now. This show will lead to more."

I desperately wanted to believe that was true. She was right that my teaching here earned me less money than I could make in Lancaster, and at twice the cost of living. My income merely slowed the alarming decline in my savings. But here it was a means to an end. This show was proof of that.

"I know," she said. "*If you can make it here* and all that."

Involuntarily, I remembered Jay Z's song, with the line, *City is a pity, half of y'all won't make it*. It was Sinatra's line that inspired me to come here. It was Jay Z's that warned me how tough it would be to stay.

Chapter Four

· ·

1986

"I've missed you, son. I can't believe it's been a month since you boys moved out and this is the first time you've come to see me."

"I know. I'm sorry." Tom put his arm around his mother, but she wriggled free to fuss in the kitchen. "Relax, Mama. I told you I already ate."

"Shush. I see how skinny you are."

Tom walked back into the living room and sat down on the old green couch. The room looked no different after his brief time away. Most of the pictures on the walls had been there for ten years or more. One of the newer ones was of himself, wearing his only suit at his first classical concert the year before. Tom smiled looking at the picture, noticing the way the corners of his lips curved down. That day he desperately tried *not* to smile. On the blue chest next to the kitchen entrance was the same glass dish that had been there for years, holding a few necklaces, coins and the little card-sized picture of Jesus propped against the wall, curling backward a little more each year.

He wondered if his mother would leave this third-floor apartment now that her sons were gone. It was an awfully big place for only one.

She looked the same. She had always been a lovely woman, but hardship aged her beyond her years in her twenties and early thirties. Her true age had caught up to her appearance as life settled down once Tom's father left for good. Tom noticed she had done her hair that day, probably for his benefit.

"This place is so quiet now without you boys, but I know how it is. You got to make your own way."

"I've been doing fine, Mama. I'm getting the hang of playing for the ballet. It's a good job. And I got a jazz gig with Art the very first night. We're playing every weekend. Funny thing— that gig pays better than my ballet job."

His mother squinted her eyes at him. "Course it does. That's real playin'. That's how you're gonna make it down there. Don't get too big for your britches and start thinking you're gonna be playing with the symphony just because you know how to read Mozart."

Tom knew well enough to keep his mouth shut. His own mother was just like all the others. Even Art and the guys they played with laughed at him for thinking his day job could lead him anywhere.

"You still singin', Mama?"

"Only in church. I don't have no one to sing with now that you boys are gone. I miss you. I'm glad Art went with you, but I miss you both. I know you'll be back, though."

Maybe his mother wouldn't leave this apartment, forever waiting for her sons to return. Tom again held his tongue. He loved his mother. Seeing her reminded him how much he missed being with her every day. But his new life could become so much more. His mother would come to accept it over time. She'd need to discover the next chapter in her life as well.

"You know it's Pentecost this Sunday," she said, looking at him from the kitchen doorway. "Do you remember the Spirit Fire concert last year? What a night that was."

"Yeah, that was fun." Tom smiled. The night before Pentecost was the biggest musical night of the year at the little neighborhood church where he'd grown up.

"You could come back for it, couldn't you? Just the concert and Sunday morning. Be back in the city in no time."

Tom shook his head. "Art and I play with the band on Saturday nights. And there are ballet classes on Sunday."

"Even Sunday?"

"That's why my day off's today. Besides, Reverend Carson must have gotten a new piano player now."

"No one there can play like you."

His mother returned to the kitchen.

Tom's eyes fell on the closed lid of the piano that used to make music in this home, first through his father, more recently through himself. Now the lid stayed closed. Art had taken his saxophone. This apartment used to ring with music every day. Now he could practically hear the echoing silence of the walls.

"How's Art?" she asked. "Is he happy?"

"Hard to say." Tom mentally noted that she hadn't asked if *he* was happy. "He always seems happy, but you never know with him."

Even though Art was the boy who always got into trouble, he was also the more personable of the brothers while Tom often kept to himself. Both boys were close to their mother, but Tom knew she had more of a friendship with Art.

She sighed. "I would have liked to have seen him, but it was probably best you came alone." She paused. "D's out. He's been asking around about Art."

Tom felt a wave of nervous energy. D was Damien Lockett, who for a time had cornered the heroin market in the nearby projects. Art ran product for him for several months. Tom knew Art had been there when D got busted, but he got lucky and walked away. From D's perspective, Art might still owe him a favor or two. That was only three years ago. Tom was amazed that D was already out.

Seeing her concern made Tom realize that he had been unfair with his mother. She wasn't more interested in Art's happiness, but she was more concerned for him and for good reason. Tom naturally looked at it differently, believing that they, as brothers, had had the same opportunities and the same choices to make. But it wasn't that simple. It made sense that their mother was more desperate for a second chance for Art than she was for him.

Tom stayed with his mother into the late afternoon. On the step outside her apartment as he left, he looked around. All the four and five story brick apartment buildings with their welcoming stoops and stubby-grassed yards were intimately familiar. Still, he felt strangely detached from this place. He had chosen Manhattan as his home; though strange and even terrifying, he never intended to leave it.

He bounded down the steps and turned into the first alley— the short-cut to the subway station. He stopped cold with a shudder and a wobble in his knees. Damien Lockett leaned against the side of the brick building, his cap pulled low and a cigarette hanging from his lips. He wore a tight silk shirt unbuttoned to his mid-torso, tucked into sleek brown slacks that looked like they still had the crease from the store. His shoes were perfectly shined. D looked up and smiled at Tom, then took his time taking one more drag and stamping out his cigarette on the alley gravel.

"Piano Man!"

"Hey D." Tom tried to stay cool, though he had never been a good actor. "I heard you were out."

D looked amused. "Come on now, don't pretend you're happy to see me. I saw your look when you came around the corner."

"Just surprised."

D ambled toward him. "Well, I'm happy to see *you*, Piano Man! Where you living now?"

Tom had always been a terrible liar. He knew it would do him no good to lie now. Enough people around here knew where he was.

"I'm in the city. Trying to make a career playing."

"Good for you." D tapped Tom's chest with his finger. "And what about that brother of yours?"

Again, what would be the use? "He's down there, too."

"That's fine. Good for you boys. You be sure to give Art my best. I always liked him. I'll never forget he stood by me in tough times. But he better not forget I stood by him, too. I could have said a lot when I was in the big house."

D's words and expressions feigned friendship, but he couldn't disguise the hate in his eyes.

"Yeah, I'll tell him I ran into you."

"I'm going to come visit you boys one day. Glad to hear you're making the most of your opportunities. There's *lots* of opportunity in the city."

D lifted his hand and offered it. Tom clasped it in a brotherly gesture, but there was nothing brotherly in the energy that passed between their hands. Tom hurried away toward the subway station. Art hadn't gone nearly far enough to escape the debts of his past, and it seemed like Tom was on the hook for them too.

He reached the subway station and boarded a train, realizing that the old habits of looking over his shoulder had returned. He knew how the game worked. Once you owed something to that world, you always owed it. Tom had worked his whole life not to owe anything. He had never touched drugs or the money that came from them. Art, on the other hand, really did owe his debt. How many lumps would he be able to take before getting pulled back in?

Reaching Columbus Circle, he didn't want to go back to the apartment. He doubted D would have followed him, but there was no sense taking a chance. Many people back home knew he had come to Manhattan, but only his mother knew the actual address. He went into an arcade and put some coins into a game.

His eyes followed the screen of the game, but his mind was elsewhere. He didn't even like arcade games. As a teenager, he played them because it was the thing his friends did. At least now it served to keep his hands busy while his brain turned, though a piano would have been better.

A Knicks game blared on the TV behind him, but he tuned it out. Sports didn't interest him either.

Tom had never felt like he fit in, not with his friends, not with his family. He was never into the same stuff. Wanting to be a classical musician was just one of the ways. In school he had many acquaintances but few close friends. It was easy to find a thing or two he had in common with someone, but rare for him to really bond. The longer he was here, the more acquaintances he would develop. He already had a few. But once again the people around him had thoughts and interests far different from his own. His brother most of all. Tom loved Art, but sometimes he felt they had nothing in common besides music... and even there they had a disconnect.

He glanced around the noisy arcade. The place seemed to be full of small groups, some high-schoolers who didn't want to go home yet, some adults who had nothing better to do. He was the only loner. He left and walked west to Ninth Avenue, confident that he had not been followed.

The streets were just beginning their dramatic shift from the business-like bustle of daytime toward the beautiful chaos of night. From a window several stories above him, Tom heard the tinny sound of a badly-tuned, upright piano. Someone was practicing on a rundown instrument they surely felt lucky to have. Tom would have given just about anything for a piano of his own. From another window around the corner came the sound of a trumpet. He paused and looked up at the various windows, wondering how many other artists were in those decaying rooms, working hard on their craft. Walking on he heard a young voice learning a song that he imagined might be from a musical he didn't recognize.

Tom loved his new neighborhood. He fed off its energy. He could feel that talent was everywhere around him. He felt kinship with these people. *These* were his friends, even if he didn't know them yet. They were all working toward similar goals, facing similar obstacles. Hearing the sounds of people he understood helped him not to feel so alone.

Here were the next generation of New York City's artists— poor and struggling just like him. Some would make it big. Most would fall short, either giving up their art for steady work or succumbing to the city's underbelly that hardly bothered to hide in the shadows. Tom's heart filled with sorrow when he wondered how many of the stoned or drunk homeless he saw in alleyways or on the subway platforms were the talented artists from a few years ago. It was hard to take your chances here. It got harder with each lump you took.

Chapter Five

....

June 2019

awoke bewildered. Nothing looked or felt familiar. I was in
a strange bed, wearing something strange to sleep in. The
breathing I heard wasn't a sound I was used to. Was it still
night or already day? Where was my little apartment, my
comfortable (expensive!) pillows that I had bought as one of my
only luxuries in the city?

My eyes popped open in the dark and I remembered that I
was in my mother's hotel room. That was her breathing in the
bed beside me. I recognized the sound after all, though I hadn't
heard it in a long time. Only city lights danced through the cracks
in the blinds, so I knew it was still deep in the night. I needed to
go back to sleep. I had another performance tomorrow... or today
... and it was a matinee. The final show. I couldn't sleep in.

This bewildered awakening could have been another
morning, back in January, when I awoke in Tom's bed...
wearing something strange, hearing another's sleeping breath.
But that morning the sun already shown brightly into the room
onto the foot of his bed.

I vividly remembered Tom's essence as I lay there awake
in my mother's hotel room, the sound of her steady breathing
rising from the other double bed. He wasn't a man whose scents

you noticed. He didn't wear cologne or use products that had distinct odors. But his *essence* was unmistakable, at least to me. Tonight, I noticed its absence. It wasn't unusual for us to sleep apart. I only spent two or three nights a week at his apartment and he'd never been to mine. Still, I missed him tonight. I missed his touch and his warmth.

I remembered the first night I had slept beside him, noticing those subtle scents of his. Looking back, it was one of the most romantic and even erotic nights of my life, even though there was no sex and not so much as a kiss. By the time I lay there beside him, awake just like I was awake now, I wanted him desperately, and wished I had not stated so bluntly earlier in the night that I wouldn't hook up with him. He acted as the true gentleman I soon learned him to be, and I stubbornly kept my word.

That was the only time I had ever slept in bed with a man I hadn't had sex with. But it was, strangely, one of the most intimate experiences I've ever shared with someone. If we had made love that first night, I might not have noticed the subtler things about Tom which I soon grew to cherish. Nor would it have been as explosive once we did become lovers.

●　　●　　●

It was shortly after the New Year of 2019, and I felt feisty. That morning it had snowed, but the sky was clear now and a three-quarter moon had risen above the top stairs and wooden water-tanks of the uptown brownstones. The streets had been plowed. It never took long to get snow off the streets of this town.

I convinced my roommate, Nikki, to come out on the town with me. Nikki worked as a bank teller while taking night classes in fashion design at a small school in midtown. I had been in the city about three months. We shared the apartment for convenience and economics, but we weren't close. Still, we hung out together at least as often as we bickered, so it wasn't a bad arrangement.

"Don't get all dressed up," I said. "Just throw something on. We'll go hear some jazz or something."

I only half followed my own advice. I put on my best-fitting jeans, a silk top that showed off my collar bones and a nice sweater. My eyes and my collar bones were my favorite features. My hair was actually cooperating with me that day—a rare wonder for a curly-haired girl. I let it stay loose and full, though I put a band in my purse just in case. Over my jeans I pulled bulky snow boots. It wasn't a night for pretty shoes.

Nikki clearly thought I looked okay, because when I came out of my room she huffed, "Not fair, you look too cute." She turned back to change and re-do her makeup, which cost us forty-five minutes when we could have been out on the town.

We took the C train to 50th Street where I claimed we could find good jazz. I had heard about some swanky restaurants with good music in Hell's Kitchen but had never actually been there.

"You better know where this place is," said Nikki. "I can't walk around all night in these boots."

Acting more confident than I felt, I guided us down Eighth Avenue and turned right on a street in the upper 40s. The sounds on this block were promising. We passed a couple of doors, then I ran down the steps of one, heard a silky male voice singing, *"It Had to be You,"* and motioned Nikki to follow me in, pretending to let her in on a secret I'd known for years. We perched at the marble bar beneath the hanging row of Art Deco lamps and ordered cocktails. I looked toward the singer on the raised platform, and the piano player accompanying him from an unobtrusive spot beside the tiny stage on the parquet floor.

I recognized Tom right away. How could I ever forget that magical day at Lincoln Center?

The rest of the room seemed to fade away. I lost Nikki, the bartender, the singer, everybody and everything except this beautiful man at the piano and my memory of the gift he'd given me some four years before. I didn't feel nervous; my heart didn't skip a beat. I just felt full and warm.

He didn't look my way while he played, and I didn't intend to go up to him after the set. I doubted he'd notice and recognize me sitting there in a sweater, jeans and snow boots. I must have looked so different back then, sweating in my leotard with my hair pulled back. It was enough to be there and enjoy the music, remembering how gentle and subtle he was when he played for me. I must have had a silly smile on my face.

After several songs, he stood up and said something to the singer. The singer looked back at him, then nodded, reluctantly I thought, based on his expression. Tom began to play. At first, I didn't recognize the song, but once I placed the melody, my heart *skipped* a beat. The young man began to sing a song I recognized—I later learned it was *No Other Love*, made famous by Jo Stafford in the 1940s. I didn't recognize the words at the time, but I knew the melody well. It was the tune of Chopin's *Etude No. 3 in E Major*, the piece he had played for me that day in Lincoln Center.

There was no way to tell myself it was a coincidence. I sensed that his notes held more meaning, compared to the previous songs. He was playing for me, and the young man was singing a love song *to me*, even though he didn't know it. Nothing like that had ever happened to me before. I felt so special and attractive through the span of that song. They slowed down through the final notes. When it finished, Tom finally looked at me, directly in the eyes, gave his irresistible smile, and nodded. I put both hands over my heart and beamed at him.

Tom came over during their next break. We talked awkwardly—a real contrast with the romantic moment we had just shared. During their final set, I sent Nikki home alone. After the music finished, Tom and I talked and flirted at the bar until it closed. Crassly I told him I wasn't going to sleep with him but walked with him to his nearby apartment anyway. Once there I finally stopped to ask myself: *What the hell am I doing?*

I was deeply attracted to this man in a way that was artistic and spiritual as much as it was physical. Yet I couldn't help but follow the same mating patterns that I had learned as a teenager, and that had let me down in my twenties. I hated myself for it but couldn't stop it. Tom took it all in stride. His mating patterns were from a different era, and not only because he was so much older than me—something I barely even noticed that night. He likely would have seemed a man of a different time even if he had been younger than me. I wanted to be of his era, too. Subconsciously I met him there, once I got over my twenty-first century dating conditioning.

Being alone with a guy in his apartment is always a nerve-wracking experience, especially for the first time. Not only is there the obvious vulnerability, there are practical considerations that make it difficult and embarrassing. Conventional wisdom said a hook up was best done at *his* place... you know, so you could leave if things didn't work out, and he wouldn't know where you lived if he ended up being a creep. But if it *did* work out, it was better to do it at home where you could be comfortable. Here I was with a man I liked, was attracted to, and felt comfortable with, all things considered. But I came close to completely freaking myself out.

My first moment alone was in his bathroom. For a bachelor, his bathroom was really clean. I figured he probably hired a cleaner, which was kind of hot. Or maybe he wasn't a bachelor? I didn't even know. He could have had a wife and children outside the city, blissfully unaware of this secret apartment. He could be a psychopath or a rapist for all I knew, and here I was. Or he could be a slow killer nursing me along until the right moment. There I sat, in the bathroom, freaking out, missing Nikki of all people... until the piano sounded.

I would learn that he had a song for everything. I already knew how he could romance a woman with the perfect song. I was about to find out that music was also the outlet for his humor.

He played the Sinatra song, *Nice and Easy*. It was a little joke. Most people wouldn't have gotten it. It wasn't one of the more famous of Sinatra's tunes, but I knew it and it put me at ease. The subject of the song was about sexual energy waiting for the right time. What could be more perfect? I couldn't help but laugh.

Pretty soon, there I was, in bed with him, sleeping in nothing but my silk blouse and panties, wanting him so badly, but I had told him not to try anything. Now I'm glad it happened that way. I came to appreciate and know him that night in a way that never would have happened if we had just had sex in our exhaustion, at three o'clock in the morning after a few too many drinks.

That morning, once I had realized where I was, I got up quickly and went into the bathroom. I lingered trying to tame my huge morning mop. I ran my hands through it a few times, but there was no helping it. When I returned, Tom was sitting half up in bed with his phone in hand. Damn, he looked sexy! Just a bit of gray hair on his dark chest, half exposed out of the sheets.

"What would you like?" he asked, pulling the phone away from his face.

"Scrambled eggs with spinach and cheese."

He gave my order.

"And tortillas," I added.

He lifted his eyebrows.

"Corn tortillas."

I suddenly realized that I was standing there in his bedroom doorway without any pants on, with wild hair, making my bizarre request, and I grew shy.

I hurried back into bed. He looked so inviting. I wanted to be beside him, but it was so weird. We were so new together. We had skipped to the intimacy of sharing a morning, when we had not yet so much as kissed. But despite myself I cuddled up to him. The warmth and strength of his ribs pulsed through the razor thin silk of my top. His arm squeezed around me. I felt his breath rise and fall against the press of my breasts, and his hipbone against my stomach. My bare leg felt the rough hair of his and the edge of his boxer-briefs. I knew he wouldn't make the first move after what I'd said last night, but I wanted him to. I felt desperately aroused.

I surely would have started something if his door buzzer hadn't sounded, heralding the delivered breakfast. I sat up in the bed.

"Confession time," I said after he had returned with the food. "I like to turn everything into tacos… especially breakfast."

Once we had eaten, I washed up, twisted my hair into a low bun and made myself as presentable as I could without the comforts of home. Tom proposed a walk in Central Park.

It had snowed again during the night, but now the sky was clear. Out on the sidewalk, the sunlight and the cold, crisp urban air hit my senses. I felt grounded for a moment again, as if waking up from the dream of Tom.

He took and held my hand. My small hand in its thin cotton glove disappeared into his firm, leather-gloved hand. My hand in his felt like a natural fit. There was none of the questioning hesitation with which a younger man might have showed. Tom gave me no chance to even think of pulling my hand away. I loved it!

He pulled me back into the dream.

The streets were clear until we got to the south end of the park. The snow spread clean and clear in the bright sun of midmorning. The meadows were perfectly smooth except for the rare cut of footsteps crossing at varying angles. In the sun the whiteness was almost blinding. A two-inch layer of snow covered the Literary Walk through the park. The bronzes of Shakespeare and Sir Walter Scott looked somber with their heads crowned in white.

I had never cared much for snow. Sure, it had been fun to play in as a kid, but growing up in central Pennsylvania, the novelty had worn off fast. Snow was an annoyance more than anything. Plus, I hated being cold. That all changed there in Central Park with Tom, walking hand in hand, talking and laughing together, learning about each other, ourselves part of a beautiful winter scene. And when, standing on the bridge overlooking the pond, he took me in his arms and kissed me, I knew I would cherish the memory for the rest of my life.

Later, we were eating sandwiches and drinking coffee at a window table in the Europan Café on Seventh Avenue. My feet were tired. I was still in yesterday's clothes, not to mention last night's makeup. I didn't care.

Through the day I had talked a lot about myself. I told him all about my past and the dreams that had led me to New York City. I tended to talk a lot when I was nervous. But I was quiet now. I wasn't nervous anymore now that he had kissed me. Sometimes a girl just needs to be kissed for everything in life to become clear.

Tom was looking out the window down the avenue with a distant smile.

"What are you thinking?" I asked.

"I always feel sentimental when I am near Carnegie Hall," he said. "I played there once... a long time ago."

I looked and could hardly believe I had failed to notice the great hall across the street and further down the block. Midtown was so full of spectacular old buildings that you sometimes just walked right by them, oblivious to the historic events and wonderful moments that had taken place there. At least I did.

"Tell me about it?" I asked, gazing at him with bright eyes. I wanted to learn so much about this man.

"There's not a whole lot to tell, really. It was a concert of Shubert's music. I accompanied a baritone who sang the *Winterreise Lieder*, and I played in the piano quintet to conclude the evening. My name barely made it into the program."

"You're downplaying it. It clearly meant something to you."

"Yes. It did. It was a lifetime dream to play at Carnegie Hall."

"When was that?"

"My first year in the city."

"You never got another chance to play there?"

He shook his head. "Life went in other directions. Music did, too. I would have taken more time to appreciate the experience had I known. I thought it was just the first of many times I'd play there. I was awfully confident and awfully stubborn back then."

He paused. "That's how life works sometimes. The moments that become the highlights of your life are only clear afterwards. In the moment, you're so focused on making something wonderful happen that you don't stop to savor the miracle that *you* are there living out your dream. Then once your moment is over, it's gone. There's nothing to hold onto and say, *See, look what beauty I created*."

I was silent for a while. I had never had a really big success with my dancing, so I didn't know how I would feel in that moment. A glance at his face told me that his mind was suddenly far off.

"There's still time," I said, smiling. "Maybe you'll play there again sometime."

"Yeah," he agreed, a slight smile playing across his lips. He slid his hand across the table and gently caressed my hand with his long fingers. "There's still all the time in the world."

After he paid the bill, he asked, "Would you like to go back to my place for a little while?" It would have been easy to say goodbye after lunch, hop on an uptown B train and wait for him to ask me out on a proper date. But the intimacy we had shared was very real. I was through with playing games.

So back I went, unsure what would happen but knowing what I wanted. Now I was fully awake and sober. I knew the meaning of my choice to be there again, in the middle of a winter afternoon. I had craved it for eighteen hours now. After less than a full day I felt more intimate and trusting with Tom than I had with almost anyone my entire life, even the man, who had been my husband of five years.

As I walked up the stairs to his apartment again, anticipating what was about to happen, a wave of anxiety swept over me. It threatened to smother the libido that moments before had been firing in my every nerve. I had not been with a man since my divorce... had dreaded this moment actually, even while I missed the intimacy and craved being touched. I knew it would be emotionally complex in a way I wouldn't dare explain to a new man in my life. *What if I start crying or something?*

Tom opened the door, and we went inside. He turned and took both my hands, then kissed me for the second time that day. I immediately felt better. Tom knew why I was there too, but he didn't rush things. He made me feel comfortable and confident. His touch made me feel cherished. His eyes made me feel beautiful and sexy.

I didn't panic. I didn't cry. Making love with Tom felt so natural. He brought me so fully into the moment with him that I forgot everything else.

He touched me with curiosity and wonder, embraced me with passion, loved me with a boyish thrill that belied his age. He knew what he wanted and wasn't shy about it. Why should he be, when he was giving me the best sex of my life?

We stayed in his bed the whole afternoon, talking, laughing, making love again and again. When we got hungry, he ordered food, putting on a robe long enough to pay the delivery man at the door. We ate dinner and drank wine naked in his bed. Finally, we slept.

When I awoke in his arms the next morning, I felt so happy. I didn't know what would come of this, but I didn't dare disturb the delicate beauty of what we had shared by trying to find out too soon. No matter what came next, I would remember that day and two nights with Tom as the most romantic weekend of my life.

●　　●　　●

When I awoke again, my mother was already up, and the sun streamed into the room. She had opened the blinds for some ungodly reason. I rose and dressed. There was a lot to do and limited hours before show time.

Mom and I had breakfast together at the hotel. I had offered to take her to a nice brunch, but she reminded me that the hotel breakfast was free. I was secretly relieved, because I didn't have extra money to splurge on a fancy Sunday brunch with perfectly poached eggs, artisan this or that, gruyere and micro-greens. For that matter, neither did she.

Morning sun streamed in through the west-facing windows of the hotel restaurant. In the urban canyon, light didn't always come from the direction nature intended. I looked out the window. The view stretched no further than the next tall building, with sunlight glancing off the steel and glass. I looked across the white tablecloth and studied my mother as she drank her coffee, always a higher priority at breakfast for her than the food.

"You're right." I said. "This is nice. I would have liked to show you more of the city though."

"I've been to New York before. Those experiences are for you now, not for me."

I turned my knobby knees to my right so they wouldn't hit hers. Her legs were short, but the tables were smaller than she was used to, even at a hotel like this. Everything tangible— tables, doorways, bathrooms, sidewalks—were a hair smaller here, while everything intangible—hopes, fears, egos—were bigger. My extended-knees and tall head (as a dancer I prided myself on good posture) frequently bumped up against the compactness of this city.

It was good to catch up and laugh together over our meal. Yesterday had been strained, between my focus on the show, and her need to talk to me about Andrea. Finally, at breakfast, we were both ourselves again, a mother and daughter who had shared so much and knew each other so well.

"Thank you, Mom."

She smiled. "Of course, dear. I wanted to see your show."

"I meant more than that. Thanks for all you've done for me— for us—over the years. You've always given *us* the experiences, never asked for them for yourself."

Mom squirmed in her seat. Her smile still curved her lips, but she looked uncomfortable.

"You've given both me and Andrea the chance to be artists even when we neglected more practical things."

"You got it from your father. He was the artistic one."

"You stayed strong and supported all three of us."

"I love each of you so much."

"I love you too, Mom."

I had been unfair in focusing on the ways my choices disappointed her. Maybe it was a lot to ask her to be proud of me, when I had done little to make her proud. She had high expectations for me. I wouldn't want it any other way.

"I wish you could stay longer."

"Next time *you* visit *me*."

"Deal."

We walked to Penn Station, wheeling her small suitcase through the Sunday morning crowd. I waited for her while she bought her ticket, distractedly watching the maze of people wrapping toward and away from each other in all directions. A jumble of announcements sounded in concert on the disparate loudspeakers.

She came back, and I saw that she held two tickets. She extended one toward me. My hands remained at my sides.

"It's for tomorrow's train." She extended the second ticket toward me. "I know you have another show today. You don't have to come home, but I want you to consider it. It would mean a lot to Andrea... and to me."

I was stung. Sure, it would help Andrea but what about me? That ticket was dangerous for me. It cracked open a box I had left safely shut under my foot for a long time. Already, the eye of my demon peered out from the crack.

I lashed my hand out like a snake and took the ticket. I dropped it into my purse, hoping to forget about it.

We hugged. I watched her walk toward the escalator and descend out of sight.

Chapter Six

....

1986

No one was at the ballet studio yet when Tom arrived. The door was unlocked—a first—so he went in and lifted the lid of the upright piano. For a moment he bent down and looked across the length of black and white keys, then ran his finger softly along them. A piano's keyboard was a sensual thing to him. The tedium of the ballet class had made him forget how honored he used to always feel to make music on such a beautiful instrument. This was a good piano too, deserving of respect and love.

He sat down on the bench. He put one of his own scores on the stand—Chopin's G minor *Ballade*—a piece much too intense and rhythmically varied for ballet class. He'd first heard this piece when listening to classical radio in his boyhood bedroom. He had rushed out to the music store to buy the sheet music even though it would be years before he could play well enough to do it justice. He started hesitantly, the piano sounding loud in the empty room. Gradually he grew bolder and lost himself in the exquisite melodies. The piano gave back to him—strength for strength, softness for softness.

He stopped mid-piece, sensing a presence behind him. He turned and saw the ballet master standing in the doorway.

"Mm hm," said Charles. He waited another moment, then walked in and dropped his bag by the mirror.

"I know I shouldn't be..." said Tom, feeling as if he had been caught committing a crime.

"Don't apologize. It was beautiful." Charles sat down and began to change his shoes. Tom thought Charles seemed different—less fierce than before. But it was Charles who asked, "You okay, guy?"

"Tough day yesterday, I guess." He was still bothered by his encounter with D. "But no big deal."

The first group of girls rushed in. It took Charles a moment longer than usual to hop to his feet.

During the class, as Tom played a flavorless version of classical pieces, he remembered his brief moment before class with Chopin. He had almost forgotten how good it felt. He also remembered the envy he felt yesterday when he heard the sound of someone's tinny upright in an apartment above the street, even the lust of looking at the closed piano in his mother's apartment. Though he played all day and all night, he had not actually *practiced* in over a month. He was scraping together a career from playing, which was a dream come true. But he had different dreams—bigger dreams.

He decided to ask Charles for a favor. He was nervous. Charles had always made him feel nervous. But he also felt a subtle understanding growing between them. He trusted Charles as much as he did anyone else in this strange artistic world.

The classes progressed one after another for four hours. Tom's fingers grew tired while Charles seemed never to miss a beat. Finally, it was just the two of them left in the studio.

"I've been thinking," said Tom once all the girls had left. "It felt so good to really play today before class. "Most of the time in the mornings there's no classes. What do you say if I came in some mornings to practice? Learn some new music."

Charles looked him straight in the eye and smiled when he finished his request.

"I'm glad you asked. I don't own this room you know. But I'll try to find a way to make it work for you. Geez, I never really thought about it, but of course you wouldn't have a piano at home."

Tom shook his head.

"There's nothing more frustrating than being an artist and having no opportunity to work on your craft. I suppose it would be worse if you couldn't play at all. At least you have this. But I get it. You want more than this. I could tell from the moment you first walked in here." He paused. "Yeah, we'll figure it out."

"Thanks."

Charles spun around and stared at himself in the mirror. Tom replaced the stack of sheet music, in order, on top of the piano.

"What's your goal?" Charles asked.

"Well," Tom only hesitated for a moment. "I want to get really good playing classical. I think I'm pretty good, but I've still got more work to do."

"We all want to get really good. What's your *dream*?"

Tom considered for a moment before answering.

"I've always dreamed about playing at Carnegie Hall. Walked by it a couple times since I moved here."

Charles smiled.

"I've never told that particular dream to anyone," said Tom. "Everyone else would say it was foolish. I saw my mama yesterday, and she doesn't get it. Neither does my brother. They only hear me when I play jazz. But my heart is in classical. I know I can be good at it if I have the chance."

"And what do *you* think?" Charles asked. "Do you think you can be good enough to play at a place like Carnegie Hall? Do *you* think it's a foolish dream?"

Tom didn't reply. It was hard to think he was good enough.

"You know the difference between your art and your job," said Charles, turning away from the mirror with one hand on the barre. "That distinction is tough for some. It's been tough for me over the years, so it's good that you know it now, and don't ever let yourself forget it when you grow older. Making a living in an artistic field is very different from making art."

Charles' words clearly summed up the thoughts Tom had not yet been able to articulate himself.

"I've never asked you before," Tom said, "but I imagine you must have been a performer before you started teaching."

"Yes!" Charles declared. "I had my days of glory with New York City Ballet."

"And you miss it."

"I should have enjoyed it more. But I was always working toward the next thing. That's the tragedy, right? What we create is so fleeting, and when our careers are over, we disappear. If I had been a choreographer, I could go see my works performed. You will have the same predicament, however well you do. You're not a composer. You may be able to play Chopin better than anyone, but Chopin's music will never be *your* music.

"Performance artists are like athletes in a way. You have to work so hard in the moment of your success. A composer can work hard in private and then bask in his success once his piece becomes a hit. But we only have that brief moment in our exhaustion to savor the audience's applause. Then it's on to the next performance. There's nothing in the world that can beat that moment when you're bowing on stage as the audience stands to applaud. But it's over so soon and then you realize it's over forever. There will be other shows but not *that* show, *that* moment. At least for an athlete, if he wins a championship, he has the validation of knowing he reached the pinnacle of his endeavor. But for us, there's always a bigger stage, a new challenge, a louder round of applause. You'll see one day. Don't let that discourage you. Just know the tragedy you have created for yourself by choosing to be a performer."

Tom smiled, sitting back down on the piano bench.

"You'll always have your art," Charles continued. "Art is a difficult but faithful lover. It is *you* who must remain faithful. Every artist has times when they want to quit, or when they don't think they deserve their success, or worst of all, when people in your life discourage you, even if they don't know they're doing it."

Tom already knew that was true.

"Don't ever let anyone take your art away from you. But more importantly, don't *ever* take it away from yourself."

"What do you mean by that?"

"People like to brag that they're their own harshest critic. Fine. Tell yourself you need to improve. Tell yourself you need to work harder. Take no pleasure from your successes. But *never* tell yourself you can't."

Tom nodded.

"So come here in the mornings and work. Work on what you love. A lot of people are artists in their heads. They have a great idea of what they could create. Or they recognize their talent and get drunk on it. But the ones who succeed are the ones who are willing to work and thrive on that work. It's not always fun, but it *is* wonderful, because the work of an artist is to create something beautiful and offer it on a platter to the world. What greater calling could there be?"

"Do you still feel that, now that you're not onstage anymore?"

"Absolutely. Especially as I grow older. I'm feeling especially old today. Soon no one will remember me. Sure, a few students will remember that they studied with me, but most of them will waste their talent. Even those who saw my best performances won't remember that it was me. Yet I'm still happy to know I've contributed to the beauty of the world."

The two men were silent for several long minutes, but neither was ready to leave. Tom had all but forgotten about yesterday's events, significant as they had seemed a few hours ago. He felt newly inspired. He also felt a new connection to Charles—this man who had been so hard on him from the day they met.

He looked at the ballet master. He saw something new on his face. Surprisingly, Charles met his gaze, practically *asking* Tom to read the new pain on his face.

"You've got something on your mind too, don't you?"

"You don't miss a lot."

"It's all over your face, man,"

Charles sighed. "I heard this morning that two friends died—good friends from a few years back. Hearing about one would have been tough, but both of them... on the same day. It's hard to make sense of it all."

Tom nodded.

"You're so sheltered. I don't know how much you know about AIDS and what it's doing, but it's tearing *my* community apart." He paused, swirling a little pattern with his foot on the floor. "There's no way you could possibly imagine how this feels to someone like me. Imagine there's a professional killer out there, picking off people just like you one at a time, at random. I can't help but think it's only a matter of time before it comes for me. I live my life like normal, but there literally is never a moment when AIDS is not on my mind."

Charles turned back toward the mirror. He gazed into his own reflection for the second time that evening.

"Hearing about those guys today hit me hard. It makes me think about a lot of things in new ways. My dancing has been everything to me. I'd never thought much about death before—at least not until recently, because now I *have* to think about it. I guess I could look back and know that I have lived well. But I've also pushed a lot of people away—my family, friends, one person who was especially dear to me."

"You don't think you have it, do you?"

Charles shrugged. "Seems all the gay men get it eventually. The doctors still don't seem to agree what's going on. I feel great, but those two friends of mine were pictures of health and suddenly they're gone. It's confusing. It's unfair and confusing."

"What are you going to do?"

Charles smiled and turned back toward Tom. "That's such a childish question. I'll do what I've always done. Keep living, keep dancing. If anything, perhaps I'll appreciate the people in my life more now, whether that's for another thirty years or only one."

Charles hopped away from the barre and picked his bag up off the floor in a fluid motion.

"Come. I want to show you something."

Tom followed the ballet master out of the studio into the main square of Lincoln Center, encased by the three great theatres. The evening air was thick and warm.

"Can you feel it, guy—all the greatness oozing out of these walls?" asked Charles, pointing at the New York State Theatre on the south side of the square. People were beginning to file in for the evening performance.

"That's where I had my glory. My first show was *Giselle*. I was only eighteen the first time, dancing in the *corps de ballet*. But the next time New York City Ballet did *Giselle* I was Albrecht!"

Tom laughed. He'd never heard of Giselle and no idea what an Albrecht was. Charles ignored him.

"Opening night was the greatest night of my life. But it only lasted till the next show, when it would be replaced by another 'greatest night' and then another. I danced with NYCB for fourteen years and performed the leads in all the major ballets and enough new choreographies that I couldn't even count. But *Giselle* was always special for me."

Tom looked at the theatre. He could easily picture Charles on stage.

"In the story," Charles said, "the character Albrecht is forced to dance himself to death by evil spirits. How perfectly morbid is that?" He laughed sharply. "I remember that first night how I reveled in my exhaustion in that final scene, when the dawn rescues Albrecht at the verge of death. I plan to live my life like Albrecht, dancing until my body can dance no more."

Charles smiled distantly, his eyes still on the theatre. Finally, he turned back to Tom.

"Thanks for letting me talk. It helps. I know I'm being dramatic. But I brought you here so you could visualize great things for yourself. Go back to Carnegie Hall and picture yourself inside. Then come here to practice. Tomorrow I'll have a key for you so you can come in the mornings. Don't tell anyone, or we'll both get fired. Nothing will make me happier than seeing you put in the work to bring about your dream. Who knows, maybe I can help make it happen."

Chapter Seven

....

June 2019

he first notes of the finale excited all my senses. I could see the same joy in the other faces standing with me at stage-right. This afternoon, for the third and final show, we were absolutely nailing it. One more song and our triumph would be complete. Sadly, it would also be over.

The whole ensemble rushed the stage, our lines long, our steps sharp. Percy and Paula stepped forward and sang with crisp pitch and rhythm. The rest of us danced and danced, savoring each moment. We lined up behind the two leads and joined in song, slowing into the final cadence. Then it ended.

The audience stood as we bowed and smiled, ran backstage, then came out for another bow, then another. The stage lights were hot on my flushed face. Nothing in the world could beat that moment, but it was over too soon. I realized it was over forever. There would (hopefully) be other shows, but not *this* show. Not this wonderful moment.

Back in the green room I changed and packed up my things, taking a little more time than on the other days. The green room sweltered, heavy with the smell of bodies and powder. The theatre was air conditioned but if there was a vent back here it hardly worked. Still, I delayed, savoring the moments, not wanting it all to end. Paula was changing beside me. I reached out and gave her a hug. She squeezed me tight. Percy came over and hugged us both, whispering *"Thank you!"* in each of our ears.

In a pretty blue dress, with my big dance bag slung over my shoulder, I stepped back out onto the stage and through the house. Tom smiled at me from across the room. I started toward him but Robert, the bartender, met me first, handing me a glass of bubbly along with my flip-flops.

"Great job, Cammie," he said. I smiled and thanked him.

I knew I was Robert's favorite in the cast and guessed that he would be disappointed when he saw me go to Tom in a second.

I rushed to my man and kissed him on the lips.

"That was wonderful," he said.

I clutched his arm and led him toward the others, who were also collecting their boyfriends and girlfriends for our cast dinner. I was glad they all saw me kiss Tom. I hadn't mentioned a boyfriend. I didn't even call Tom that. But as I brought him forward, I felt proud of him. He was handsome, engaging and a brilliant musician. Who better could a girl want for a cast dinner date?

Before leaving the theatre, I took one final moment to take it in, knowing I would likely never be in that space again. What an odd little hall it was, with its not quite square stage, brick walls and low ceilings. The dark red carpet beneath my feet was stained. So was the gross purple stage curtain. There were high quality stage lights, but now that only the house lights were on, it seemed poorly lit, as if the electricity couldn't fully power all of the bulbs at once. I would remember this place fondly for the rest of my life.

Our group, now numbering fifteen, walked a few blocks to an old neighborhood Italian restaurant where Percy had reserved us the downstairs banquet room. Percy and Paula were each accompanied by their respective boyfriends, Jonathan and Jonah. We all knew Jonathan, who had been around as a smiling and funny support pillar throughout rehearsals and preparation. Jonah was exactly who I would have expected for Paula—impossibly good looking and stylish, but clearly still wet behind his ears. Darnell came with his girlfriend Tiffany. Nick, the guitarist, had his girlfriend Molly. She was exactly who I would have cast as his love interest: young with a cute face and tattoos down her arms, mirroring Nick's body art. They looked like they belonged more in L.A. than New York. It turned out Heather and Elly were a couple. I had absolutely no idea until then and felt embarrassed for not knowing, especially since Heather had become my best friend in the cast. Only Cleopatro and Brian were dateless.

The restaurant was classic Manhattan Italian. It had been there since the thirties and was now run by the grandson of its original founder, though Carlo was an old man in his own right. He greeted us like family as we crowded through the undersized door beneath a faded red awning. Black and white tiles led past the granite bar-top and down a flight of narrow stairs to the banquet room where we followed Carlo. Although there were no windows in the room, plush red curtains hung on the walls. The candles on the long table cast a deep glow against the curtains and ceiling. An upright piano stood against one wall covered in books and menus, with a layer of dust on the keys. Almost as soon as we nestled into our uncomfortable wood chairs, wine appeared at the table and began to flow.

Percy stood with his glass.

"To each of you, my lovelies! You made my dream come true this weekend. It was a lot of work. And it was worth every minute. I love you all."

We clinked as many glasses as we could reach.

Jonathan, who always encouraged Percy to dream big, added "Next stop, Broadway!"

We hooted and clinked glasses again.

"If only some of the producers had been there this weekend," said Percy.

"Are you complaining?" asked Jonathan, elbowing his boyfriend in the ribs. "After that great show?"

"No, I…"

"Check your phone, darling. Thanks to your whining, you're probably getting banner ads for tissues and tiny violins."

We all roared with laughter. Even Percy.

I squeezed Tom's hand under the table. He leaned toward me.

"It really was a good show," he said.

I smiled at him, inviting him to elaborate. I hadn't planned to ask him what he thought if he didn't volunteer it. He had seen too much. I knew it was a small show, and I wasn't even the lead. He didn't give compliments lightly. This meant a lot coming from him.

"I obviously *have* seen you dance before," he said with emphasis, "but this is the first time I've seen you perform. You're a wonderful dancer and singer."

I smiled and kissed him quickly. "Thank you, darling. Thank you."

Big plates of pasta appeared, as we talked loudly across the long tables, reliving the glories of this and other shows from our pasts, and dreaming about the future.

The drinks kept flowing after dinner. I'm not sure if it was Elly or Tom who first dusted off the keys of the piano, but soon they were sitting together at the keyboard, banging away on an instrument that probably hadn't been tuned in twenty years as Percy and others sang. Unable to resist the merriment, Carlo came back down. He sat with us and called for grappa and limoncello on the house. We drank up and listened to his stories of the restaurant's past when he bussed tables as a boy, listing all the famous artists, politicians and gangsters he had served. Later Tom accompanied him as he sang an Italian aria in full voice, every bit as out of tune as his old piano.

Pretty soon we were all giddy from the wine. Some handled it better than others. Poor Jonah wobbled badly as he ascended the stairs to the restroom. On his return, we all worried for his safety on the steep descent, but no one wanted to compound his embarrassment by getting up to help him. He made it back to his seat and tried to pretend he was fine.

We sobered up when the bill came and began the awkward arithmetic dance around the astronomical total that was sadly necessary for adult artists to perform. Carlo had conveniently disappeared.

Paula and Jonah left quickly after the sum had been settled. The rest of us lingered with hugs, kisses, promises to keep in touch, and wine-fueled dreams of a reunion show. For a dinner after a matinee, it was astonishingly late once we all left.

The party had allowed me to remain on the high from the show and to avoid thinking about what would happen next, coming all too soon the next morning. In the run up to the show I had neglected to line up other work. I had nothing scheduled for the next two weeks. My savings were getting low. I needed more teaching work—soon. I had done everything I could to forget it, but the ticket to Pennsylvania festered in my purse.

I thought for a moment about joining Tom as he called a taxi to take him home, but instead I kissed him goodbye on the street outside the restaurant. I was tired and had a lot on my mind. But I felt the energy of the city giving me a second wind as I walked toward Times Square with Heather and Ellie, where they'd catch the No. 2 train to Brooklyn, and I'd take it in the other direction. Heather and I were giggly from the wine. Ellie still seemed pretty steady.

"Wait." Heather stopped on the corner, a few paces back from where Ellie and I watched for the traffic light to change. "I want a hot dog."

"No, you don't," said Ellie. "Come on."

"Look, there's a hot dog stand right here. Don't they smell good?"

"There's a hot dog stand on every corner and they all smell disgusting."

Heather started toward it. Ellie rolled her eyes and turned back. I followed, not sure if I should laugh or turn away.

"Heather, you're drunk. I'm not letting you get a hot dog."

Heather turned back with her jaw open. "You're not *letting* me?"

The man working the late-night hot dog stand seemed like he hoped this little domestic dispute would keep on moving down the block.

"How are you even hungry after that gigantic meal we just had? Come on, you're a dancer. You can't go eating any crap you want."

"Oh, no, you're fat shaming me. *You*, fat shaming *me*?"

"That was low."

"Cammie, back me up. I can have a hot dog if I want one."

"I am *so* staying out of this."

Somehow, we all three started laughing. Inexplicably, now I kind of wanted a hot dog, too. I couldn't believe I was hungry again either.

"Fine." Ellie huffed, then stepped past Heather to the hot dog stand and ordered *two* hot dogs. I covered my mouth in my hand to muffle how much I was laughing. Then I reached into my purse for two one-dollar bills and ordered myself a hot dog. The hot dog man smiled brightly as he handed me my treat. A meal cheaper than a subway fare; who said New York was expensive?

"Mmm." Heather wiggled with delight. "Now aren't you glad I made us get hot dogs?"

Heather and I stood eating against the closest locked and gated door-front, as late night pedestrians passed on the sidewalk. Ellie was back by the hot dog stand.

I was so used to hearing any and every language spoken on the streets of New York, so the fact that there was a conversation with unfamiliar words happening nearby didn't even register for me. Not until I realized that it was Ellie I heard, her Brooklyn voice transformed. She and the hot dog man were growing enthusiastic in their conversation, in what must have been Arabic. I stepped closer with wonder.

"Happens all the time," Heather said to me.

Ellie turned back to us, smiling. "This is Amir. He's from Lebanon. I've actually been to the town where he grew up."

I was about to ask, but Heather explained as Ellie and Amir returned to their conversation.

"Ellie's a quarter Lebanese. She learned both Arabic and French growing up. She's not close to her family here. The Lebanese side is very traditional as you might imagine, so they don't accept her for who she is. But she loves the culture. She went to Lebanon a couple times as a kid with her family. She returned solo after high school and made what she loved about it her own, free from all the negativity that her grandmother's family had brought with it. Ellie's connection with her heritage is beautiful when I think about it."

I thought so, too. I loved seeing the smile on her face as she spoke with Amir. I loved the look on his face, too. His English had been passable, but as hee spoke his native language, it became clear that he was vibrant and highly educated.

It was so easy to misjudge people in New York—to sell them short. Everyone had so many facets to them, that often remained hidden by the difficulty of making a life here. Although I couldn't understand his words, the depth of Amir's character showed through his eyes as he spoke. I had misjudged Ellie, too—the piano player in our little show—who, it turned out, spoke at least three languages and had traveled the world. Somehow, through this fascinating life she had led, she found the time to become a pretty mean piano player. The piano players in my life always turned out to be more interesting than they first seemed.

I finished my hot dog with a sensuous mix of pleasure and guilt. Ellie turned toward us.

"You want to go to a Lebanese night club?"

"Seriously?" said Heather.

"Right now?" I asked.

"Amir's cousin runs a club. It's only three blocks from here."

I was about to point out that it was midnight on a Sunday but remembered in time how ridiculously *small town* of me that would have sounded. "Let's go!" I said instead.

First there was the matter of closing up the hot dog cart. Amir was quick about it, turning off the heat, folding flaps up, locking and securing it together, changing it from a small restaurant into a vehicle as if it were a transformer toy. We helped him push and steer the thing three blocks north through the late-night pedestrians who didn't think this whole production seemed strange at all. Heather and I were in cocktail dresses and high heels and still had our stage makeup on.

We arrived at a 1960s high-rise, sheltered between the bustle of the Avenues. Nobody would have suspected there was a night club anywhere on the block. Amir unlocked a gate, and we pushed the hot dog cart into a narrow alley. He undid the padlock on a garage door and lifted it up by hand. We wheeled the thing in and locked it in for the night. We returned to the front of the building and went inside. The security manager recognized Amir and smiled. We took the elevator to the ninth floor.

I wasn't at all prepared for what greeted us when the elevator doors opened. We stepped into a festive room, dimly lit and loud with laughter and music. It smelled of hookah and spice and perfume. It was night club music playing, but with a distinctly Arabic twist. I'd never heard anything quite like it, but I loved it, and it made my body want to move. Everyone was dancing. When they saw the four of us enter, they pulled us right in. I had been feeling tired when we left the restaurant, but now I thought I might dance all night.

Those elevator doors seemed to have teleported us straight from New York to Beirut. The style of the dancing was different, but Heather and I caught on quickly to dance movements of other women in the club. The two of us had been learning choreographies with only one or two reps since we were little girls. Ellie didn't pick up the dance, but she spoke the language, so she fit in just fine. Best of all, the people were so welcoming. We were there to celebrate life with them, and that was enough.

I don't know how long we danced—it must have been at least two hours. It was only afterwards that I thought about the fact that—as far as I could tell—there had been no alcohol served at this Lebanese club, and I hadn't even missed it. The energy of the people, the music, the movement and the joy for living had been a far better buzz than drinking.

I had to take a local train back uptown after we said goodnight to our new friends. As the train lurched to a stop every six or eight blocks underground, I felt my energy dwindle, and my eyelids grew heavy.

Finally, back in my uptown apartment, I stood in our closet-sized kitchen gulping down a glass of water. The dancing had sobered me up, but I'd had way too much wine and champagne earlier. What a night!

I set the glass down and began to collect the pins from my hair. Once my mane was set free, I shook it out and massaged my throbbing scalp.

This had been exactly why I moved to New York City. I had already succeeded —no matter what happened next. Still, I wanted to dance in bigger shows on bigger stages with brighter lights. I wanted to get paid to perform, not just to teach. I needed to get back out there and sign up for some auditions. But right now—my feet aching from dancing, my head buzzing from music and wine, my heart emotional—I savored the moment.

I had lived a season in lights. Whatever came next, no one could ever take that away from me.

Act II

....

Chapter Eight

....

2019

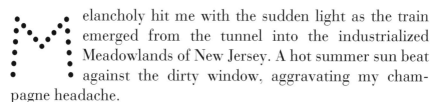elancholy hit me with the sudden light as the train emerged from the tunnel into the industrialized Meadowlands of New Jersey. A hot summer sun beat against the dirty window, aggravating my champagne headache.

Here I was, unable to resist the pull of that damned train ticket my mother forced on me, or my own guilt sending me back to be with my little sister. I told Nikki I'd probably be back in a few days. I texted Tom from the train telling him maybe a week or two. It was hard to say when I didn't know myself. I'm not even sure what my mother expected. Yes, I owed it to Andrea, but surely she had moved past all that by now. Had I?

The uncertainty worried me as the ruthless city I loved and struggled against faded behind me. I was afraid to give up, afraid to feel satisfied with the small successes. It was the wrong time to take a rest from the city, although as soon as I reached Lancaster taking a rest would be awfully tempting.

I closed my eyes against the painful sun and dull landscape. My mind drifted ahead of the train toward home. My father might be a little rounder than the last time I saw him. I loved him more than any person in the world, and yet it had been important for me to get away from him too. His poor health and lack of ambition (I always wondered which came first) created an energy I didn't want to absorb, as much as I cared for him.

Andrea would surely look even more beautiful than when I last saw her, despite whatever destructiveness she was up to. I'd find out if Mom's worries had been warranted, or just a way for her to pull me back home. I would be able to tell quickly if Andrea was really in danger or just blowing off steam… if she needed an intervention, or just a friend. If it came to it, I could handle another intervention if needed. Being a friend was somehow harder. With us, it was pretty complicated.

I wasn't proud of the feelings I'd had about my sister growing up, but at least I finally understood them. It would have been hard for anyone, after being an only child for seven years, to welcome a new sibling into her life. Then to watch that sibling be fawned over as the cutest baby and most adorable little girl. Meanwhile I grew into a gangly teenager with unruly hair who the boys laughed at. All I had was my dancing, but at least I felt I was getting pretty good. Then Andrea, barely ten, began to show a talent for drawing. This caught everyone's attention. As I became a grown woman, Andrea emerged into a rare beauty, with the prettiest face and a perfect, petite feminine figure.

None of this was Andrea's fault. She *was* talented, yet I resented her successes, convinced that her looks were the real reason doors opened for her. No one ever knew how I felt. I'd gotten really good at burying it inside. Certainly, my little sister had no idea; she who had always looked up to me with the admiration I craved from everyone else. Not until I sabotaged her big chance with my own recklessness, leaving us both with a bitter price to pay.

My jealousy came to a head as Andrea finished high school. I had been dating Alex, my ex-husband, for almost two years at the time. We talked about getting married, but I had reservations—ones I should have heeded. At twenty-four, in a steady relationship with a good guy, marriage felt like the next step. Could I really hope for anything better?

Andrea had never done much with her art. She never let her paintings be displayed, always saying she wasn't quite finished with them. But the teachers saw her talent and recommended her for a prestigious painting intensive in Paris the summer after her graduation. It was a big chance for her, and though expensive, our parents tried to figure out a way to make it happen.

I was furious. When had my parents offered me a chance to do something like that with my dancing? There were ballet academies every summer in Philadelphia, close to home. No one ever thought of sending me to those. And now they were going to pay for Andrea to go to Paris? I had always dreamed of going to Europe. It was so unfair. I took it personally.

While they were still trying to work out the details, I pushed Alex to propose, then joyously announced that we were getting married that fall. Neither Alex nor I had any money, so the bill fell to my parents. How could they have said no? I didn't demand a huge wedding, but there was still no way they could pay for both a wedding and a trip to Paris. Andrea's big chance was snatched away.

She knew what I had done, but what could she say? Who would deny their sister a wedding?

"Couldn't you have waited one more year to get married?" Andrea finally asked. It was the only time we would ever discuss it.

"But I'm in love!" I declared, still trying to convince myself. "Isn't my happiness more important than a vacation?"

"It's not a vacation," she snapped. "This could have been my big chance as a painter."

"You're never going to be a painter and you know it. You can't finish a single piece."

They were cruel words. The kind of painful barbs only a sibling could muster, piercing straight to the heart of my sister's worst insecurities.

The wedding happened in October, just after my twenty-fifth birthday. My enjoyment of it was tinged with guilt, and fear that I had rushed things. This obviously proved true as Alex and I only lasted five years. Meanwhile Andrea went to Temple and flamed out of the art program.

Sometimes, during my worst bouts of depression, I had wondered if my failed, miserable marriage was my repayment for what I'd done to Andrea.

I was finished with the resentment. The years had helped me see the pointlessness. I wanted to be glad for Andrea's beauty and talent. I wanted her to succeed as an artist. I wish I could have learned by my mid-twenties what I knew now, at almost thirty-four. Sadly, by the time life's lessons are learned, the damage of life is often already done. I hoped for the chance to make up to Andrea for the wrong I had done her.

As the train began to slow, I looked out and saw everything as I remembered it. Houses, cars, even the shapes of the trees looked familiar. I breathed in deeply as I stepped out through the train door into the summer heat. Despite the proximity of the trains, the air was a lot cleaner than in the city. I could smell the hot cut grass of nearby lawns and the more distant odors of farms. I could hear individual cars as they drove by, and words as people talked with each other on the adjacent street. I had grown used to the traffic noise and my neighbors' voices merging into a cacophony. The way people talked, even the speed at which they drove, felt familiar.

It was all intoxicatingly comfortable.

The comfort was part of the danger for me. Without a purpose, without activity, without dancing, would I be able to keep my demon at bay? Already I imagined I could hear it laughing with delight, waiting to take me back into its clutches.

It would be so easy to slip back into the old life and the old resentments. The old and familiar depression. I wanted to be back as soon as possible in my Upper West Side apartment with Nikki... or even better, in Tom's Hell's Kitchen flat. I wanted to arrange more work, maybe set up auditions for another show. Most of all I wanted to be where everybody was busy with their own thing and had no time to worry about other people's problems.

I'm stronger now, I told myself, *I'm a New Yorker.* This trip had a purpose, a good one, and in two weeks, three at the most, I'd be back in the city auditioning for another show, back in the city that had finally given me a sliver of a chance.

Nine months was the longest I had ever been away from this house. Even during my married years, I lived so close that I stopped by here once a week or more. I noticed that the bushes below the front porch looked smaller than I remembered, even though they should have grown bigger. I noticed that the neighbors had painted their house, and my parents probably should have thought about painting their own. Opening the door, I noticed the smell. It wasn't a bad smell, or a good one either; it was simply the house's essence. I had never noticed it before, but now I knew that it had been the unique smell of this house for longer than I could remember. All the little things I noticed when I walked into my childhood home surprised me.

Dad was alone in the living room.

"There she is, my big Broadway star!"

"In my dreams! Hi Dad."

He beamed at me from his chair. I had been prepared to smile as if I didn't see that he looked worse than when I left. But he only looked *a little* worse and that pleased me. I hurried to hug his broad shoulders before he tried to stand.

"It's so good to see you, honey. I've missed you so much."

"I've missed you too, Dad."

"I would have come last weekend, but your mother wouldn't let me."

"She was right. It would have been a tough trip and that crazy little theatre isn't exactly handicap accessible."

"Oh, whatever!"

"Would you like to see a clip from the show?"

I pulled up Facebook on my phone and found the video of the number I danced with Darnell. His girlfriend Tiffany had filmed it and posted it earlier. I stood behind Dad, with one arm around his shoulder and the other held in front of him with the phone. So close to him, I noticed how thin his hair was. It was the same color as mine, but while my hair was thick and curly, his was wispy, with not quite enough of it to cover his scalp.

We talked for about half an hour, then I asked Dad if there was anything he wanted. He asked if I'd take him to the Giant. Going to a grocery store was the last thing I wanted to do. I could have used a nap. But I really had nothing but time, so I helped him into the car, put his walker into the trunk, and backed out of the garage.

I couldn't understand why my parents still kept this old Plymouth when my mom had her Honda. I suppose it would be hard for my dad to admit that his driving days had ended. And why not, with a two-car garage and all. Here I was thinking like a New Yorker, where every square inch was worth its weight in gold and extra stuff had to be continually purged. I was glad they still had the second car, so I could use it while I was here.

Much as it had surprised me that going to the Giant was Dad's first request, once I was following him as he pushed his walker down the aisles, I understood. He probably hadn't been to a grocery store in ages. Mom was so busy, working all day, doing all the cooking, cleaning, caring for him, and yes, shopping on her own. It had been a small ordeal getting him in and out of the car. No way she would bring him with her when she did her errands. She wouldn't have the time and he would feel guilty asking. The whole errand would take her twice as long. Such a small thing, but I realized the gift I had given my dad just to get him out of the house to do something familiar— something normal.

I got myself a coconut water and drank it as I followed Dad through the store. It helped my headache right away.

Andrea texted me as Dad and I were on our way home. I glanced at it even though I was driving and shouldn't have. I had texted her from the train to tell her I was coming back.

"Come to the house," I quickly typed and sent from the next stoplight, then stuck my phone back into my purse between the two front seats. When it buzzed again a moment later, I resisted the urge to look until we were parked in front of the house.

An hour later Andrea came over. I had started unpacking my bag in my old bedroom, which was now a guest room. None of my childhood things were there anymore, but the bed, dresser and desk were the same. It was all familiar yet odd.

I hugged my sister tight, her chin lifted onto my shoulder, my nose in her dark hair. She looked amazing, yet like she didn't care, just as always. But I could see a little of what my mom had alluded to. There was weariness in her eyes. It may have partly been caused by late nights, too much alcohol and maybe some other stuff—who knows? But that wasn't the real problem. It was the exhaustion of a monotonous life. I recognized it all too well from the last few years of my marriage.

"Want to get out of here for a while?" she asked. "There's a fun new brewery at Penn Square. We could catch happy hour if we go now."

"Sure. Why not?"

"Don't change into something fancy or anything. You look great. That t-shirt's super cute."

"Okay."

Now that I was settled, I had thought about changing out of my jeans, which I had worn for the air-conditioned train car. Despite the heat of the day, I would probably be glad to keep them on because wherever we went would likely blast cold air at me, too.

"Just let me touch up my face so I don't look like I rolled off a train car. Even though I did."

She followed me into the bathroom while I got out my makeup.

"Let me guess, when Mom was up in the City she asked you to come back to be a good influence on me?"

I laughed. I had anticipated this question and was ready with a response.

"She said you could use a friend. Couldn't we all? But it's also for Dad. It's hard for him to have me away."

She nodded.

"Timing's good," I added. "My show just ended and nothing much happens in the city in the summer. Everyone who can afford it goes off to the Hamptons."

"I wish I'd come up to see your show. I'll come for the next one."

"I hope there is a next one."

"There will be."

We were both silent for a few minutes. I was looking forward to telling Andrea all about the show, the crazy cast, the magic of last night at the Italian restaurant and Lebanese nightclub. I'd save all that for later.

"So how *are* you, really?" I asked her. "I heard what Mom says, but I want to hear it from you. I'm sorry I'm so bad about calling to catch up."

"Not like I'm any better. What did Mom say?"

"Can't you guess after you passed out wasted on her couch, when you don't even live here?"

She laughed. "That night was cray-cray! I don't even know what the hell happened or how I got back here. But it was just once. I'm not really like that, you know."

"Oh." I paused with my brush and looked at her. She knew what I was thinking, I didn't have to say it.

"It wasn't like that other time, when you took me to the E.R. *Trust me*, I know. I may not remember, but I know. Mom's just a worry wart."

She went back to the bedroom.

"You been painting at all?" I asked.

"Actually yeah."

"Really, can I see?"

"Uh, no."

I laughed. "Fine, be that way."

I almost had my face to a place where I didn't mind looking back at it in the mirror.

"Are you dating anyone?" she asked.

"I guess. Not exactly."

"What do you mean? Either you are or you aren't. Or are you trying to say you're just fucking someone?"

Damn her. She made it sound so crass.

"Sure. Yeah." It was easier to just agree than to try to explain right now, even though there was nothing crass about what I had with Tom.

"Good for you. Glad to hear you're lightening up a bit post-marriage. Got a picture?"

"I'll show you one later."

I hoped she'd forget because I actually didn't want to show her a picture of Tom. The only one I had on my phone was his professional headshot, which I'd found online. He wasn't on Facebook. I didn't want Andrea to comment on his age—obvious in his distinguished headshot—or on the fact that I was seeing a black man as if it was some kind of novelty. Maybe I was judging her unfairly, but I didn't want to find out right then.

"I'm ready. Let's go" I grabbed my purse and started down the stairs.

As I lay in bed that night, I tried to think about New York, but all my senses were bluntly reminded of where I was. The faint smells of the room, and of the yard through the cracked window were just like they were in my childhood. So were the sounds of the town outside, even the crunch of the gravel of the alley as the neighbor brought his car around to the garage, just like he had done every night for 20 years.

I couldn't believe I had gone out again—on a Monday no less!—after my escapades of the night before. But it was good to spend time with Andrea. We started laughing together after we got a few sips into our beers. I'd say it was like old times, but it was better, since we were different people now. There was so much history between the two of us that it was hard not to remember old hurts, even little annoyances from the past. I tried instead to hang out with her as if she was a new friend, despite the shared stories we were laughing about that evening. Unfairly, you tend to be more forgiving of a stranger than of family. I would try to forgive Andrea for everything. I hoped she would be as generous to me.

I closed my eyes, trying to recall what it felt like to fall asleep in Tom's arms. It had only been a few nights, but it felt like much longer. So much had happened since I went back to his apartment on Friday after my opening show.

Was he thinking about me too? I thought about calling him. It wasn't that late. But I didn't know what I would say, or what I wanted him to say to me. That wasn't the type of relationship we had. There was no way that me calling him at a time like this, in this kind of mood, would in any way make him think better of me, or be more attracted to me. I just had to get back to the City before he forgot about me.

I slept in the next morning, so I didn't see my mom until she got home from work on Tuesday. She asked me if Andrea and I had "talked" when we went out. I just laughed. We had talked for hours, but not the way Mom meant. It had been clear to me when my mom asked me to come home, that Andrea needed a friend, not someone to "talk" to. Deep inside, I think Mom knew that as well.

I was ready to start fresh with Mom, too. What would any of us—Andrea, Dad, me—do without her being there for us? She rubbed us all the wrong way sometimes, but she knew what we needed. She even had the wisdom to know when our needs required someone other than herself. Right now, she knew that what Andrea and Dad both needed was me.

Chapter Nine

· ·

Summer 1986

o this is when it starts to get tough, thought Tom. The rent on his apartment had remained constant, but by the fourth check he wrote, it felt like the sum had been raised each month. In April and May, he and his brother made a little more than they spent. June and July were another matter.

The restless pace of New York City slowed dramatically as the summer sun blasted its sticky heat onto the concrete and steel. Those with means went on vacation in Europe, or to spend their weekends in the Hamptons or at the Cape.

Tom and Art's regular gig was suspended until the fall. They worked to arrange one-off shows, but restaurants weren't hiring musicians as often in the summer. They were lucky to get a paying gig once every couple of weeks. Ballet classes were less regular in the summer, too. With all the tourists in town, Art did pretty well playing his sax in Central Park, but the brothers struggled to meet their expenses.

The light schedule gave Tom several hours each morning to practice at the ballet studio before classes. He appreciated the blessing and tried to trust that his work would eventually have a financial reward. He didn't have money to buy sheet music and scores, but there was more music in the under-belly of Lincoln

Center than anyone knew what to do with. Charles knew enough people to allow him to borrow as much as he wanted.

Tom and Art had kept in touch with the man who first gave them their first jazz gig. Though Marcus was a small-time talent agent, he was nonetheless popular with musicians in the City desperate for work.

After ballet class on a Tuesday evening in July, Tom walked down to 72nd Street to meet Art for yet another audition. This one was for a Midtown steakhouse experimenting with live music on the weekends. The proprietor didn't have anything specific in mind, so Marcus lined up musicians of various styles to play for him. Tom and Art walked up four narrow flights of stairs and waited on a cramped landing between two studios for the prior act to finish.

It was a multi-purpose art studio, with a ballet barre and mirror on one side, and the piano on the other. Bins of costume pieces and props were piled high on the near wall by the door. It was a hot night. A fan whirred laboriously in the corner. The windows on the far wall were all thrown open, looking straight across the narrow street to fourth floor apartments. Small decks dotted the building across at haphazard angles. It was like the dance studio was sitting in five or six different living rooms. Two TVs shined obtrusively into the studio. If Tom had looked hard enough, he could have seen what was on. One couple was sitting down to dinner. A haggard woman stood on her deck in a satin slip with a cigarette, shamelessly watching them. Surely what she saw here night after night was better than what her neighbors could find on their TVs.

Marcus and the restaurant proprietor sat down as Tom and Art began to play. After the first song, the proprietor leaned toward Marcus and commented that their music would sound better with drums and bass. Marcus reminded him that four musicians were out of his budget. Tom and Art caught each other's eyes. No words needed to be said.

Of course, they would sound better with drums and bass! They could have brought the guys they played with in the spring, but you could only cut a show check so many ways if everyone still wanted to eat. But what would you be willing to do to get the gig? Marcus asked them to play one more song, then they packed up. The proprietor shook both their hands, seeming to have liked their music. You never really knew until you got that phone call.

As they walked back through the waiting area between studios, a girl with a stack of music under her arm stood up to follow them in. Tom couldn't help but turn and look at her. Her summer dress revealed smooth dark skin and a striking figure. Her pretty face was framed by thick curly hair. She was black, but Tom could tell she wasn't local. An unmistakable breath of the islands hovered about her. His eyes caught hers for a moment before she looked away.

Tom and Art were halfway down the stairs when Marcus came running after them.

"Tom, hold up." He turned as Marcus caught up and paused to catch his breath. "That little lady who came in after you… her pianist stood her up. Can you come back up and play for her?"

"She a singer? What style?"

"Yeah. She's Dominican. Sings Latin jazz. I know that's not really your thing, but you could manage a couple tunes. Help a sister out."

Playing a couple tunes for that lovely girl was the thing Tom wanted to do most in life right then, even if he knew nothing about Latin music. He and Art followed Marcus back upstairs.

Back in the studio Tom extended his hand and introduced himself.

"*Hola.* I'm Vallia." She gave him her hand and smiled. She handed him a lead sheet for *Begin the Biguine.* "Do you know this one?"

"Sure."

He sat down on the piano bench. Vallia leaned forward. "Like so," she snapped her fingers and began swaying to the rhythm she wanted. Tom smelled coconut and hibiscus in her hair. She was intoxicating.

As he started playing, she stepped away from the piano, still swaying her body, and began to sing. The old woman on the deck across the street lit another cigarette and watched with interest. Art relaxed into a chair with one leg draped over the other. Tom worked hard to follow the girl's feel of the song and give her room to interpret it. Her voice was good, and her sensual stage presence alone would get her work. But her style was undeveloped. With training she could really be something.

He could already guess her story. Back home in the DR she was probably the best singer in her little town. Maybe she had even earned a living performing in Santo Domingo. Like so many others, she thought she could come to New York, get discovered, and hit the big time. But what she really needed was a voice coach to develop her style and who had money for music lessons? There were so many good musicians here and only the very best got the breaks. It was the same for him and Art. Unless Tom committed to working his jazz chops, they would be stuck working for these small-time gigs. But Tom was only practicing his classical music, hoping his break would come there.

Vallia sang one more song, then Marcus thanked her, and she left the room, followed by Tom and Art. Another act had been waiting and ducked inside.

"Thank you so much," she said at the top of the stairs, kissing Tom on the cheek. He felt the wisps of her hair brush his neck, felt her chest press slightly against his own. "You saved me."

"My pleasure," Tom replied. "Say, can I call you sometime. I'd love to get to know you."

She laughed pleasantly. "Sorry, *chico*. I have no time for love."

She was already half a flight down the stairs. Art grinned and jabbed Tom in the ribs.

The brothers walked home in the twilight, zigzagging the short blocks south and long blocks west. Whenever they walked west, the low sun was in their eyes, shining orange against the brick buildings. Art talked most of the way, but Tom only half listened. His thoughts were of Vallia: her silky, accented voice, the scent of her hair when she leaned low toward him at the piano, the smooth glow of her skin. She was right, neither of them had time for love. He had no money to date either. But he would have liked to find a way with her.

Turning onto their block, the garbage from each apartment building was piled in organized mounds in front of each brownstone, ready for the morning pickup. Tom glanced at their own pile, amazed at how much garbage the city produced and somehow eliminated each and every day.

All his life Tom had tried to carve a life for himself different from the one destiny offered to him. Yet much as he rebelled against the drug-ruled street life that ruined his father and pulled at his brother, Tom's instincts knew and recognized the evil even when it lurked in the shadows. As the last beam of western sun shot down the sidewalk, Tom's eyes didn't miss the flash against a thin slice of metal in the garbage bag he recognized as their own.

He stooped to look closer. It was a needle that had worked itself free and punctured the plastic garbage bag. He began to tear at the bag. His brother had continued down the steps toward their door.

"What the hell is this?"

Tom pulled out a small syringe, the kind sold on the street for single hits of heroin. Two more syringes fell out of a makeshift wrapper of paper towels.

"Whoa, whoa." Art scampered back up the steps, his hands outstretched. "Careful with those."

Tom was furious but forced himself not to shout on the sidewalk. Art took the syringe from his brother, stuck it back in the hole in the bag and tied up the tear in a careless knot. As soon as they walked into the apartment, Tom grabbed his arm, pulled him inside and roughly shoved him in a chair.

"What the hell is wrong with you? You can't be using. Not here!"

Tom could see Art had been trying to think up a lie but now he reverted to self-defense.

"I've only done it a couple times. I'm no junky or nothing."

"Look how easily I found out. What if the garbage man saw it and called the cops?"

"I'll be more careful."

"Damn it, no you won't because you won't do it again! If you ever take one more hit here, you're out."

Art lurched to his feet. "The hell you'd kick me out. How'd you pay rent on your own? I earn more in a day in the park than you do with your faggot dancers. You can't afford to kick me out. Mama wouldn't let you either. What's it to you if I spend my own money to feel good once in a while?"

Tom took a deep breath to calm down, then looked his brother straight in the eyes.

"Look, I'm not upset that you're spending money. That shit'll ruin you, but it's not even that either."

He paused to make sure Art was listening.

"The thing you gotta know is if you're buying on the streets, D will find you."

"He could find us if he tried hard enough whether I'm buying or not. Look how easily he found you when you went home to visit Mama. How do you know he didn't follow you back?"

"Maybe he did. But as long as you're clean he'll probably leave us alone. Once word gets to him that you're using, it'll be time for you to pay your debts. He'll have that on you to pull you back in."

Art stood up and walked into the kitchen. His attitude was dismissive, but Tom could tell he was hearing him.

"He'll never find out," said Art. "I was careful."

"It's his job to find out. A man like D makes it his business to know who's buying and who's selling. Even all the way down here. That's why I won't have it as long as you're living here. You can do whatever the hell you like with your own life, but don't pull me down with you."

"Fine. I'll quit."

Art said it in a tone that forced the conversation closed. Tom was unconvinced. He didn't know how often his brother had used… he never seemed high. But even if it was a rare thing, quitting heroin was no easy task. He didn't expect his brother to be motivated by health and sobriety alone. But he sure hoped Art took seriously the threat of being pulled back into the dark world he narrowly escaped several years ago.

●　　●　　●

"I hate summer," Charles snapped as soon as the final students had left the studio.

Tom leaned his elbows down on the piano.

"You saw them today," Charles continued. "How am I supposed to teach a group of tourists like that? Every girl at a different level. I'll never see a single one of them again, so I'll never even know if they improve."

"Is that why you do it?"

"I want to create something beautiful. If I can create something beautiful in one of these girls, that satisfies me." Charles reached behind himself to the barre and absently made little circles with the point of his toe while he spoke. "I need every day to mean something and today sure didn't seem to mean much."

"Maybe it did, though. Maybe you did inspire something beautiful in one of those girls."

"But I'll never know. They'll be back in Topeka and I'll be here."

Tom smiled. "So that's what it is. You want the satisfaction of *knowing* what you did."

Charles smirked. "I am an egotistical old man."

"Stop calling yourself an old man. What are you, forty-five? Look at it this way. Those girls today came from all over the country. This class may have been the highlight of their summer. They'll go home to their small town ballet studio and tell about the time they got to dance at Lincoln Center just the way they always imagined it …with a grouchy gay teacher who yelled at them."

Charles laughed aloud.

"Think about it. Maybe this experience today inspires one girl to work harder, and she becomes a star. You will have created something beautiful, just the same as with the girls you've worked with for years."

Charles spun in place, then rested in third position. It surprised Tom to recognize the ballet positions and movements by name now, even though he'd never danced a step in his life.

"Is that what you think about to be able to stand playing this soulless music you hate?"

Now Tom laughed. "I actually hadn't thought of it. This is just a means to an end. Any playing is valuable practice. I'm egotistical too. I still hope for my day on stage."

Charles looked Tom intently in the eyes. "You *hope* for your day on stage. But have you really visualized it?"

Tom didn't answer.

"What did you think, that night when I took you out to the square and we looked at the theatres? Did you see yourself on those stages?"

"It's hard to visualize myself being part of that world…"

Charles walked over to the piano and set his hand on Tom's back.

"Let me tell you something about New York City. This is one of the few places, maybe the only place left in the country where the class system is still alive and well. When you're in one New York City you don't even see people, who are in a different class than you, even though they're brushing shoulders with you every day. You and I are the subway class. I bet everyone you know is in the subway class. Artists and workers, just struggling to make ends meet.

"There's another class going to work in their cars, splashing you as you walk on the sidewalk. But you never see them, and they never see you. They're in their own world. There's another class altogether who don't work at all, up in the penthouses of the buildings you walk by every day without thinking about it. They come to shows here at Lincoln Center every week. You don't think about them, because they don't touch your world and they don't even see you walking below their perch in the sky. Have you ever been to the top of one of the really tall buildings?"

Tom shook his head.

"You can't even imagine it, the lights spread out as far as you can see."

"I've seen some pictures."

"So you *think* you can imagine it, but you can't. Not until you've really been up there. That's where some people live every day of their lives.

"There's one more class in this city. Down below the subways, in the gutters—the New York of crime and chaos and despair. Maybe you see this world, but you don't touch it and it leaves you alone. But you better believe the class of New York that drives on the streets or hovers in the sky doesn't see it any more than it sees you."

Tom knew this part wasn't entirely true for him. He wouldn't be left alone. Just as that needle of Art's poked through the trash bag, the underbelly of the city would always be reaching out of the gutters, grasping at his ankles.

"Here's something Koch and the rest of those assholes won't tell you about this town: You get to choose your class here. It's not determined by your upbringing. It doesn't matter that you're black or that I'm gay. It doesn't even matter how much money you have. All you've got to do is convince people that you belong. You've got to tell them who you are before they tell you."

Tom sure wanted to believe that was true.

"So, guy, if you believe you belong playing the piano in those theatres, or living up in those penthouses, then that's who you can be. But if you believe you belong playing the cheap jazz clubs in the Village, then *that's* who you will be."

They fell silent.

"I have a confession to make," Charles said at length. "I've stood outside and listened to you practice a few mornings. You're good."

"Thank you." The compliment meant a great deal to Tom coming from a man like Charles, who was usually so critical.

"I took the liberty of mentioning you to a friend of mine whose regular pianist is in Europe. It turns out there are a couple jobs they could use you for. The first is playing background music for some stuffy house party in The Hamptons. Standards, light jazz. Not your favorite stuff, I know, but it pays well. And it'd do you good to see another class in their playground."

"Yeah, of course I'll try out for it."

"No need to audition," said Charles as he walked back to the barre. "They already hired you on my recommendation."

Tom could hardly believe his ears, or the generosity of Charles to think of him.

"The second gig you will have to audition for, but I think you'll get it. They need an accompanist for a Shubert recital a few days after the party."

The sound of many feet echoed in the hall outside. It was time for the next class to begin.

"Where's the recital?" Tom asked.

Charles looked him in the eyes, a small smile creasing his lips.

"Carnegie Hall."

Chapter Ten

·····················

Summer 2019

t took me less than a week in Lancaster to fall back into the clutches of my demon.

I should have seen it coming. Why the hell didn't I see it coming? My depression was as familiar to me as everything else in this damn town. Hadn't I known the danger the moment Mom stretched out her hand with that train ticket?

By the third day home I was questioning my choice. Why had I allowed myself to be pressured into it? Andrea was fine. That was clear to me right away. She was a little down about the current state of her life, and drinking a little too much to compensate, but she wasn't going off the rails, or to the ER again. No wonder she felt down; she was *here*. Now I was too.

I had to get back to New York. I needed to schedule classes, auditions, anything. It would have to be something that made at least a little money. But it was summer now, and there wasn't much work for dancers. Before I could pick up my computer and my phone and try, I felt exhausted. I'd do it tomorrow, I told myself. One day wouldn't make such a difference. But the next day I was even more exhausted. It was my fifth day back and I spent most of it on my bed.

There in my room, all my worries crashed in on me at once. They crushed me with weight that felt physical, pressing down on my chest, and pressing in on the sides of my head. Would I ever have another show in New York? Would I even get back to New York? It had been five days but felt like an uncrossable chasm had opened. By the time I did make it back, would Tom have found another girl to have fun with? Because that's all I really was to him, right? He didn't love me, not in the way that really meant something. We'd never marry. We'd never have children together, so what was I doing? Didn't I still want those things? I did, didn't I? Or did I want the easy joy of what I'd shared with Tom?

I called him, thinking the sound of his voice might quiet the tirade within me, but he didn't answer. I didn't leave a message but as soon as I hung up, I wondered if I should have. What kind of girl calls and hangs up? But it would have been worse to leave a message in my current state. I would have said something, or even just let my tone of voice give me away as a total mess. What would he think of me? God, why did I overthink it so much? He probably didn't think of me at all. Now I really wanted to leave a message. It was all I could do to keep my finger from hitting the call button again.

I started crying.

What was the point of any of it? How long could I live like this, always only a dollar better than broke? What if I got hurt and couldn't dance? Then I *would* be broke and broken and the dream would be over. It already was, wasn't it?

I was down the rabbit-hole, lost and panicked.

At dinnertime, I claimed a headache and stayed in my room. By the next morning the crying phase was over, and the worst part had begun. I recognized every stage in the process, but I still couldn't stop it. The only part I never seemed to remember was how to come out of it.

My demon had beaten me again. For how long, I couldn't know. Days? Months? Never yet years, but close.

That was what I called my depression—my demon. It helped me to think of it as an *other* that possessed me.

I have struggled with depression since I was about fourteen. It comes and goes. When it comes back, it cripples me on the inside, even as I function normally in public.

After the worries came the regrets. If regret had stopped at my decision to come here on Monday, I could have fixed it, boarded a night train and been back in the city by dawn. But my regret ran deeper, twisting into the mud of past decisions that could never be undone.

Why hadn't I taken a chance on my dancing years ago, when I had more margin for error? Why did I marry Alex? Why did I divorce him? Why did I sabotage Andrea? How could I have been so stupid as to leave my fun, well-paying teaching gig at the local college to follow a pipe dream to New York, taking such satisfaction in an unpaid show in a crumbling theatre no one had heard of? How different might my life be if I had done things differently back in my early twenties? There was no going back though, and there would be no chance for a do-over because life didn't work that way. Maybe my time in New York this year was my chance and even that hadn't been much of one and what was even the point?

That next day I wanted to stay in my room, but I knew that would make things worse. Mom would have worried and become over-caring. Just my luck, she was home that day. I always had that kind of bad luck. I lugged myself out of bed, took twice as long as normal to make myself presentable, then went downstairs with a smile on my face and a silent scream in my chest.

Mom talked about Andrea all day, asking me how she was doing and what we had talked about. By the time I escaped to my room at night, I was furious. When had she asked how *I* was doing, or really looked at me long enough to see that I was crushed by depression and loneliness? Shouldn't she have been able to see it in her own daughter. I knew it was grossly unfair of me, even though I was angry about it. Mom didn't know because I was so damn good at hiding it. I had been a master at hiding my depression for nearly two decades.

I've never told anyone. I probably never will. I've never trusted someone enough to talk about it. I suspect there are a lot of people like me out there, but I'll never know—none of us will, because we don't tell each other what we're going through. The truth is, I'm embarrassed. I don't have any excuse to be depressed. I had a good childhood as childhoods go. My marriage was unfulfilling but other women have had it far worse. My husband never inflicted physical or serious emotional damage on me. I've been healthy my whole life and I've followed my dreams. I imagine anybody, whom I told about my depression would tell me to buck up and get over it; think of all the people who are really suffering. So I don't tell anybody.

Depression is tied to unhappiness, but it's not a direct link. It's not as simple as cause and effect. Trust me, I've spent way too much time thinking about it. I've been unhappy without being depressed and I've been depressed a lot more often than I've been unhappy. For a while I thought it was tied to a lack of hope, but that doesn't explain it either.

It felt like a thick cloud, cold and wet, had descended upon and enveloped my heart. It was like the fog that covers a lake or a bay, oppressive and endless. The fog had weight to it. I would long for a sliver of sun to shoot through, heralding a clear afternoon. But the break wouldn't come. The fog got thicker and colder.

I was exhausted but couldn't sleep.

I tried to hide my tired eyes the next day with a smile. Conversation made my skin crawl. When I couldn't stand smiling any longer, I went outside. It was too hot for a walk, the air thick and choking. Each step was an effort. Was I the same girl who leaped lightly across a New York City stage only a week ago? I didn't feel like that girl as I labored one step in front of the next.

Every block had a memory. These were the streets where Andrea and I had ridden our bikes as kids, always a little farther than what we considered the arbitrary boundaries set by our parents. Lancaster was a good town to grow up in. But it wasn't a town to stay in. I wish I'd realized that sooner than I did. Everything was so quiet, so quaint. I never thought about my hometown that way growing up. Most people referred to Lancaster as a small city, but now I had the real city to compare it to. I envied Tom the lifetime he had lived in New York City. He must have seen me as such a small-town girl.

Maybe that's who I really was. Maybe I didn't have the toughness to work my way to a successful career in the city, the way Tom had.

Before long I was drenched in sweat and exhausted like I'd run a marathon. I turned around, dismayed that I had three blocks to go back to my parents' house. It was tempting to just sit down on the curb and try to wait it out. Even if that took forever. If there had been any shade, I might have done just that.

Finally, I was back at the house, intending to return to the seclusion of my room, but I could tell Dad wanted to talk … poor Dad, who had so many actual reasons to be depressed, yet took on each exhausting day with joy. I sat down, smiled and talked, overcome with guilt. The guilt made me all the more determined to hide my despair.

Then I was back to the seclusion of my room, where I could curl into a ball on my bed and wait for life to go passing by. I thought about getting out my laptop and watching a movie or a show. TV had been a reliable distraction for me in the past, but this afternoon it felt like too much of an effort to pick something to watch. It was easier just to lie there.

I didn't take a shower that day. I didn't have the energy for it. The next day, I really needed one, especially because of that ill-advised walk in the heat, but it took me an hour of thinking about it before I could make myself do it. Even then I wondered if I could get away with not washing my hair, which would cut the task by half. But I did wash it, and dry it, and go downstairs again with a smile on my face, because that's what I do. That's how I hide. I've been doing it for years.

What was the point? I'd have to shower again tomorrow and a thousand more times just to keep from descending into the filth and chaos that was always reaching out for us. Because life itself was little more than a slow-motion race to the bottom, an effort to hold back death and decay which was doomed to fail.

How did a shower become an existential crisis? I really needed to get a hold of myself.

How long had it been? Almost two years, I thought. It lasted a couple months that time and when it was over—when I finally danced my way out of it—I immediately made plans to move to New York. My demon never bothered me there.

The worst time was the middle year of my marriage. My depression lasted nearly a full year that time. I remember mornings when I would put up a good show until Alex left for work, then nearly collapse from exhaustion. I had to leave two hours later than him (they never scheduled college dance classes early) and it would be all I could do to drag one foot in front of the other to the garage and into my car. Most nights I'd watch TV for hours, until the distraction no longer worked. I could have quit. Alex could have supported us. But I couldn't let that happen for two reasons. First, because then he would know that something was wrong with me. And second, I needed to get into that car each day, because my work was dancing.

Dancing was my only escape, my only joy. So naturally, it became a point of contention between Alex and me. He wanted children, but I didn't want to take time off from dancing. Not yet. I asked him to give me a few more years as a compromise.

The truth was I was terrified to stop dancing. When I was depressed I danced to escape and when I wasn't depressed I danced to keep it at bay. I couldn't tell Alex about that. Instead, I told him that dancing was my career and reminded him that I made almost as much as he did. Why should I have to give up a successful career so he could have a baby? He said I only had to take a break, one quarter off from my classes. But I knew how it would go. I would be pressured to continue to stay home with the baby. Everyone would agree that it was *frivolous* to pay for day care. So I'd take a year off instead of a quarter and then there would be another baby and pretty soon I'd be a stay at home mom who *used to be a dancer.* Always the wife giving up her career.

Then my demon would have me in its clutches, maybe irrevocably. If I ever told anyone after that, they'd assume it was the babies that caused my depression and then I'd be labeled a shitty woman. The worst kind. A mother who resented her kids. Only I'd know that wasn't true. It would be the dancing feet that had been stilled. So I never would have told. I would have suffered alone. Eventually, I probably *would* have started resenting my own kids.

Alex agreed to give me a few years. Then we got divorced. Some compromise.

He had always feared I would choose my dancing over family. In the end, I suppose he was right. Except it was way more complicated than he ever knew.

The worst thing now was not knowing when I'd have the chance to dance again. The very thought of dancing was exhausting. After only a week, I wondered if I still remembered how. Percy's show seemed like a memory from years in my past.

The days began to pass, one after another. I spent them longing for bed. The nights I spent awake and waiting for dawn, with my mind racing through despairing *what ifs.* Whenever I was with my parents or sister, I'd long to be alone. Then when I was alone, often curled in a fetal ball on my bed on a hot afternoon, I'd feel crushingly lonely.

Every time this had happened to me, it felt like the fog of my depression would never lift, and maybe this time it wouldn't. Eventually, surely, the time would come when it wouldn't lift. I started wondering if I should finally give in and seek help, medication, even though I only had something that barely passed as health insurance. But that would require me to tell someone what I was going through, and I couldn't do that, even if it was a doctor. I was too embarrassed. I was scared to take medication, even if it helped. What else might it do to me? If it took away the clouds of depression and replaced them with clouds of lethargy, wouldn't that be worse? I'd read about the stuff people used and the side effects—like bloating and fatigue—killers for a dancer. What if I got hooked on the stuff and the copays were more than I could afford? As long as I could still put on a good face and function normally in public, then I figured I was better off handling this demon on my own.

That middle year of my marriage, when my depression almost didn't ever lift, it was Andrea's episode in the E.R. that snapped me out of it. I didn't know it at the time. Even as I drove her there, passed out and poisoned, I felt the full weight of it. As I sped to the hospital, the worries assailed me the same as always. I was afraid my sister would die and that I would blame myself. It might even be partly deserved. How would I recover from that? Why not just end it all if that happened?

Even in the worst of my depression I've never been suicidal. I was always depressed because I wanted my life to be better, not because I wanted to escape it. But that night, as I anticipated the guilt I'd feel from Andrea's death, I thought about how easy it would be to end the pain. Bring on oblivion!

My sister didn't die though. In the days and weeks that followed, as she rebounded first physically and then emotionally, I had been forced to think less about myself and more about her. She needed me. I was determined to protect her secret. As embarrassed as I was of my own fault, I understood how desperate she was not to let anyone else know how far she'd fallen. Once she was back to normal, and we were both back to our normal lives—maybe even a week after that—I remember waking up and realizing I wasn't depressed anymore. The fog had lifted. I was free again after nearly a year.

Whatever Andrea was going through now didn't require that sort of all-consuming effort. Nothing could distract me from my own misery. I was stupid to come back to Lancaster, this town that swallowed my dreams and crushed my heart. I was supposed to be here to help Andrea through another rough spell, but it was me who needed help. What good would I be to her, or Dad, or anyone like this? I had unraveled quickly.

Maybe it was fitting then, that it was Andrea who ended up providing that help. Back then, it was her crisis that pulled me out of depression. This time, it would be her gift.

My two allotted weeks in Lancaster were almost up before Andrea let me see any of her new work. After a rough first week, the second had been absolute hell for me.

We stood in the alley behind her high school art teacher's house, where concrete steps descended to a basement. Andrea took a key out of her purse and leaned toward the lock of the heavy metal door. Her fine black hair fell straight off the side of her delicate face.

"Promise you'll be kind," she said, before pulling on the door. Her childlike tone touched my heart. It saddened me that she would have to say that, but I had been very cruel to her in the past. Fresh guilt washed over me, with sadness in its wake.

We went inside. She switched on fluorescent lights, giving a harsh yellowness to the broad room. The one small window was half stuffed with an air conditioner, hardly letting in any natural light, even though it was a bright summer day. Andrea turned it on, but I was skeptical that it would be able to tamp down the heat. My eyes first noticed the smooth wood floor and the mirrors that covered one wall, the first things a dancer always observed when entering a room. With stacks of boxes and closed paint buckets in front, the mirror didn't reflect much.

I almost missed the main objects in the chamber: three easels standing at irregular angles, each draped with a sheet that refracted the florescent yellow. They blended in so easily. Beneath the sheets I could now see the shapes of canvases on easels. A paint-bespeckled tarp lay on the floor beneath them. Several blank, prepared canvases leaned against the wall opposite from the mirror. Despite the paint splatters, the entire room seemed to blend into the yellow hue.

"Peter was so generous to let me use the space and his easels," Andrea said. It took me a moment to realize that Peter

was our old high school art teacher, whom I still thought of as
"Mr. Robinson."

"So you *have* been painting."

"Yeah."

Andrea had no idea how much effort it had taken to get me
here today. As much as I hated the monotony of depression, it
took a lot of willpower to step out of the fatigue. I was really
glad now that I had come. I was curious, and curiosity was a
nice change of emotion.

First, I was curious about this beautiful wood floor.

I walked to the center and couldn't help myself. I did a
pirouette and then a double *fouetté* turn. I realized with some
wonder that the dance step had felt easy—less effort than
putting one foot in front of the other.

"That's really why I wanted to bring you here," Andrea said.
"I don't use the whole room. You could practice here. You said
yesterday how much you need to dance. I would enjoy seeing
you dance while I work."

Even though I had just popped off a couple *fouettés* in street
shoes, now that I thought about it, I was nervous. I don't know
why. I needed dancing. But something in me was clinging to the
depression, almost like I didn't want to chase it away.

"Now that I'm here, will you show me what you've been
working on?"

I knew I shouldn't push her. She was clearly shy about it.
Still, she only hesitated for a moment. Bringing me here must
have been the hardest step. She walked to one of the easels and
pulled away the sheet.

I gasped.

Into the drab yellow room shot an explosion of dark color.
Andrea pulled the sheets off the other easels and more vibrance
illuminated the room, transforming the space instantly. My
eyes darted between the three paintings. They were similar
but totally unique. I could see hints of the style I remembered
from Andrea's youth, but this was something new and amazing.
The style was mostly abstract, but with suggestions of human

form and motion. Her mastery of color was incredible. To have painted such dark works that exploded as if with light... it was like nothing I had ever seen before.

"I'm still working on them," she said.

"No, you're not! Don't touch any of these. They're wonderful."

"I was thinking," she stepped over to the first one she had disrobed, "I need a little more blue here."

"No. It's perfect. What you've done with the color... I don't even know how to describe it. Don't risk losing the effect by adding something else. Put your blue on a new one."

"You really think so?"

Andrea always had trouble seeing a project as finished. I used to use that against her. I think today my genuine awe was clear because soon she let me help her take the first painting down and replace it with a fresh canvas. I realized what a big step this was.

I wasn't finished pushing my sister from her comfort zone.

"You need to show these," I said. "Would you be open to selling them?"

"I guess. But who would buy them?"

"You'd be surprised. Just promise me you'll show them. We could find somewhere to hang them for next month's art walk."

"Are three pictures enough for a show?"

I extended my arm toward the blank canvas we had just attached to the easel. "There's number four."

She smiled and began mixing paint. I dashed to the other side of the room and changed my shoes. I always kept a pair of ballet slippers in my purse. I still felt the weight of depression, but I wanted to dance too. I didn't want to give in. I wanted to feel alive again. I slipped to the floor and put on my pointe shoes.

I danced until I was dripping with sweat. When we left, locking up the studio and going to feed our famished bellies, we were already both looking forward to coming back tomorrow. That anticipation was the shaft of sunlight, breaking through the thick clouds over the pool of my heart.

Chapter Eleven

....

1986

hen Tom arrived at the ballet studio, Charles was standing outside the closed door. He pulled off the note that had been taped to the door and handed it to Tom.

"What did I tell you, guy? Summer."

The note said that the 4:00 class had been canceled. The note added that there was a message for Charles in the office.

"Labor Day's next week," said Charles, "then things will be back to normal, thank God."

He started back down the hall. "Let's see what this message is about. We've got an hour to kill."

Tom followed him, remembering the first time he had been at the ballet school's office, the day he auditioned for the job. Since then, he had stopped in every second Friday for his paycheck, but he hadn't seen the school manager since that first day.

"This is your big week," said Charles as they walked the close-walled hall of Lincoln Center. "Two big gigs. I'm happy for you."

Tom smiled.

"I hope you've got something to wear."

"I've got a suit." Tom wished there was money to have it cleaned and pressed, along with the black dress shirt he planned to wear with it. He'd hang it in the shower and run the water hot. That would at least get the wrinkles out.

"A suit?" Charles scowled at him. "You think they'll let you into that Hamptons house in your old high school suit? That's what it is, right? And what about Carnegie Hall, where you've dreamed of playing for years? Do you want to walk in there as the accompanist, or the king? If you want to be a classical pianist, you need a tux."

Tom was embarrassed.

"We'll talk about this later."

They walked into the office. It was a sparse room. A clean desk with a couple of chairs, a wall with a slot for each employee, though nothing but his paycheck ever appeared there for Tom. It was somehow not at all surprising not to see a barre along the wall.

Charles pulled the note out of his slot and sat behind the desk. Tom sat in one of the chairs in front of it. He watched as Charles opened the folded piece of paper and read. A strange, distant look appeared on Charles's face. The note, which looked to not be much more than a name and a phone number, had clearly stirred a memory. Tom couldn't tell if it was a good memory or not, but it was significant.

"I need to make a call."

"Should I..." Tom pointed toward the door.

"No, please stay. I want you here."

Charles picked up the receiver and deliberately dialed the number on his note. Tom thought he was taking his time to gather his nerve for what would await once that last number swung back home on the dial. Tom wished he hadn't been asked to stay. He would have rather spent the hour in the studio practicing.

"Hi Mary. It's Charles."

There was a pause.

"Thank you for calling," said the woman's voice on the phone. Her voice was sharp, clearly audible to Tom where he sat a few feet away. "I tried the old number I had for you, but you must have moved. I thought I could reach you here."

Tom felt more uncomfortable hearing both sides of the conversation.

"Did you call about Julian?" asked Charles.

Another pause.

"Yes."

"It's been over four years."

"He's dying, Charles."

Charles put his hand slowly to his forehead. Tom could see the news wasn't surprising, even though he looked devastated.

"He's trying to stay positive, but it's hard. How can anyone make sense of all this? My brother's a sensitive man, as you know. He's not ready to die."

"Who ever is?"

"How are you, Charles?"

Tom could tell, from the change in her tone, and in Charles's expression, that there was surprise in this question. He imagined that Charles and Mary were not each other's favorite person.

"I'm fine," said Charles. "I'm scared though. I keep wondering if I'll be the next guy down. I had thought about Julian a lot, but I was afraid to call. It's tough after so long."

"He's talked about you lately. He's been thinking more about the good times. He talks about his time with you like it was the best time of his life. I know there was a lot of hurt at the end, but at a time like this, the good memories come through."

"I really loved him."

"He knows that." She paused. "I know that, too."

Tom thought about getting up and leaving. He didn't feel it was right for him to listen to this. As he was about to stand up, Charles reached across the desk and grabbed his hand. Tom hesitated for a second, then squeezed down around Charles's fingers. He couldn't get up from his chair now. Uncomfortable or not, Charles needed a friend, and Tom was the only friend around.

"We took him to St. Vincent's on Thursday. They have a good AIDS ward there. It was becoming too hard to care for him at home. There's not a lot they can do for him at the hospital, but at least they can keep him more comfortable, with people who aren't afraid to care for him. I hope you'll come and see him. It would mean a lot."

"Yeah."

"Call me again to let me know."

Charles was crying softly when he hung up the phone. Tom continued to squeeze his hand. Eventually Charles let go, took a handkerchief out of his pocket and wiped his eyes.

"I'm sorry."

"Don't be, it's okay."

"You probably heard everything?"

Tom nodded.

"Julian and I were together for five years. We were in love. But I screwed it up. We parted on bad terms and haven't spoken since."

Tom squirmed in his seat, and as soon as he realized it, sat very still, hoping Charles hadn't noticed. Tom had considered himself open-minded having a gay friend like Charles but hadn't wanted to think about what that really meant. It was hard for him to think about love between two men, but he had been with a couple girls before. He couldn't imagine thinking of one of those girls dying so young. He tried to think what Charles was feeling, knowing someone he had loved for years was dying. But try as he might, Tom knew there was no way he could understand. It was all too foreign.

Finally, he asked, "Will you go and see him?"

"I'm scared to."

"Because of the past?"

"I'm afraid to see him fading away. He was so beautiful. I'm afraid of that happening to me."

"This ain't about you, man."

Charles sighed. "When I told you I didn't have the virus, I stretched the truth a little bit. The truth is, I don't know. I haven't had the courage to get myself tested." He drew in a deep breath and then added, "I'm afraid to know."

"It would be better to know, one way or the other."

"Would it?" Charles looked at him pointedly. "There's no cure, so what's the good of knowing I'm going to die before I get sick?"

"Well, if you don't have it, then you can stop worrying about it."

"I suppose I'm just sure I do have it, especially now. They say it's transmitted by sex. I had sex with Julian, and Julian has it."

Tom squirmed again. Charles saw it.

"This is the world you live in. Get used to it."

"I'm sorry."

"It's okay, guy. You've come a long way."

Charles looked off toward the upper corner of the room. Tom waited.

"Julian was the last man I was with," Charles said. "I broke his heart, and my heart ended up broken as well. But since I was the one who screwed up the relationship, I was never able to feel sorry for myself. It took me a long time even to acknowledge that the heartache was there.

"After we broke up, I mostly gave up on love. I gave up on my group of friends, too. I tried to find my joy in ballet, though it was hard, because that was only a year after I retired from New York City Ballet and began teaching, so my identity was sort of lost in the desert. Who was I? I was a dancer, but no longer performing. I was gay, but I was separated from the community. But I guess I've been tied to the community this whole time, whether I wanted to be or not. I never really could step away. That only made me lonely. It didn't protect me from everything that's happening. I tried to turn a blind eye to what's happening but that was never possible. It's too horrible and I'm tied to closely to it. There's no escape. I should never even have tried."

Tom took a deep breath. "You've got to get tested. Otherwise, the worry will kill you."

"You think it's that easy?" Chares suddenly had venom in his voice. Tom lurched back in his chair. "Just go and get a fucking test like it's no big deal. Come on! It's a death sentence. Do you get that? A fucking death sentence!"

"I'll go with you if that makes it easier," Tom said. "There's a clinic that I walk by every day on my way here. I've seen a sign there just since the last month or so, saying they do free HIV testing."

"You being there would NOT make it easier. Maybe a half a bottle of gin would help. But I doubt it."

Tom was silent for a minute. He saw something in Charles's eyes, beneath the veil of anger.

"You've been thinking about it though, haven't you? Part of you has wanted to get tested for a long time. Secretly, you want to know. Don't you?"

Charles said nothing, but the anger had left his eyes.

"Let's walk down there after the 5:00 class," Tom pressed.

"I'll think about it."

"Thinking's the problem. You've been thinking about it for a long time. I can tell. Now you've got to just go and do it. I'll be there with you. It'll be scary. But stuff like this, it's always better to know."

Charles exhaled.

"Then, you need to go see your friend," Tom said. "For his sake, not for yours."

Tom was amazed how composed Charles seemed during class. Perhaps it was the routine of what he loved that allowed Charles to be himself. He snapped at the girls when their lines weren't right and even banged on the piano once. It had been a long time since Tom's playing had been considered less than adequate. He supposed he had been practicing too much for the upcoming Shubert concert. No room for rubato here! It was a better class than usual for the summer, and Charles seemed energized.

But after the girls had changed back out of their pointe shoes and left, Tom saw that Charles was exhausted. He packed up his own things quickly.

"Come on, man, let's get it over with. We can walk to the clinic in ten minutes."

"I'd rather do it tomorrow." Charles wouldn't look him in the eyes. "I'm too emotional thinking about Julian."

Tom walked over to him and took his shoulders, forcing him to look him in the eyes.

"Trust me—you'll be glad after you go. I'll be right there with you."

Charles looked at him with unconcealed disdain. In that moment, Tom finally understood. For Charles, AIDS didn't feel like an *if*, but a *when*, and wouldn't a test only confirm that... confirm that HIV was lying in his blood and waiting for its hour to strike? What was the point of getting tested? Maybe it was better to stay in the dark a while longer.

But Charles was already nearly out the door. Tom sensed that he had only given Charles a gentle nudge today, assisted by Julian's sister. He had been wanting to do this for a while, but it had remained too easy to wait till tomorrow. Always tomorrow.

They walked wordlessly south on Eighth Avenue. Tom thought it was best not to talk. There was nothing more to say about *this* and Charles was too smart to be distracted by talk about something else. He would have only been annoyed if Tom had tried.

"You're a good friend, Tom." It was the first thing Charles said during their walk. "After this is done, we're going downtown to get you a tux and a nice pair of shoes. I recommended you for those jobs, so it's my reputation too. I can't have you walking in there looking like a slob from South Bronx."

Tom laughed, glad that Charles had broken the heavy silence of their walk. "I ain't got money for a new shirt, much less a tux and shoes."

"I know. It will be my gift, to give your career a good start."

"You ain't rich either. We're both in the subway class, remember?"

"And always will be with that attitude. What have I got to save my money for?"

Tom stopped. "Here's the place."

Charles hadn't stopped. He was already two steps ahead toward the door of the clinic. It seemed he was done second-guessing. Yet when Tom caught up, he saw the dread in Charles's eyes. He himself had felt dread before: waiting to find out if his father would go to prison, or if his brother would be implicated after D was caught. He had felt the dread of hunger, of the danger of their streets. But he had never felt the dread of a personal death sentence that might be waiting a few steps away—and having the courage to walk in and find out.

The inside of the clinic didn't look like a hospital, as Tom had expected it would. It was colorful and inviting. It looked almost like a children's clinic, and indeed, there were a couple of colorful pictures on the walls that had obviously been drawn by children. Tom's heart sank with the realization of it all. He had only really heard about AIDS as a "gay disease." That's what the newspapers said, and the only people he knew of who were affected were Charles's friends. But he now realized the kids who had drawn those pictures might be dead or dying.

"Yes, we can test both of you right away."

Tom's attention was brought back to the desk where the middle-aged woman was looking at him. Charles was there at the desk writing on a page of paper.

"Oh no," Tom came forward. "I just came with my friend. Moral support."

"If your friend is at risk, don't you think it would be a good idea to have yourself tested as well? It's free."

"Oh no, we're not, I mean…"

Charles had looked up from his page with amusement.

"There's no judgement here," said the woman. "But isn't it always better to know?"

He had told Charles the same thing only two hours ago.

"What the hell." He began filling out a form too. He told Charles he would be there all the way.

Only once the needle went in to draw blood did Tom really start to feel nervous. Maybe he was at risk. He had been around

Charles a lot, had even touched him today. You could get the flu by being in the same room with someone, maybe you could get AIDS too. How much did they really know about the disease? And here he was in a place where AIDS patients came in and out every day, sitting in the same chair, breathing the same air. He hoped they cleaned everything well. Who else had this needle poked?

The needle came out.

"How long does the test take?"

"About a week, sometimes a little longer. Come back next Wednesday and we should have your results."

"A week!" He had expected minutes, maybe an hour.

The woman smiled. "We have to send it to the lab for analysis. If there's a positive result, they send it out for a second confirmation."

Back outside the clinic, Tom and Charles stood for a minute on the sidewalk.

"Sorry you have to wait so long," Tom said. "I didn't know it would be like that."

"I did. Well the hardest part's done. You were right, I've been trying to do this for a long time."

"It was brave of you, man."

"You've got to wait now too."

"Shit, I only did it for you."

"The look on your face when that woman assumed we were lovers! Some cradle-robber I must look."

"Hey now!"

Charles laughed. "It was very kind of you to take the test too. It did make it easier, and now you have to come with me next week."

"You know I would have either way."

Charles started walking toward the subway entrance across the street.

"Uptown's on this side," Tom called after him.

"We're not going uptown. Come on. It's time to get you some new threads."

As Tom followed Charles into the subway tunnel and sat beside him on the downtown A Train, he made plans for how to tell Charles that the price of the clothes would be a loan. He didn't know quite what it would cost, but it would surely be enough that it would take him a long time to pay it back. It would probably cost more than he was about to earn with these next two gigs. That money was needed for rent as it was. It would be good to have performing clothes, and maybe that, in itself, would help him earn the money back more quickly.

"I'd say you're probably a 38 or a 40," said Charles on the train. He was excited. Tom figured it was good for him to have a distraction after that test.

"It shouldn't take much tailoring. I'm taking you to my favorite men's wear store. It's been years since I've gone—I don't really need suits anymore. I hope Juan Carlos still works there. He should be able to do any alterations while we wait."

"Will they still be open? It's almost eight o'clock."

"You must be joking. This is New York City, remember?"

"I don't like the direction we're going. This is the high-roller neighborhood."

"You don't need to worry about that. I told you, it's my gift."

"My mama taught me not to take handouts."

"Now I'm offended. A gift from a friend isn't a handout. Especially not after what you did for me today."

Looking at Charles and seeing the pleasure in his eyes as he anticipated shopping together, Tom changed his mind. Allowing Charles the joy of giving was a gift in itself. After what Charles had gone through today, Tom had no business hanging onto his pride. Mama would understand, if she knew the whole story.

Sometime well after nine o'clock, Tom stepped out of the glass doors of the menswear shop, as the lock clicked behind him and the lights started going out inside. He had a big paper bag with handles and three boxes inside: the biggest one for the tux, the heaviest one for the patent leather shoes, and the most delicate one holding his new shirt, bow tie and studs. Man, was he going to look like some kind of cool!

"Thank you, Charles. This is really some gift."

"Thank *you*, for letting me. I've got nothing to save for, with one foot in the grave."

"Hey, stop that. We're having a good time tonight. We got through the tough stuff earlier. Don't spoil it."

Charles's expression had changed. He had been so excited on the train, and in the shop, catching up with his friend Juan Carlos after many years. But when the fun was over, he would have to take the train back home, trying to sleep while remembering that his former lover was dying in a bed at St. Vincent's Hospital, and that his own blood was on its way to a lab to determine if he would share the fate of so many of his friends.

The look on Charles's face reminded Tom of when he and his friends used to come down to the city from The Bronx to party. Poor as they were, the price for a drink, or to get into a nightclub was crippling. They only came down once or twice a year. Toward the end of the night, some of them would have that look of knowing the night was about done, checking their pockets to see if they had enough for one more club cover, or one more drink, and still have 90 cents for subway tokens back to The Bronx. Charles had that look now. He didn't want the night to end. He didn't want to go home to be alone with his thoughts.

"You hungry?" asked Tom.

"Famished! I know a place just around the corner from here."

Charles hurried around the next block. Tom followed.

"It's the best restaurant in town. I've only been there once in my life."

Tom looked across the street as several plump men in striped, double-breasted suits guffawed their way out the door. One glance was all it took to see that this was a restaurant for those who oozed money.

"My treat."

Now Charles was just being reckless and Tom had had enough. This wasn't what he had in mind when he suggested eating. He grabbed Charles's arm.

"No man, I ain't going into that place with you. You can't afford it. I'm accepting these clothes and these shoes because you gave me something that's important, that I can use over and over again, and that I'll use to earn money so I can pay that turn forward to another young fella who needs a chance one day. But now you're just being reckless because you think you're gonna die. You ain't dying, Charles. Whatever that test says, you're gonna dance yourself healthy. They've got no cure now, but they will one day, or medicine that can keep you alive, and some of the guys who are testing positive are gonna make it to that day. If you wanna go to dinner, there's a diner on 14th that's awfully good. Just as good as this high-class joint for a penny to the dollar. Priced for guys living for another day—you and me."

Chapter Twelve

....

2019

ndrea and I began to spend our days at the basement studio.

As soon as I knew she was off work I took the Plymouth and met her at the art teacher's house. I plugged in my laptop in the corner and danced to my music collection while Andrea painted. It was a good arrangement. We both enjoyed the company but were each focused on our own thing. I didn't get shy having someone watch me practice, and she didn't feel as self-conscious as she would if I had been looking over her shoulder at her work.

I cleared the junk away from the mirror and borrowed a standing barre from the school. It made a decent little ballet studio. I didn't know what I was dancing half the time, but it felt good to move. I started making up little choreographies as a way to focus and practice the harder movements of the repertoire. It was actually the hardest I had danced on a daily basis in years. It was invigorating.

Sometimes we would start shortly after 5:00, painting and dancing while the poor little air conditioner worked to bring the summer night down from sweltering. Without natural light, we wouldn't realize how much time had passed until we were starving. Opening the door, we would be shocked to find it completely dark outside.

It gave me something to look forward to each day, a reason to get out of bed, get dressed and go through the motions of the day. The desire to dance, and yes, the desire for this new companionship with my sister was stronger than the pull of depression. After a few days, I was cautiously optimistic that the worst was over. The longer I danced that day, the better I felt. The mornings were still pretty rough. It was hard to get out of bed. But as sad as I felt, I dragged myself out each afternoon, with the memory that dancing had made me feel better the day before. Soon I began to sleep better—good, hard dancing always helped for sleep—and that made the mornings a little easier.

The days became weeks. I mailed Nikki a check for the next month's rent, which slashed an alarming percentage off my remaining bank balance. I took the summer teaching job at Encore Studios. It was good for me to have something else to fill the early parts of my days.

The more I danced, the freer I felt until the clouds had lifted from my heart. I felt hopeful again. It had been one of my shorter spells and that was encouraging, though even after the depression was gone, I felt wounded and worried. I tried to avoid thoughts that might be a trigger, anything that would send me back into the destructive spiral of *what ifs.*

I set Andrea the goal of showing her work at the Lancaster art walk, which happened the first Friday of every month. July was right on top of us, but August seemed realistic. As far as I knew, she hadn't yet made any phone calls to find a place to hang her paintings. I could only push her so much. I didn't want to risk setting her off, which might in turn set me off again. At least she was painting again. Her fourth painting was quickly coming together, in the same vein as the other three. She had also put up another blank canvas, but from what I could tell hadn't started on it yet.

I missed Tom a lot. We talked a couple times, and texted, but it didn't feel natural. We needed to be in each other's presence for the magic to be there. Our relationship had never been serious enough to try to talk on the phone every day. He wasn't much of a phone talker to begin with. Once I got back, I figured things would pick up with Tom right where they left off. He was that kind of guy. As long as I didn't wait *too* long.

What had been so great about our affair was that it always remained in the moment. If I thought too much about it, I would ruin the beauty. Because of course I knew it couldn't last forever. When I was in New York I wasn't worried about that. But now that I was back here it seemed important that a relationship should be able to last. Wasn't that the point? But then, that was also the kind of thinking that had gotten me into a worthless marriage.

How can I describe those summer weeks in Lancaster? The truth is, once the depression was gone, I felt relaxed and comfortable. It had knocked me for a loop and now that I was on the other side of it, I savored the simple pleasure of the studio and my blossoming friendship with my sister. I hated the comfort of being home, even as it felt good to have a mental rest from the pressure. It scared me to dream too big right now, lest I send my mind back into worry and regret. Even so, I reminded myself that while I had been in the pressure-cooker of New York City, my demon had stayed down. As long as I stayed in Lancaster, I would be in danger. Was it only a matter of time?

New York City always emptied out in the summer. I reminded myself of this. Those who could afford to leave got out. Nobody wanted to be in Manhattan in July, when every sunbeam got magnified off ten walls of steel and the garbage melted in great piles on the sidewalk. As I had found from my searches, there would have been no work for me. I told myself this too, even though deep down I remembered the intensity with which I had scrounged for work my first months in the city. Comparatively, my current effort was laughable.

I wondered how many people even noticed I was gone. Tom did, obviously, but his life would go on the same as it had for thirty years. If I didn't come back, there would be other girls.

Maybe there already were. Nikki wouldn't care as long as I paid rent. The only people I really kept in touch with were Heather and Elly, who had invited me to their place in Brooklyn and seemed genuinely disappointed that I wasn't in town. We had bonded that night over hotdogs and at the Lebanese night club.

New York wasn't a city that waited for you to get your shit together. It was moving ahead with or without me. When I returned, I would have to squeeze into my role in the city with the same effort it took the first time. Truly, to fit into New York City, you had to make that same effort every single day. Did I still have that in me?

Meanwhile, here in Lancaster, my acquaintances took my return with a sense of inevitability, as if I was just returning from a long vacation.

I had dropped off Facebook, at least in that I wasn't *posting* anything. I still checked it every day on my phone, looking at other people's posts with the voyeurism that had made Facebook a national addiction. So I saw the brunch invitation—from Kate, one of my former dancer friends who had come with me on a couple of those New York trips in my twenties. Someone must have told her I was in town.

I can't believe I actually went. I convinced myself it would be good for me, another thing to keep my mind off darker thoughts. I regretted going as soon as I was there. Kate's food was fine, but the atmosphere at the brunch was horrible. It reminded me of all the reasons I had shed my marriage like an ill-fitting coat and high-tailed it out of this town. Other than a couple of brief questions, none of the ladies were very interested in my New York adventure. They just wanted to complain about their husbands and commiserate about the stress of childrearing—while giving themselves permission to drink cheap champagne at 11:00 on a Sunday morning. Broke Percy had brought armloads of better champagne for our post-rehearsal extravagances!

I debated between offending them by leaving almost as soon as I'd gotten there or glugging down enough of the bad champagne to endure it, despite the headache it would cause. I had to worry about myself, not them. I couldn't stay if it would trigger me and release my demon again, now that I had finally locked it away.

I snuck away to Kate's bathroom, then went farther down the hall. I don't know why I did that. I had no interest in snooping around Kate's house. Something drew me, and before I knew it, I was face to face in the hall with a little girl.

She was a chunky little thing, in the way girls sometimes were at that age (eight or so, I think—that would have made sense, remembering that Kate was pregnant at my wedding). One good growth spurt would thin her out as she morphed into a preteen. Her hair was brown and stringy.

"Wait, don't tell me," I said. "I remember when you were born. Celeste, right? I've known your mother for a long time. I thought that was such a pretty name when she told me. Like the stars."

Celeste smiled and it was a great smile, despite the teeth that were still coming in. That smile surprised me because children usually had a different reaction when encountering an unfamiliar adult. I knew from her smile that she would become an attractive woman, although she surely doubted it, now at perhaps the most awkward stage through which her development would ever have to go.

"Are you the dancer from New York?" she asked.

I was taken aback, but said yes because... well, I was.

"Mommy told me about you. I want to come see one of your shows."

"I would love that. Do you dance too?"

"I take ballet class on Tuesdays, but I'm not very good at it. I can't keep my balance."

"That was hard for me when I was your age too. It does get easier. I promise."

I smiled, but felt I had nothing more to say. I wasn't very good with children. I felt shy, realizing that this little girl was star-struck by me. I said goodbye to Celeste and went back to the living room.

I didn't mind the horrible conversation and lack of commonality anymore. I drank coffee instead of champagne. I was flattered. I'd gotten a badly needed stroke on my tenuous self-esteem, even if it wasn't deserved. I was nobody and had done nothing. I didn't deserve her admiration.

But maybe the encounter meant something different. Maybe it was about her rather than me. I remembered once when I was about her age, dancing in the local Christmas production of *The Nutcracker*. I was one of the little girls at the Christmas party in Act I, whisked out of the theater and to bed before the real drama started. One night my parents let me stay up to see the rest of the show. We had imported the two leads that year from the Pittsburgh Ballet. I was backstage that night, and the Sugar Plum Fairy brushed by me in the hallway and had the decency to smile at me. She was tiny in her purple tutu, barely taller than me. But she was a star to me, larger than life, an inspiration to keep working my young butt off in those tedious technique classes. Maybe I could hope to have inspired young Celeste in a similar way, tipping the scale toward her sticking with it, away from quitting because the other girls made fun of her for not, at this particularly fickle time of childhood, looking much like a ballerina.

I was really moved by my encounter with Celeste, and afterwards, it motivated me to live up to the image she had of me. Having shaken free of my depression, now I had to shake free of my complacency.

The next day, I left my father early in the afternoon, thinking a change of environment might help shake me out of my rut so I'd buckle down to really search for work. I needed something, anything, in the city with a firm date. A show audition would be ideal, but even the beginning of a class series to teach would work. I needed a goal and an end date to this sabbatical. I took my laptop to a coffee shop on Duke Street and settled in at a table in the corner. It was a chic café with high, unfinished ceilings and an exposed brick wall behind me. The day was hot but with the air conditioning inside I pulled my wrap around my shoulders. I was glad I had opted for a hot latte even though I almost asked for iced.

Despite my renewed focus, my search mostly brought up the same things I had seen before. I began to understand that you didn't find the good things online. This held true whether you were looking for the best restaurant or the next hot show to hit Broadway. The good auditions—the ones I really wanted— weren't advertised. You needed to be there, rubbing shoulders with people in the know. All my efforts may have made me feel better by thinking I was doing something, but I was just spinning my wheels. I never could have found out about Percy's show without being in the city, and I would never find my next show until I was back. After fifteen minutes my mind started to wander. Still, it felt good to be somewhere other than my parents' house or Andrea's studio.

A group of guys came into the café laughing and talking loudly. I glanced at them, then returned to my half-hearted efforts. After the men had their drinks and began to pass by me one of them paused.

"Cammie, is that you?"

I looked up. At first, I didn't recognize him. His eyes were familiar, but I couldn't place him.

"Imagine without the beard," he said.

I stared for a moment more as my mind raced back fifteen years.

"Oh my God… Jason?"

I hopped up and gave him a big hug.

"Hey guys, I'll catch up with you later," he called to his friends, then sat down at the table across from me without waiting to be invited.

"You look great," I said. I meant it. He had a strong forehead under neat reddish-brown hair. He had crisp blue eyes and a thin, well-toned body. He wore a tailored dress shirt, skinny jeans and designer shoes. I wasn't really into full beards on guys, but Jason wore his well. I'd had a big crush on him back in high school, but nothing ever came of it. I'm sure Jason knew I liked him, but in my mind—perhaps also in his—he was out of my league.

"You haven't been in Lancaster this whole time, have you?" I asked.

"I've been back almost three years." He crossed his legs on the small, wood-topped stool. "I started my own IT business. It's going great."

"Why'd you decide to come back?"

"After grad school, I worked for a couple years in Charlotte and a year and a half with a start-up out in Seattle. When I came back to visit, I discovered there were hardly any decent network engineers in Lancaster. I've had more business than I can handle. I hired a second guy last year so now I have a little more free time."

"Convenient for chatting up girls at coffee shops on a Monday afternoon."

We both laughed. I surprised myself with my flirtatiousness but enjoyed it.

"What about you?" he asked.

Nobody had asked me why I was back. I could say whatever I wanted, so I did, and loved hearing my own answer.

"I teach dance. I actually moved to New York City. I'm only back for the summer. I'm here to help my sister get ready to display her paintings in a show."

"Wow, look at you! That's fantastic."

I smiled. Yes, it sounded fantastic put that way.

"What's next for you?" Jason asked. "Think you'll open a dance studio here in Lancaster?"

It was a typical question. Everyone assumed New York was a temporary excursion.

"I like it there," I said. "I'm planning to stay."

Jason and I sat together for almost an hour. He was a good talker, and I didn't mind that he talked mostly about himself. I felt flattered for a busy man to suddenly drop everything for me, particularly someone I'd once liked from afar.

My heart reminded me of Tom, but from the beginning I knew what Tom and I were... and what we were not. Our age gap may have been the only thing that allowed me to open myself up to a man like him. The timing was also perfect, only three years out from my divorce. I wasn't ready for anything too serious. But I was going to be thirty-four soon. I couldn't know how long my romance with Tom would last—or if it might already be over. Eventually I would want a life-partner, someone I could have a family with. I had tried to want that with Alex, but now I saw those years as wasted. If I had gone to New York then, instead of getting married, so many things might have been different now.

All these thoughts made me curious about Jason as he sat across the small table from me. He seemed to check every box of what I *should* want if I tried to seriously date again: handsome, successful, witty, and we had some shared history together. My mother had always wanted to see me and Andrea with men like Jason, who had made their own success, unlike the man she had married. Would it be so bad to live in Lancaster with a man like him?

I tried to stop myself from getting so far ahead. How terrified would Jason be to know I was marrying him and bearing his children in my mind when we had only been reacquainted an hour? Besides, these were small thoughts and dreams of other people... not *my* dreams. New York had taught me to dream big. Whether or not I could sustain my life there, I couldn't let this small town inflict its ambitions on me.

Jason must not have been too terrified of me, because at the end of the afternoon he invited me to a party at his condo that weekend. I asked if I could bring my sister and he said yes.

That night, after spending the evening with Andrea at the studio, I looked at my phone and saw a Facebook friend request from him, which made me smile.

After teaching the summer class at Encore the next day, I decided to skip the studio with Andrea and head home to keep looking for opportunities in New York. I sat at the kitchen table with my laptop, while Dad sat nearby. We chatted while I worked. I told him the types of shows I wanted to audition for, and he asked me to tell him stories about Percy's show. I had an easiness talking with Dad, like he was an old friend, a peer rather than a parent. I almost even slipped up and started to tell him about Tom, but I remembered that he was actually my dad and that Tom was closer to his age than mine. Better to keep that story to myself.

When Dad got tired, I helped him out of his chair and he walked to the bedroom, where he had a more comfortable setup. I returned to the kitchen and sent off a few e-mails.

I felt pretty good about myself. Maybe I really could be whoever I wanted to be. Celeste thought I was. So did Jason. As long as I believed it myself, what could stop me? I was almost ready to head back to New York with or without work lined up. I had a month or two of savings left and if I really believed in myself, that could be enough. Even if I did eventually come back here to settle down, it wasn't time yet.

It surprised me when I heard the garage door open, meaning Mom was home from work. I'd been at it longer than I thought.

"Hi Cammie," she said with a note of surprise as she walked into the kitchen. "I thought you'd be at the studio."

"I had some work I wanted to get done."

"Oh." A note of question in her voice.

"Logistics for my classes in the city." For whatever reason, I didn't want to tell her the details I had just shared with Dad.

I closed my laptop and stood up. Mom took a glass from the cupboard and filled it with water at the fridge.

"I was just finishing. I'm going back to my room. Let me know if I can help with dinner."

I started down the hall toward the stairs, my laptop tucked under my arm, but stopped. It dawned on me how rude I was being. I didn't ask my mother about her day, or if she was tired from her work. I should have asked her if she wanted a glass of water, not sit there while she got it for herself. Telling her she could ask me to help with dinner. Not offering. Not once since I returned had I actually made dinner for my parents, like a good unemployed daughter.

I walked back to the kitchen but stopped in the entryway. Mom sat in one of the high-backed dining chairs, her eyes closed and an expression on her face I had never seen before. Her untouched water glass sat on the table in front of her. I stood motionless in the kitchen doorway. Her expression was so unfamiliar she didn't even look like my mother. It was a look of pure exhaustion. She looked ten years older. Only five minutes earlier, she had come home from her workday seeming chipper and energized. I must have returned to the kitchen on my best dancer's feet, because I knew she wouldn't let herself look so exhausted if she knew I was there. I darted away, not wanting her to open her eyes and know that she had told me her secret. Tomorrow, I would have dinner ready when she got home.

I couldn't shake the way Mom's face broke my heart. How often had I done just that through the years, letting my smile disappear as soon as I thought I was alone? I had known, and appreciated, how much Mom did for us all these years, with Dad unable to work and me and Andrea chasing our dreams. I'd been better about verbally expressing that appreciation, as I did that morning with her at the hotel restaurant after my show. It made me sick to my stomach, though, to see what it really did to her. And I had gotten up and left as soon as she walked in like a petulant teenager—sullen and unappreciative. The fact that I *did* know all she did made the way I lived my own life that much worse.

She would be sixty in a couple of years. She couldn't keep up with the pace of her construction job forever. But there was no retirement on the horizon for her. Hers wasn't the type of job to offer a pension or 401K, and while the union's health insurance would cover her and Dad until Medicare took over, she didn't have much in the way of savings—not the kind you could live on for any number of years. Once she retired, social security and Dad's disability payments would be it. She didn't want the rest of us to think about those things. She didn't want any of us thinking her body might be slowing down—that her inevitable retirement might be forced rather than chosen.

Back in my room, my first thought was that support of my parents would one day fall to me. The thought filled me with dread. A moment later, the dread filled me with shame. Everything I had done as an adult was for *me*. The very thought of caring for someone else filled me with dread. Why should it have? I felt so alone sometimes. Why not welcome others' need for me as a joy?

The last decade rushed past me, with all the selfish things I had done. How I sabotaged Andrea's big chance because I wanted a wedding. How I checked out of my marriage because it didn't fit my storybook script. How I ran off to New York, blowing my own savings because I deserved my shot in the city while I was still young. How in doing so, I left the beginnings of a good career here in Lancaster, one that in time could have taken the pressure off my mother—the pressure that was aging her beyond her years.

At least that career had been doing what I loved—dancing— unlike Andrea, who worked as an accountant and hated every minute of it.

Mom was exhausted and worried. She had hidden it well. But I doubted she was depressed, at least not in the same way I was, because all her work had been for us. She loved us that much. Maybe that was part of my problem. I always focused on what I wanted and thought I deserved, yet it still wasn't good enough. Therein laid the root of all my regrets. Maybe my depression wouldn't cripple me so badly when it came, if I took as much time thinking about my family as myself. Mom, Dad, Andrea... none of them had gotten the lives they probably thought they deserved either.

In retrospect, I had a pretty good life here before I blew it up and ran off to New York. A stable teaching job, a few local shows a year—more if I wanted them. But I never appreciated it because it was *here*. In my twenties, dancing was always complicated by so much else. Doing it as a career changed the way it felt. I let that happen more than I should have.

I looked out the window at the old trees and rooftops of my little town.

Back in New York, what was my best case for a life? I could dance in some more shows, possibly for money, but considering all the rehearsal hours it would make for a pittance. My classes could grow, and I could make a name for myself, but with more competition and higher expenses. Ultimately, a *good* life for a dancer in New York would amount to scraping by and enjoying it. There would never be money to send home to my aging parents, or even to craft some sort of retirement plan for myself. I'd be lucky to have an extra month or two of rent in the bank for an emergency.

For a lot of artists, that worked just fine. It was even a dream come true. It had worked out pretty well for Tom. But after what I had just seen on my mom's face, it would be hard for me to embrace that kind of future without burying a large dose of guilt.

Chapter Thirteen

....

Summer 1986

Tom stepped off the train and ran his hands slowly down the front of his tuxedo jacket. He glanced down to admire his new threads, all the way to his shiny shoes. Then he looked up at the unfamiliar surroundings with a big smile. The house for the party was a mile from the station. He relished the walk on such a fine summer evening. The hot sun was still out, though low to the west. Feeling sharp in his tux, he didn't even worry about walking through such a wealthy white neighborhood alone, which would have terrified him under most circumstances.

He walked between pristine green lawns cased in immaculately trimmed hedges, with shimmering houses nestled in the background. Tom walked confidently, remembering the things Charles had said and imagining that he belonged. Sure enough, the people he passed seemed to believe he did. A few even smiled and nodded. Somehow, a tuxedo changed everything.

In the Hamptons the scents that filled the air were new yet recognizable: fresh cut grass, floral perfumes, less natural perfumes emanating from the houses, and through it all the sharp scent of the sea. The heat of the day enhanced all these beautiful smells. Tom savored the experience, knowing how rare it was for a man like him to be welcomed in a place like this. He sensed a magical evening might be in store.

He had seen places like this in the movies but hardly believed they really existed, especially just a couple hours by train outside the city. It made him think of *The Great Gatsby*. Although he blew off reading the book in high school, he had seen the movie with Robert Redford.

Impressive as the homes along his walk from the station had been, Tom was unprepared for the sheer majesty of his destination. He double checked the address on the card in his pocket to be sure. Yes, this was the place. It was a mansion, set well back from the street past sloping green lawns and twisting garden paths. Ten white columns lined the front of the tall house. A hedge blocked the view from the sidewalk, except where two driveways cut toward a large parking area just off the street. There were some of the fanciest cars Tom had ever seen, attended by two valets. The parking area was made of individually laid stones. A wide stone path lined with flowers led through the lawns to the house.

Tom knew better than to waltz up that stone path, but he took a moment to gaze admiringly at the scene before walking around to what had been graciously labeled "Vendors' Entrance." Two white vans were parked in the alley with their back doors thrown open. The words "Clausen's Catering" were emblazoned in red along the side of each van, the way red frosting would be scripted on a white cake.

He came into the kitchen, which looked more like a restaurant kitchen than somebody's house. Workers from the contracted caterer buzzed about. Trays of hors d'oeuvres accumulated on tiered carts while odors of more substantial food emanated from ovens and stoves. The blast of central air-conditioning waged a valiant battle against the heat of summer, the heat of cooking, and of a fast-moving crowd in the kitchen.

While Tom had never played for an event like his, he felt comfortable and knew his role. The kitchen was like a large green room, or even an elaborate backstage. The "stage" would be the main area of the house, which he wouldn't see until it was time to sit down at an unfamiliar piano and play.

He sometimes envied his brother with his sax, or a violinist or guitarist who always had their own instrument—even a singer whose instrument was their own body. He never knew how a piano would feel until he began to play it. They were all different. Some had a light touch, some were heavy. Sometimes the keys stuck, making it hard to play fast passages. All piano keys were the same size, but some pianos had keys that went down farther than others to strike the string, which increased the stretch of his finger from one key to the next.

He stood and waited in an area of the kitchen that felt out of the way of the caterers, expecting someone to find him and give instructions. He wouldn't be hard to spot—a black man in a tuxedo amongst all the buzzing workers in white. The person who found him first was the last person in the world he expected to see right then.

"*Hola, chico,*" rang a musical voice in his ear. Despite all the smells of the kitchen, he caught the remembered scent of hibiscus and coconut. His senses tingled.

He turned and smiled with delight. Vallia, the Dominican singer he had played for weeks ago stood there in a caterer's white shirt and black pants, one hand on her hip. Her hair was clipped tight against her head.

"Nice place to play," she said. "Clearly, we'll both do whatever it takes to be invited to this kind of party."

He laughed. Though surprised to see her, it made sense. All the struggling musicians had other jobs, many of them in the service industry. He was a lucky one to have a job where he still got to play.

"Did you boys get the job from that audition?" she asked.

"No. I thought maybe I shot myself in the foot by helping you get it."

She laughed. "I didn't get it either."

"Got anything else lined up?"

"One more. The night after tomorrow." Tom mentally noted that was the same night he would play at Carnegie Hall. "That will be my last show in New York."

"Why?"

"Between what I earn tonight and what I earn for that show I can either pay rent for one more month or buy a plane ticket home to Santo Domingo. If I pay rent, I might not be able to pay for either in a month."

"Don't you want to stay?"

Her lips curled in a distant smile. "I gave it my best shot." Their eyes met with understanding.

She touched his arm, not softly the way American girls did, but with a firm palm. "Back to work for me. I'll see you out there." She began to walk away.

"Yes, Vallia."

Hearing her name, she turned and smiled over her shoulder at him, then continued back to her work. So that was what she meant when she said she had no time for love. He felt a touch of sadness for her and wondered how long it would be until he needed to make a similar decision. For him the old life was only an hour away on the D Train — a blessing or a curse.

The event coordinator found Tom and escorted him to the main hall of the house.

Seeing the grand hall brought a quick gasp out of Tom before he could stop himself. What had appeared from the street to be a two or even three-story house, turned out to be a single hall with thirty-foot high ceilings and tall windows rounded at the top. White columns, similar to the ones Tom had seen out front, lined inside as well. To the south, wide glass doors were thrown open to a stone terrace. Past a hundred feet or so of sloping lawn, the sea shown orange in the setting sun. It was the last weekend of the summer season.

Guests were beginning to arrive. It was time for the entertainment to begin. Tom went straight to the grand piano and arranged his folder of lead sheets.

The piano was well-tuned, its sound was good, but the keys were sticky. Tom had learned that this hinted at how infrequently the piano was played. This one served more as decorative furniture than musical instrument. It hadn't seen enough hands to adequately loosen the keys. It made little difference. Tonight's music was easy, effortless. His instincts playing the jazz standards were flawless. He had been playing this music since before he could remember.

As more people arrived and booze began to flow, Tom's music became more a part of the overall noise than the main attraction. He didn't mind. He played as expressively as he wanted. Some of the guests stayed close by him, enjoying his music, while those who didn't care went about their evening only vaguely aware of the pleasant musical background.

The guests were dressed impressively, but Tom noticed there were only a handful of other men in tuxedos. Most wore fashionable suits and ties. It was a middle-aged to older crowd trying to pretend they were still young. The women all wore fancy dresses, many of which would have been better worn by their daughters. As voices rose from too much champagne, what had at first appeared as a party of immense class started to show a few cracks. Tom thoroughly enjoyed the spectacle.

His eyes kept wandering to the kitchen entry, waiting for Vallia's next appearance. Whenever she emerged into the room, first with trays, later with plates or pitchers, he followed her around the room with his eyes. Even in an unflattering uniform, he easily remembered how she had looked and moved that night at the studio, with a light summer dress falling over her swaying hips. She often looked toward him as well, and he didn't mind that she knew he was watching her. He was fascinated by her. He wanted her to know.

Twice she took an extra moment on her return to the kitchen to come by him at the piano. The first time she whispered in his ear, "you play beautifully," the last word with each syllable drawn out in her delicious accent. The second time she just ran her hand over the back of his shoulders as she passed. Again, he noticed the firmness of her touch. She looked back as she passed with a smile that had been growing more flirtatious each time. Yes, he assured himself, she was fascinated, too.

Tom had little sense of the time or how long he played, but eventually the party began to wind down. As the guests' senses dulled, he felt his own sharpening in anticipation. He felt sure his adventure wouldn't end when the last guest went home.

The event planner appeared at his side and struck out his hand. Tom, mid-song, understood that his job was done. He took the man's hand and shook it.

"You played fine tonight. Thank you." Out of his breast pocket he pulled an envelope and handed it to Tom." He could feel that the envelope contained both a check and a business card. That was a good sign that this gig might lead to more. By the time Tom had the envelope in his own pocket, the man had moved on.

Though some of the more obnoxious guests still mingled, cutting the music was meant as a reminder that the party was now over. The message was received by all but the few for whom it was intended. But that wasn't Tom's problem. He packed up his music folder and made his way back to the kitchen. It appeared some of the caterers had already departed. Most of the cleanup had already been done. A few workers still patrolled the front, serving and retrieving the last of the drinks. He didn't see Vallia.

An ignition sounded in the alley, followed by the crunch of wheels on gravel. Tom stepped to the window to see the first Clausen's Catering van pull away. His heart fell. Was she already heading back to the city? He chided himself for reading too much into their few interactions.

He walked slowly to the back door of the kitchen and stood in the alley. He realized that in his excitement to come here tonight he failed to check the schedule for the last train back to Manhattan. If he walked all the way to the station he might have to sleep on the bench. He supposed, if he asked, they'd let him catch a lift back to the city in the second catering van.

He smelled coconut and hibiscus without seeing Vallia approach. Then she was beside him in the shadow of the rear of the house.

"Come with me." She took his hand with a firm grip.

Her hair had been shaken loose. Her apron was gone. She wore a white tank top tucked into her uniform pants with her dress shirt slung over one shoulder.

As soon as they were away from the kitchen windows the night was dark. The curve of the shore positioned the light from the dying party away from them. Ahead, the ocean glimmered with a few lights. The grass and beach in between looked black. Tom followed, guided by the white of Vallia's shirt against the dark of the surrounding night. By the time his feet reached the grass, his eyes began to grow accustomed to the dark. He could see the wispy strands of her hair and her firm left shoulder-blade, pulled back by the arm that guided him. He saw shapes on the wide lawn of the property and other houses in the distance. Far to the east, a rounded yellow glow on the horizon preceded the moon's eventual rise.

Vallia led him to one of the shapes on the lawn—a canopied beach couch facing the ocean. The sand was only steps away. By the time she turned toward him, his night-sight had adjusted so that he could clearly see her brown eyes, her full lips, curved nose and slender neck. He could see the shape of her breasts, dark and full, through the thin tank top.

She guided him down to sit on the cushion beneath the canopy. Even if anyone came from the house, they wouldn't have seen them there unless they actually walked down to the beach. Vallia lowered her knees down on either side of Tom and brought his face up to kiss her. Tom wrapped his arms around her lower back, enraptured by the taste of her warm, moist lips. She pressed her waist into his as they kissed, not giving him the chance to try to hide his excitement.

She pulled her lips away and pushed him down to the chaise, still sitting atop him. She slowly pulled at his tie, then meticulously at each stud of his shirt. She pulled off his shirt and coat in one motion, the arms of the one still inside the other. Just as deliberately, she eased her own tank top up over her head. Tom pulled her down on top of him, feeling her firm nipples and the soft cushions of her breasts as he held her warm body close. A cool breeze lifted off the water.

The sound of the second catering van rose and then disappeared. Tom barely heard it, as if it was a distant reminder of a past life.

They made love tenderly, slowly. They had the luxury of knowing there was no need to hurry—they had all night. Yet they also felt the urgency of knowing they might *only* have this night together.

A late, waning moon—big and soft—had risen out of the Atlantic. It reclined on its side with sensual, rounded edges. The surf and sand glittered in her gentle beams.

Vallia lay with her head on Tom's chest looking at the path of moonlight across the water. Her finger traced across his stomach. After the darkness, the night suddenly seemed incredibly bright. It was still warm, but pleasant. The stickiness of the humid day had passed. Tom's hand ran slowly down the length of her side, over her hip and then back up to her shoulder. Finally, she stood. Tom stared at her beautiful body, poised confidently. The moon made soft shadows against her.

"Come," she said. He obeyed, himself feeling much more self-conscious in his nakedness than she seemed to be. Vallia walked into the water until the waves lapped above her knees, then dove in, reappearing ten feet farther on, gasping and laughing. Tom splashed in after her. The water was cold but felt good. Before he reached her, she swam, finally pausing about fifty feet from shore. Tom went after her and pulled her into his arms, kissing her salty lips as they bobbed in the cool water. The surface of the water was translucent in moonlight. The lights of the house where they had spent their evening were still on. All the houses of the Hamptons seemed distant and forgotten. They were entirely alone with each other, the sea and the moon.

Eventually they swam back and walked dripping back to their couch. Laying with their limbs wrapped together, with salt drying on their skin and their toes caked with sand, they were happy and carefree. Without heed for the world, they dozed off.

● ● ●

"Tom, Tom."

He woke, and tried to open his eyes, eventually breaking his lids apart through dried salt into the heat of daylight. Remembering where he was, his head popped up and he was wide awake. The first thing he saw, besides the brightness of the day, was his own body as he lay on his back, stark naked in the sunshine for all the world to see. From their canopied couch, he only saw a small stretch of beach. Yet in the periphery he sensed movement.

Vallia saw his reaction and began to laugh. Tom couldn't help himself and laughed too. For all the romance of the night before, their situation was now precarious, even dangerous. Yet the humor in it could not be ignored.

"Well won't this be a sight." Tom reached for his pants. "A couple of naked negroes camped out on the lawn... in the Hamptons of all places."

Vallia had hardly stopped laughing since Tom awoke. She also started to get dressed, but more slowly and deliberately than Tom.

"You think we'll get arrested?" she asked.

"We might get shot."

At that, Vallia finished her dressing with more urgency. The day was already hot, but Tom put on his coat and Vallia her dress shirt anyway, both trying to make themselves as presentable as possible. Tom's bow tie went in his pocket. No sense trying to tie it again. Charles had shown him how but he wasn't sure he remembered.

They stood and looked at each other again once dressed, making sure the canopy still shielded them from the house. After a moment, they both burst out laughing. Tom's tuxedo was impossibly wrinkled, as were Vallia's shirt and pants. She had tried to tie her hair back, but it was all over the place. His own hair was a knotty mess and anyone who looked closely could see the dried salt on both of their skin. Vallia grabbed Tom's head and kissed him.

"Come on, *chico*. There's nothing to do but walk tall and black and proud."

As soon as they were in the open, a landscaper in a neighboring yard stopped his work and looked at them. Once on the street they kept their eyes focused forward, feeling eyes on them from passing cars and pedestrians that seemed somehow always to be on the other side of the street. They walked hand in hand as if they belonged in this strange neighborhood full of money and prestige. The mile to the station felt like an eternity. Waiting for the train, people eyed them cautiously. The benches to the immediate right and left of their chosen seat remained vacant, even though the station was crowded.

On the train they shared a good laugh again but didn't feel comfortable. They were the only non-white people in their car— disheveled and salty. After what seemed like an eternity, the train came into Queens and they breathed easier when they saw black and Hispanic folks boarding at Jamaica and Woodside.

Vallia's apartment was in Long Island City, just across the East River from Manhattan.

"Will you come with me?" she asked.

"I have a rehearsal at five for the Carnegie Hall concert. I need to get cleaned up."

"Shower at my place. We'll have a little lunch. Then I'll come with you. I'd like to hear you play again. I can't come to the concert tomorrow, so hearing you tonight is next best."

"I can hardly show up wearing this."

"Why not? I have an iron. Tell them you thought it was a dress rehearsal."

Tom laughed, delighted with the boldness of this woman he was just getting to know, who would soon leave forever.

This fact was graphically evident when he stepped into her studio apartment. The only piece of furniture was a bed. Two suitcases lay open on the floor and a box of kitchen things sat open on the counter.

"You really do have one foot out the door."

"I sold all my furniture last week. No turning back now."

"Gave notice already?"

She laughed. "Tried to. They won't let me break my lease, so I'll just leave. They'll never know till I'm gone."

She laid her head ever so briefly on the back of Tom's shoulder. In her voice he heard a tinge of the regret that probably hadn't bothered her until now, already starting to miss New York.

"You could still stay," Tom said.

"How?" Vallia asked, unbuttoning her shirt as she walked toward the bathroom. "Are you going to support me, *chico*?"

Tom smarted at her blunt honesty. She was right. It only paid to be a dreamer if you could find a way, or find someone, to pay for your dreams.

He stood for a moment in the middle of the empty room, hearing the sound of the shower coming on. A few lonely nails poked out from the bare, brick walls.

"Get in here," shouted Vallia. "The hot water won't last all afternoon!"

The day went by faster than either of them realized. By the time they had dressed and eaten lunch, it was time to go to Tom's rehearsal. He was glad he had the foresight to put his concert music in his folio along with the music he played at the party. He still wore his tux but felt better about it in a clean body and after the pass of an iron over the shirt and pants. Vallia wore a floral blouse and jean shorts. They took the E train into the city, arriving at Carnegie Hall with hardly a minute to spare.

Tom should have expected it, but he still didn't get his chance to see the famous auditorium, or the backstage that was reserved for only the lucky few. That would have to wait until tomorrow night. The rehearsal was in the small recital hall. There was another concert happening on the main stage that evening. He would have to guess as to the feel of the piano, too, but had little doubt the touch and tuning would be perfect.

Vallia sat by herself at the exact mid-point of the theatre. He saw her patiently watching as the musicians stopped and started their way through concert order. Tom didn't get much individual attention. He was the accompanist for most of the music. Only on the last piece—Shubert's grand piano quintet—did he have a more prominent part.

It was a long practice. Tom liked that Vallia was in the room. She didn't seem to mind how long it took and probably liked being close to him too. Neither wanted to hasten the inevitable conclusion of their time together. Tomorrow they would both perform their concerts—separately—and after that would probably never see each other again.

When the rehearsal ended, Tom was tired. Even by his standards, he had been playing a lot. But there were no breaks. He couldn't afford to take a break. Tomorrow he would play the biggest concert of his life, and the next day the regular fall ballet classes began. The best thing he could do was get a good night's sleep.

But tired as he was, sleep wasn't what he wanted that night. He wanted Vallia.

They walked together down Sixth Avenue to 51st Street and then toward his apartment. It was just starting to get dark. She hung on his arm, tired too. Neither had said anything, but the understanding was clear that she was coming back to his apartment. Tom wondered if Art would give him a hard time for bringing home a girl. Neither of them had yet. They stepped down from the sidewalk and he opened the door.

Tom gasped in horror. Vallia clutched his arm.

Art sat meekly in the corner.

In the center of the room, with his hands on their table and his eyes fixed on Tom, sat Damien Lockett. Several guns were spread out on the table in front of him.

Chapter Fourteen

....

Late Summer 2019

"What are people like in New York?" Andrea asked. "Are the things you hear really true?"

"You've been there. What do you think?"

We were at my sister's apartment, getting ready for Jason's party. I had only brought a couple dresses down with me from the city. I had already been in Lancaster longer than I intended. I wore the same blue dress I had changed into after the closing show.

"You've lived there, though," Andrea said. "You've seen a different side of people."

I paused from my makeup application.

"I don't know. People say New Yorkers are jerks. They're not, but they don't have time for bullshit. They don't do small talk—which I actually love because I'm no good at it."

Andrea laughed.

"As soon as they sense you're wasting their time they're gone. If you're used to something different, you might not like that attitude. That's all of New Yorkers tourists usually see."

I looked at her. She was still in yoga pants and a t-shirt. I was almost ready. I resisted the urge to ask when she would get dressed. It's not like we had to be at the party at any specific time.

"What's so wonderful about people in New York," I said, "is that they're all *doing* something. Nobody's in New York by accident, not even people who were born there. Being there takes effort and purpose. The only people who can afford to be there passively are the filthy rich or the homeless. When I went there it was with the ambition of doing something with my dancing. I've had a first success but that doesn't mean anything there if I can't keep it going. My roommate is working full time so she can go to school for fashion. There are thousands of other people like us, each with their own dream. We're all driven, we're all busy, but we love each other in a unique way because we all get what the others are going through."

"Is it hard to make friends?"

"No harder than anywhere else. My first month was pretty lonely, but then suddenly I met all kinds of great people. I realized that people were waiting to see if I would stay. People come through New York every day. Some stay for a week or two or a month. They try to get a taste of what it's like, but then they go home and don't really find out. I don't think it's conscious, but again, New Yorkers don't want to waste their time, so why make friends with people who are just going to leave? People in Washington Heights where I live—at the coffee shop or the bar, or the market— paid no attention to me until they saw me long enough to know I was sticking around. Then everything changed. I was there less than a year and I made so many amazing friends."

I caught myself using the past tense and it was out before I could pull it back. I realized that I was exactly the kind of temporary New Yorker I had described. I had no right to talk about New Yorkers as if I was one of them.

Andrea seemed to know my thoughts. "Are you going back?"

"Absolutely." I forced my assurance but needed a deadline. "I'll stay for your exhibit. Then I'll go back."

If only it were that simple.

I was ready for the party. I looked at Andrea who still hadn't started.

"Well, are we going to this party or not?"

"I'll be ready in ten minutes."

I sat down on the bed, doubting her, although she was now actually starting to put herself together.

"I've got to tell you about my roommate, Nikki," I said. "It's such a great example of a New York story and kind of the opposite from mine."

"Yeah?"

"We came to the city at the same time, which was why we paired up for the apartment. She's from Southern California, but not L.A. She came to New York to go to fashion school but is trying to sell some of her designs now. Anyway, I guess she had success a couple years ago with a show in whatever little town she's from. But when she came to New York, she played it up like she was a big up-and-coming fashion designer from L.A."

I stood up and followed Andrea to the bathroom sink.

"Unbelievably, people in New York bought her story. Within a couple weeks of moving to the city she was getting invited to these swanky parties and shows. I went with her to this one penthouse party overlooking Central Park with all these designers and some famous DJ."

"Who was the DJ?"

"I have no idea. I knew you were going to ask me that."

"You're useless."

"Stop it. You're missing the point. The thing is, in New York you can invent yourself, since everyone has a past, but all anyone wants to know is who's hot right now. For a couple weeks, Nikki convinced people she was the new hot thing. Of course, it couldn't last because she actually had no connections and no real body of work. Now she's just a student in fashion school and I get invited to more things than she does."

What a party that was! I remembered thinking, *this is New York*, as I sipped champagne and looked out over Central Park, knowing I was punching way above my social weight. I was putting on my own act, in a plunging sequin dress that was way sexier than what I was comfortable wearing and had cost way more than I had any business spending. I wore it confidently though, among people I would never see again, with the knowledge it would still look brand new when I returned it to Saks the next day.

"I think I'd like it there," Andrea said.

"You'd take the city by storm."

"Let me start with Lancaster. I'm ready."

"Really? I think that was under ten minutes."

"Told you."

She looked incredible. Here I had worked on myself for more than an hour and put on my cutest dress in order to feel somewhat presentable. She just threw on jeans and a pink blouse, did I-have-no-idea-what with her makeup, and ran a comb through her hair—yet she would be the one all the guys at the party would gravitate toward. I forced myself not to be jealous. What did I care about boys at a silly party in Lancaster? She wouldn't come to New York, and I *would* go back. I hadn't tried to project myself as something I wasn't like Nikki did. I really would make something of myself there. I just needed more time.

"Who is this guy, anyway?" Andrea asked as I drove toward Jason's condo by Penn Square. Her question reminded me that there was one guy there whose attention I cared a slight bit for. I would never admit it to her though.

"Jason was in my class in high school. I told you about running into him this week."

"Do you like him?"

"No."

"Does he like you?"

"I so don't care. I won't be around here long."

And that was that.

We parked a couple blocks away and walked through Central Market to Jason's building. The neighborhood was a mix of the old brick buildings that formed the backbone of downtown

Lancaster, and new construction that reflected downtown's new appeal to young professionals like Jason. His condo was in one of the new buildings. We buzzed in and took the elevator to the fourth floor of the five-story building. The party was well underway, but when Jason saw us, he dropped his conversation and came to greet us. He wore a checkered shirt with the sleeves folded up and a skinny tie.

I introduced him to Andrea.

"Nice place," she said. From the entryway, we could see toward the open deck doors which looked out over the marketplace.

"Thank you. I love living here." He stroked his coifed beard.

"How long have you had it?"

"I bought it just over a year ago. May I get you two something to drink?"

People continued to arrive until the place was crowded. I recognized a lot of people, which surprised me more than it should have. Andrea mingled effortlessly. I stood watching with my plastic cup of white wine. Despite the duties of hosting, Jason frequently came over to make sure I was having a good time. I enjoyed his attention but tried not to dwell on it.

As he and I were talking, Andrea appeared at my side.

"I was just telling Jason about our studio," I told her. "What if he came by? You said yesterday it would be good to have someone else see your paintings before you show them."

"I don't know." She glanced down. "I'm shy about them."

I saw Jason look at her with wide eyes. She looked so sweet when she wanted to; her batting brown eyes, a trace of cleavage at the top of her blouse. *No jealousy, Cammie!*

She agreed and Jason said he would come by the next day, after he had cleaned up from the party.

Andrea went back to the kitchen for another drink.

"I didn't know your sister was a painter," Jason said.

"Did you know I was a dancer?" I asked.

"Of course." He looked me straight in the eyes. I felt ashamed about my question. "It's hard to remember that far back, but I'm pretty sure I saw you sing and dance in some of the school plays. Hopefully I'll get to see you dance again sometime, although I don't make it up to New York very often."

He got pulled away by some other guests, but he had definitely said the right things.

I took my cup and stepped out to the balcony. I looked out over the town that was my home, whether I liked it or not. Was it really so bad? Was the simple life I had lived here really worse than fighting for the next month's rent in New York? I taught the same dance classes in both places but with less pressure here. I could perform here too. Whenever I wanted to dance in one of the humble Lancaster ballet productions, I was offered a big part. Now I would be even more in demand—I had danced in an off-Broadway show! If I worked the connections here the way I tried to do in New York, I could probably dance leading roles around here for years to come.

Whether or not I got married again, in a few years I could afford to buy a place like this too... maybe one or two floors lower. A place like this would cost several million in New York City. I glanced inside and saw Jason. Before I could look away, he looked back and smiled at me. I felt myself blush and was glad to be out on the dark balcony. Maybe I wouldn't even have to wait to buy my own place, if I could only wrap my head around a new set of dreams.

I chased those thoughts away. I didn't want to give it up. I had more memories to make. For the second time that night, I remembered that penthouse party overlooking Central Park, rubbing shoulders with modern day Gatsbys. Who cared if I belonged. I was *there*.

I closed my eyes for a moment. When I opened them and saw Jason's over-crowded condo, full of faces I'd been seeing since high school, I felt tired and completely over the party.

I found Andrea in the kitchen. She was good and drunk.

"I'm tired. Do you mind if we leave soon?" I asked.

"What? We can't leave yet."

She was surrounded by a group of guys, closer to her age than mine. They hardly even glanced at me. Now I wanted to leave even worse.

"You can go if you want." Andrea said. "I can get a ride home or take an Uber."

Well, she was an adult. And she certainly wasn't my responsibility. I said my goodbyes, asking Jason to make sure Andrea was okay.

"Absolutely," he said. "I have a second bedroom so if she needs to she can stay here and I'll give her a ride back when I come see her paintings tomorrow."

This made me feel better. I hugged Jason, glad that I would see him again the next day.

I drove slowly back to my parents' house, feeling sad for the thoughts I had allowed myself to indulge. I had to stop it, before I spiraled into self-pity, regret, depression.

Tired as I had felt at the party, once I was back in my parents' guestroom, I was wide awake. I probably should have just stayed. It was the most exciting thing I had gotten to do since coming to Lancaster. Why was I so bored by it, yet so tempted by the lifestyle that Jason or similar men might have offered me if I lived here. It made no sense.

I got out my laptop and started watching *Center Stage*. It was a good distraction. I had seen it at least ten times and didn't expect to get far. But I watched the whole thing and cried at the end for at least the tenth time.

I was at the studio the next morning at 11:00. I danced hard until I was drenched in sweat. My phone ringer was turned up high, but I expected it to be a couple hours before Andrea emerged into the day.

There was a taco truck that parked less than half a mile from the studio. I couldn't resist its seduction. The guys who operated it already knew me. I dashed over there for lunch and brought my three tacos back to eat at the studio. They layered little slices of radish on the flat tortilla along with the meat and salsa. Mm mm, so good!

Andrea texted me at 1:30 saying she was on her way. I hurried through my last taco, washed my face and brushed my teeth. She arrived with Jason, a little after 2:00. They were all smiles and laughs when they came in. Andrea seemed no worse for wear, still bouncing back from a night of drinking like a college student. I smiled at Jason, feeling self-conscious about my dancing sweat.

Andrea's original three paintings had all been taken off their easels. She had them set aside, covered with sheets. To my surprise, she uncovered them and set them on the floor against the wall without hesitation. I had expected her to be shy. Perhaps it was easier to reveal them quickly, like tearing off a Band-Aid.

Jason set up a folding chair and sat in it backwards looking at the paintings. He raved about them, but in a way that showed he really didn't know much about art. I smiled. It was kind of cute. I stood watching with my hand on my portable barre, my feet passing mindlessly through the dance positions. It occurred to me later that I wished Jason had asked to see me dance. But even though he looked toward me often, his attention, and the conversation, remained fixed on the paintings.

"What about these?" he said, turning toward the easels. She had two mounted right now.

"Those are the ones I'm working on."

"May I see them too?"

She pulled the sheet off of the one she started the first day she brought me to the studio. Even I would agree that she had a little further to go on it, but it was coming along nicely.

"How about that one?"

"I've only just started it." I detected the expected shyness creep into her voice, and myself became curious about the new painting which I thought she had not started at all. "I'll show it to you another time."

"At the First Friday art walk!" I said.

"If it's ready by then."

"Really?" Jason asked. "Where will you hang them?"

"I don't know yet. I still need to make some phone calls."

For the first time since we had devised this plan, I began to wonder if she really would. July was passing quickly. The venues would be looking to book artists for August soon. Meanwhile, before long, rent would be due again at my Wash Heights apartment.

Jason stayed about an hour. Though I hadn't noticed it when they first arrived, *he* was the one who looked tired. Understandable after the party he threw. I hugged him when he left despite my sweat, and he promised to come back to check on Andrea's progress.

My sister worked quietly the rest of the afternoon. I danced a little more but had already worn myself out.

Over the next couple of weeks, Jason came to the studio often, and the three of us hung out together. Nothing more than that. I enjoyed his company, but it seemed a bit odd too. Was he interested or not? Was I?

When I mailed Nikki my August rent check, I told her I wouldn't be renewing the lease. It would be up at the end of September, so that gave her two months to find someone else. She was still sore at me though. It hurt to have to pay for yet another month when I wouldn't be there, but I knew I couldn't just bail from a lease if I ever wanted to show my face in New York City again. I had heard enough horror stories and I didn't want to become one.

Andrea had mostly finished the fourth painting, but she left it up and dabbled at it from time to time. She was working on the fifth one now. She had it tucked into the back of the studio so I couldn't see it while she worked. She told me she wanted to wait and show it to me once it was finished.

Finally came the news I hadn't wanted to admit I expected. Andrea hadn't booked a place for the art walk. I lashed out at her. She threw it back at me and for one afternoon we were at each other's throats as badly as when we were kids. I made her confess that she had not made a single phone call. I stormed out of the studio, went home and cried.

The August exhibition was supposed to be my deadline. My second deadline, after my initial two week one failed. Should I just leave now anyway? I had half a mind to pack my suitcase and buy a train ticket the very next day. I was still paying for that dumpy apartment either way. Had I suddenly become scared of taking the chance? What was different now than a year ago? I'd become soft after only a month at home, first beaten down by depression and then by complacency. What did I owe Andrea; I had gotten her this far, hadn't I? Couldn't she just make a few phone calls? I could come back whenever her show happened... if it happened. What did I owe Mom and Dad? They wanted a happy daughter, didn't they?

I went back to the studio later that evening. Where else did I have to go? I could see that Andrea had been crying too and I felt bad. We embraced and forgave each other. Both of us had fresh tears in our eyes.

"I made a couple calls this afternoon," she sniffed. "One of the art galleries was looking for something for September. I texted them some pictures and they said they'd hang them for next month's art walk. I can finish the fifth painting by then."

"September," I whispered.

"Please," she pled, squeezing both my hands. "Stay till then. It's only one more month. I need you. I can't do it alone."

I sighed. I had promised her I would stay until she had her exhibit. Now she had finally made a commitment. Would I really run back to New York where I had no work lined up and no money to wait for something?

I called Tom that night and we talked for a few minutes, but it felt unnatural. Hearing his voice was nice, but I really wanted to be in his arms. His tone was warm, but I couldn't read him over the phone. Did he miss me? No doubt he had seen countless people like me over the years, who lasted a little while in New York City before the opportunities and money dried up and they were forced home. Why waste his time missing a girl he half expected never to see again?

Summer weeks continued to pass. The college called, having heard I was in town. They begged me to come back and teach ballet in the fall term. I said I'd think about it. The Lancaster Ballet sent out an e-mail with audition invitations for their October show, as well as for the holiday Nutcracker. There was a new jazz/modern dance group in town that would probably put together some interesting choreographies. It would be prudent to take all of these opportunities. The money would be decent, and I would have fun doing them—even *Nutcracker*, no matter how sick I was of every step and note of that over-performed ballet.

Would accepting work in Lancaster mean I had given up, or just that I had finally accepted reality... and responsibility?

Truthfully, I *did* owe Mom something. My own happiness wasn't enough, not after what I had seen. If it weren't for her sacrifice, I'd never even be able to ask those kinds of questions. The path to my dreams walked above the invisible safety net she'd built for me. The net showed signs of fraying. If it tore, I might be the only one with the strength left to mend it.

After that moment in the kitchen, when my mom unknowingly revealed the depth of her exhaustion to me, I began to watch her more closely and I noticed things. I noticed her reach behind to rub her own shoulder, or down to rub her knee. I noticed how for three days in a row she turned her whole body every time she needed to look to her left. I recognized the motion from a time in my early twenties when I fell awkwardly and could hardly move my neck for a week. After a few days, Mom was moving normally again. I noticed a cut on her hand, with the tell-tale sheen of super-glue sealing it up, but that she had to seal up the same cut three times, because those things didn't heal as quickly as you got older.

Maybe I didn't deserve the chance to make it or fail in the big city. Maybe my mom deserved a daughter with a good career, who could take some of the pressure off of her. Maybe she deserved a rest, after all these years.

Chapter Fifteen

....

Summer 1986

"Get lost, sugar," said D.

Tom looked at Vallia and nodded. She hesitated before leaving. There was a touch of fire in her eyes, but she left.

"Sit down, Piano Man. You're just in time."

"In time for what?" Tom remained in the doorway, as if there might still be a chance to escape this trap. He wanted to turn and run with Vallia, all the way to Santo Domingo.

He looked at his brother, furious at having been dragged into this. But Tom knew if he left now Art would be dead by morning. Tom couldn't pretend he didn't know the rules. He sat down.

D smiled. It was the kind of smile made by cruel men who saw and enjoyed fear on the face of another.

"You boys are in luck." He pushed back from the table on the back two legs of his chair. On his head was the same cap Tom remembered from their meeting in the Bronx that spring. "I have a little pick-up tonight and it's a three-man job. I chose the two of you."

"Why not bring your own guys?"

"You *are* my guys! Who else do I know in the city? This ain't my territory. Art owes me a good turn, but I'm giving *you* the good turn. Just an easy little job and you'll each earn a grand. I bet you could use the money."

The tension in the room was as thick as the late summer humidity. Tom tried not to be tempted by the money, but it was hard.

"Stop scowling, Tom. It'll be easy. And look how sharp you're dressed for the job."

"What's the job?"

"I knew you wanted in on it." D stood up. "It's damn simple. There's a vacant warehouse over by the river. One of my business rivals uses this place as a drop point when he has product to sell. He's got a partner in Jersey. They pick it up by boat. An exchange is happening tonight."

"How do you know?" Tom asked.

"That's how Art came in. You might not'a known that your brother has made the acquaintance of a few dealers here in the city. Really helped me get a feel for the product flow around here."

Tom glared at his brother. He had known Art's drug use could lead to this. Tom turned his attention back to D, watching the dealer like a poisonous snake. His anger colored his judgment, but he forced his mind to be alert. Something about D's story failed to add up. He seemed to know more than a small-time Bronx dealer should.

"While waiting for the pick-up, the stash is only guarded by a single guy. It will all happen quickly. Tom, you'll stand outside and watch for the boat. Art and I'll go in, handle the guard and take the stash. I can sell it up north no trouble. I'll pay you both tomorrow and you'll never see me again."

Tom's heart fell further the more the situation became clear to him. D's assurances rung hollow. Even if he and Art lived through this dreadful night, life might look very different by morning. If D's plan failed, they would go to prison or worse. Even if it succeeded, the chance to walk away from that life would be gone forever. His dream of playing at Carnegie Hall tomorrow night seemed dashed. Saddest of all, he doubted he would ever see Vallia again.

"Now all we have to do is wait. Me and you two boys." D sat back down with his feet on the table beside his arsenal—two pistols and a shotgun. "Relax. Have something to eat, have a smoke. Ain't we all friends? We've known each other since we was kids."

Tom couldn't sit. He paced, trying to think of some solution. But there was no way out. He was trapped and D knew it. The minutes ticked by.

"Might as well change outa them threads, Piano Man. I know you won't try to jump out the back window. You want a piece of this whether you'll admit it or not."

An hour ticked by when D suddenly stood up and announced: "It's time."

He picked up one of the pistols by the barrel and extended it to Tom.

"Take it, Piano Man."

Tom hesitated, then reached out and took the gun by its handle. He could tell it was loaded by its weight. He hated that he knew that so easily. All it would take would be to raise it an inch, flip the safety and pull the trigger to shoot D where he stood in the middle of their apartment. But Tom was no killer and D knew it.

"Know how to use it?"

"Yeah, I s'pose."

D picked up the shotgun and motioned for Art to take the second pistol, watching him closely. He wasn't about to hand Art a loaded gun by the barrel. D threw on a trench-coat to conceal the shotgun, and they walked out into the warm night. Could anything be more suspicious than a man wearing a trench coat on a night like this? Worse than if he'd stayed in his tux. D might as well have carried the shot gun out in the open.

D directed them west on 51st Street, walking behind. It was only a few blocks to the industrial riverside. They turned north and walked about ten more blocks. D stopped to look around.

"There." He pointed to a squat, aluminum-sided warehouse. Sliding doors opened to a gravel drive that led twenty feet or so to the alley, with a path and steps down to a small boat-launch on the river. A wire fence lined the rocky shore with a gate open at the bottom of the steps. The river looked black except for the silvery line where it broke against the rocks, and across where it shimmered in the lights from Weehawken. The smell of fish and exhaust hung in the air. The warehouse door was opened enough for a man to slide through. Faint light shown from within.

"He's already there," said D. "Give me a minute to scope it out."

He ran silently up the alley to the street, gazed down the front of the warehouse, then returned to the brothers at the rear.

"It's all just as it's supposed to be," he whispered.

D was looking around like a man seeing a place for the first time. A job like this should have involved meticulous planning and at least a one night stake-out. Supposedly D knew all the details of their victims' operation. But how?

D reached into his coat and pulled out a long knife. "Alright boys, let's go."

"What are you going to do?" Tom asked.

"I got this guy. Have your guns ready though, in case there's any trouble."

"Or if there's more than one guy in there."

"There won't be."

"Then we take the stash and leave?"

"It's not that simple. I don't know where they have it hid in there. Tom, you stand guard and watch for the boat while we search for the stash."

D and Art slunk to the cracked door of the warehouse. D darted through, fast and silent as a cat.

In the brief moment when they were alone outside, Tom looked at his brother, but Art wouldn't look him in the eye. If they were going to run, now was the time.

A shout sounded inside, quickly muffled. Then the sound of a brief struggle, and the quiet thump of someone being lowered to the floor. Art dashed in. Tom remained. He had been told his job. He stood there and watched the river.

Faint whispers came from inside as D and Art searched the warehouse. Tom hoped they would hurry. His heart beat faster with each moment that was lost. His eyes scanned the river. There were a few boats out there, but none seemed to be coming his way. How would he know until it was too late?

They were taking too long inside. Something wasn't right.

A figure approached from the side, too fast for Tom to see and be afraid. It was Vallia.

"What are you doing here?"

"I followed you. You've got to get out of here while you have the chance." She pulled him away from the open door, to make sure their whispers wouldn't be heard inside.

"If I leave, he'll kill my brother."

"That's better than all of us dying."

"How do you know?"

"I wasn't the only one who followed you here."

"What?"

"I listened outside your door for a few minutes, then waited at the next block till you left. I stayed in the shadows, but another boy stood on the stoop three doors down from yours the whole time: smoking, looking down toward your door, smoking some more. As soon as your door opened, he crouched down until you were gone, then he left."

"I thought you said he followed us."

"I guess he knew where you were going. He's standing out front right now with two other boys. I saw them. Here you are only watching the back like they must have known you would. They'll surprise you guys from the front."

"I'll warn them."

"Hurry."

Tom dashed inside and looked around. The first thing he saw was the prostrate man D had killed. Blood soaked the concrete floor all around him. He fought the urge to retch, horrified and ashamed at being a part of this.

He ran toward D and Art, at the far wall searching cabinets and file drawers. D's trench coat was on the floor. So was the shotgun. Everything felt suddenly clear. There was no stash in there at all. D was such a fool.

"Come on, we gotta go."

"Is the boat coming?"

"No. It's a trap. Three guys coming from the front."

"Did you see them?"

Tom paused ever so briefly before lying. "Yes."

D glared at him with hate.

"I know what you're trying to do. Get back to your post."

"You're a damn fool, D. Did it ever cross your mind this whole thing might have been a setup?"

"You lyin'."

"Think about it? You come down here messing in another crew's territory. How better to get you out of the way? Look at you two. You don't even know what you're looking for. You didn't even case this place out. I saw how you were looking around when we got here."

"And him?" He pointed at the body across the room. "Is he a setup?"

"Maybe it was his time, too."

D paused for the briefest moment. Was the truth dawning on him? Glancing at his brother, he felt Art knew it.

"Go back to your post. If I see your ugly face again the boat better be coming or else, you, your brother, your mom, and that pretty girl of yours will all be dead tomorrow."

Tom's whole body shook with anger and fear as he walked back outside. Subconsciously afraid of what he would find out there, he had pulled out the gun. Only Vallia was there.

"They didn't believe me," he whispered.

"Then walk away."

"I can't. My brother..."

She stepped in front of him, taking his head in her hands, forcing him to look her in the eyes.

"Tom, this isn't who you are. Your brother made his choice. Don't throw away your future, your dreams, your life. You can't save him now. Walk. Away."

She was right. Her belief in him made him strong. She had believed in him enough to risk her own life tonight. How he loved her in that moment.

Tom remembered something Charles told him months ago about how in New York you got to choose which class you belonged to. He had a choice tonight. He had almost been pulled down into the gutters. All the work he had done, not only through these first months in the city, but in all the years leading up to it, all his effort to stay out of the trouble that followed Art, all that would be undone if he made the wrong choice right now.

He took the first step, the hardest one, then began to jog away from the warehouse. Vallia was right beside him. Back on the riverside path he felt her take the gun out of his hand.

"Don't be startled," she whispered.

A shot rang loudly in the night as Vallia fired into the pavement. Tom jumped despite her warning. Immediately, sirens sounded in the distance, coming closer.

"What are you doing?"

"Saving your brother's life. Now run!"

She threw the gun as far as she could into the river. It splashed and disappeared. Scurrying steps could be heard near the warehouse behind them. They ran hard without looking back.

When he heard gunfire again, Tom stopped. They were four blocks away. First came three sharp shots. Then a pause and a deep, loud explosion, as if from a cannon. Then it was over except for the sirens.

Tom and Vallia continued at a fast pace, turning back toward the city. It was very late, but a few people were out on the streets. Tears began to drip from Tom's eyes. The farther he moved away from his own danger, the more his heart ached for his brother, who might already be dead. Finally, when they seemed far enough away, when the sirens had moved past them in the direction they had come, Tom couldn't go on. He sat on the nearest stoop and wept into his hands. Vallia sat beside him and laid her head on his heaving shoulder.

In time, Vallia urged Tom to his feet. "Come on. Let's get back to your place."

"Do you think that's a good idea?"

"You want to be home when the police come."

"Unless other people come first to kill us in our sleep."

"That won't happen, they got what they wanted."

He looked at her through his tear-streaked eyes.

"You risked your life for me tonight," he said. "Why? Why didn't *you* run? And how did you know to say *this isn't you?* You hardly know me at all."

She smiled. "I'm your girl, now. Only for a short time—it's true— but I am right now and that's real. A girl wants to be able to believe in her man. I do believe in you." She reached up and kissed him firmly on the lips.

"Come home. Pray for your brother. You did everything else you could. Hold me tonight and sleep well. Tomorrow is your day."

●　●　●

Tom jolted upright, startled, though neither he nor Vallia had slept at all. He looked at the bedroom clock. It was 4:00 in the morning. The knock sounded again, firmer this time.

"It's the cops," she said. "I told you they'd come."

"What if it's not the police?"

"Then they would not have knocked." She rolled her head over and smiled at him. The lights from the city came in the bedroom window enough for him to see her face. "Go on. I'm you're alibi." She winked.

He pulled on shorts and a shirt and stepped to the front door. He turned on the light, looked around quickly for signs of D's recent visit, then opened the door. Two police officers stood outside.

"Evening. Mind if we come inside?"

Tom backed away from the door, wondering if he looked sufficiently startled. The first cop, a gruff white man with a thick mustache, looked him over carefully. The second cop was very young.

"You been home tonight?"

"Yes sir. I played piano at a rehearsal earlier, then came home."

They were both inside. Tom let the door close behind them.

"You alone?"

"No. My girl, she's in there." He inclined his head toward the bedroom.

The officer seemed to consider whether he should check on this claim. The young cop took off his hat and wiped his hand against his forehead. His blonde hair stuck to his head from sweat.

"Does Arthur Haley live here?"

"Yes. That's my brother. I'm Tom Haley. It's only my name on the rental, but he's been staying with me. There." He pointed toward the mattress in the front room where Art slept. "I haven't seen him tonight."

The cop paused for another long moment. Tom doubted his lie had been convincing.

"I have some bad news for you," the policeman finally said. "Your brother was in a drug shootout down at Riverside tonight."

Tom grabbed the back of the same chair D had sat in earlier. His knees were ready to buckle. He feared the worst.

"Is he..."

"He's alive, if that's what you're wondering. Beat up pretty bad, but he'll be okay."

Tom exhaled deeply. His knees buckled anyway, and he fell into the chair. Exhaustion and relief overwhelmed him.

"Your brother is in big trouble. This was a bad scene, and he has a record. Two men are dead. Did you know about any of this?"

Tom shook his head. "I knew Art had done some things in the past," he said. "But since we moved down here from The

Bronx, we were just playing music together. Trying to make it like anyone."

The cop nodded.

Vallia emerged from the bedroom, wearing one of Tom's big white t-shirts. Tom saw the two policemen shift uncomfortably as they nodded at her. She stayed in the doorway.

"Do you know Damien Lockett?"

Tom looked up. "Yeah, I know him, but I wish I didn't." This question he could answer with complete truth.

"Why do you say that?"

"I don't want nothin' to do with men like Damien Lockett. He ran drugs in my neighborhood in South Bronx. He was locked up, but I heard he got out recently."

"Seen him since he got out?"

Tom considered his answer ever so briefly. "No."

"Well, he's dead now. He was there with your brother tonight. One shot to the back of his head."

"Shit."

"Yeah. I don't think it was your brother though. His gun had been fired three times, but Lockett was definitely killed by a different weapon."

Tom remembered the shots he had heard followed by that *boom*!

"Who else was there?"

"Three men fled as we arrived. We weren't able to make any arrests besides your brother. By the looks of things, we got there just in time or he would have been dead too."

Tom glanced over at Vallia, remembering what she said when she fired the gun. Maybe she really did save Art's life. He was sad to see him go to prison, but it was the best he could have hoped for. He hated feeling it, but he was glad that D was dead.

"When can I see my brother?"

"We took him to St. Vincent's. He'll be there a few days under guard before we transfer him to Metropolitan."

Tom nodded.

"Do you have any idea who these other men might be?" the officer asked. "Anything to help us find the men who beat up your brother and killed Lockett?"

Tom shook his head, remembering that these men *did* know how to find him. Unlike the police, they knew there had been a third man with D tonight, and even knew where he lived.

The police officer shifted uneasily. The other man, who had not said a word, looked about as tired as Tom felt. Vallia came and put her hands on the back of Tom's shoulders.

"We won't keep you anymore," said the cop. "Thank you for your cooperation. Mind if we contact you with any other questions?"

"Sure. Happy to help."

"Good night."

Tom stayed in his chair as the cops let themselves out. When Tom finally stood, he could barely hold himself up. He was weak with relief and exhaustion. Vallia guided him back to the bedroom. He was asleep almost as soon as his head hit the pillow.

Chapter Sixteen

························

Fall and Early Winter 2019

took my old teaching job back at the college. I hardly had a choice. I was good and broke.

School started the last week of August. Everyone was so happy to see me again. It felt good. It felt right and like I was home. I allowed myself to enjoy it, even as I hedged my bets and told them I wouldn't commit past the fall term.

I joined the jazz/modern dance group as well, though I refused to commit long-term. The whole cast of the new company had "heard of me." That felt strange. All my years of teaching and performing in this town had built a reputation that I never really considered. If I stayed, I could leverage what I had already done toward putting together a solid career here—maybe opening my own school or starting my own dance company. If I left for too long, that currency of my reputation might disappear.

When the Lancaster Ballet held its *Nutcracker* auditions, I went for it and was cast as the Snow Queen. That was the best part to be had other than the pros they brought in from Pittsburgh. It would make for a nice end-of-year paycheck.

My teaching hours were erratic, so I only joined Andrea at the studio two nights that first week. She made me promise to spend Saturday and Sunday with her.

"I like watching you dance when I paint. It inspires me."

"Really?" I laughed.

"I can't paint as well when you aren't there dancing."

"You painted those three paintings before I came and they're beautiful."

"Yes, but for *this* painting I need you here."

"When can I see it?"

"Soon." She smiled. "Not yet."

That weekend, I actually had tangible things to work on for the first time since New York. I practiced steps from my upcoming lesson plan and some jazz movements in preparation for the first rehearsal with the new group. I also danced the choreographies I had put together over the summer, wondering for the first time if I should do something with those ideas. I could produce a show myself. Why not?

Jason had come to the studio every weekend since his party, usually bringing something—snacks, coffee, whatever. His visits always felt a little awkward, but I also found them incredibly sweet. I had found myself thinking more and more about him during those weeks. I felt flattered by the attention of his visits.

That Saturday he didn't come. Andrea seemed not to notice. When he also failed to appear on Sunday, I texted him and asked if he was coming by. His "no" was short and terse.

I sat down on the floor against the mirror. I started to type another text but stopped myself.

"That's weird," I said.

"What?" Andrea poked her head from behind her painting.

"I just texted Jason to ask, and he seems mad."

"Oh yeah, I should have told you. Don't think Jason will be coming by anymore."

"Why not?"

"We broke up."

"Um... what?"

All the air punched out of my lungs.

"Yeah, it just didn't work out," she said.

"But... when did you... I had no idea."

"Really? I figured you knew. I mean he hung around all the time. I hooked up with him that night I stayed at his condo and then we were messing around some after that. It was fun. He's a cool guy. The sex was great! But it wasn't the kind of thing that could last long."

I was such a fool.

"Sorry, I guess I should have said something since he was your friend first." She was already back to her painting. She didn't seem to consider it all that important. "But you said you weren't interested in him."

I had said that, hadn't I? Was that supposed to make it okay?

I stood up and stormed out of the room. I drove straight back to my parents' house, went into my room, closed the door, threw myself on the bed and cried. I felt betrayed yet also knew I had no right to the feeling. Somehow that made it worse. I hadn't decided if I was interested in Jason or not but had wanted to reserve the option of being interested. Sisters should be able to understand such things.

A guy like Jason wouldn't understand. He saw the hotter sister and took his chance when she was drunk at his place. I felt repulsed by him—by his cockiness, his grin, his stupid beard and his skinny pants. Just like in high school he chose other girls instead of me. Just like always, if Andrea was around, guys didn't notice me at all.

Maybe I deserved this after my wedding and Paris. Whether intentional or not, Andrea had finally returned the blow.

I stayed in my room the rest of the day and night. I didn't come down for dinner. I heard some texts come through on my phone but didn't even look. It was probably Andrea. My tears dried up and then I felt numb.

Over the last two months I had gradually been acclimating myself to the idea of staying in Lancaster. New York seemed farther and farther away. My interest in Jason had been part of this acclimation. Yet now I saw the terrible truth: I was a divorcée in her mid-thirties in a small town where people knew me, my family and my history. How would I possibly ever marry... or even ever *date* again? Who could possibly interest me here who would also be interested in me? And how much time did I have? Even my romance with Tom seemed like a waste of time. He was a wonderful man and I cared about him. But we had no future.

I liked to think that if I had been born in another time Tom and I could have had a long and happy life together, but I didn't really know. I wondered about the girls who must have loved him and left him in the past. How had those loves shaped who he was when I met him? Would our story have been different if the years had aligned for us to meet when we were both young and naïve? I started crying again.

On Monday I dragged myself back to the studio. It was Labor Day and school was closed. Where else would I go? What would I do? The only other option would have been to get on the New York train that morning. I certainly considered it... broke as I was.

Only once I had parked and was about to go in, did it dawn on me how amazing it was that I had come. After a weekend full of tears and regrets, I was back at the scene of my despair, ready to dance and get on with life. I'd been knocked for a loop but picked myself back up before depression could wash over me. I hadn't let my demon win this time. Maybe I was getting stronger. Maybe something in me had finally shifted.

Andrea was relieved to see me. She gave me a big hug.

"I wasn't sure if you'd come back."

I said nothing.

"I'm really sorry about Jason."

I relaxed for a moment.

"I shouldn't have kept you in the dark about us. I just assumed you knew."

I stiffened again. She still didn't get it.

"But forget him now. I don't want boys to come between us. This summer has been all about us. You and me. Hasn't it been great? I feel so close to you now."

I started crying again… just a little bit. Andrea pulled away and looked at me with that sweet, gentle smile that melted all the guys' hearts. It even melted mine.

"Forgive me?"

I wanted to. I really, really wanted to forgive her.

I nodded. "Yeah, it's okay."

As soon as I said it, I *did* feel that it was okay. I meant it.

"You'll still stay for the show? It's this weekend."

"Yes. I'm staying." As I said it, I knew it meant more than just this weekend. I had to let myself be okay with that.

She smiled again, this time mischievously, and grabbed my hand. "It's time to show you the newest painting."

She led me to the corner of the studio where the last easel was set carefully back so no one would see. In the pulse of her hand in mine I felt deep love. It was a complicated love that had started in her earliest years when she looked up to me and modeled herself after me. It was a love that had been shaken by my jealousy and cruelty. It was a hurt love because of the way I betrayed her eight years ago.

Maybe subconsciously she had exacted some revenge, but she didn't mean it. Ultimately, Jason had been meaningless to her—just a good time for a few weeks. It should have been meaningless to me too. What *was* meaningful was this time we had shared at the studio. We had both been creating, with all the vulnerability that involves. Allowing someone else to share the space and the experience created a rare intimacy. Our togetherness through this time had been powerful. It dawned on me—in that short walk across the studio to the easel— that this time together had been one of, if not *the* highlight of Andrea's life.

Andrea pulled the sheet away from the canvas. I beamed.

It was another abstract roil of color, but it had a slightly different focus than the others. I could instantly tell it had been inspired by me. The light moved through the dark background the way a dancer moved. Maybe not everyone would read this in the painting, but any dancer would.

No wonder it had been so important to Andrea for me to be there with her. No wonder she wouldn't show it to me until now. She was painting *me* all along. I would have grown shy had I known and danced with less freedom. Looking at it closely, the light didn't just move like any dancer. It reflected the way *I* moved. I felt flattered and exposed all at the same time. It was easily the best of her five paintings.

"I don't know what to say." Tears were rolling down my cheeks.

Andrea hooked her arm around my waist. "I wasn't sure if you'd like it."

"Like it? It's exquisite."

"I couldn't have done it without you."

"It's good you didn't show me before." I laughed away my tears. "I would have frozen up over there."

"I know. I've never painted a model before."

"Don't they always tell art models to sit very still?"

"Maybe that's why I've never liked it. I want movement in my paintings. That's why you made the perfect model for me."

"Andrea, I... this is really special. I didn't think I would stay here this long, and it's been hard for me. I didn't want to leave New York. This makes me feel better about it though. This is really an incredible painting and now I feel like I was a part of making it happen."

"You were a part of all of them. Everything. Without you I wouldn't be doing this exhibit."

She turned toward me. We embraced. I leaned my face down onto the top of her head. All was definitely forgiven. She pulled away.

"Get over on your side and dance for me," she demanded with a twinkle in her eye. "I need to finish this thing, and I only have four more days. You and your deadlines."

That night, remembering those moments in the studio with Andrea, I knew it was a time I would cherish for the rest of my life. I didn't want to run away again. I needed my family in my life, and I wanted to show them all that they could need me too. That thought gave me a feeling of happiness that overpowered all the feelings of things not working out as I had wanted them to.

It amazed me that I could think about those good moments, because I felt sad about a lot of things. I felt sad thinking about New York, about Tom, about the shows I wouldn't dance in. I felt sad about what had happened with Andrea and Jason. It's not that I wanted him for myself, especially not now. It just saddened me that I had made myself vulnerable enough to get hurt over something so stupid, and that this would always be part of the dynamic between Andrea and me.

Things had happened, but my mind wasn't wandering through every terrible thing that might come next. I was sad, disappointed by life, but not depressed, and that was a big deal for me. I felt okay, even hopeful.

I was beginning to embrace my duty to my family, and even my duty to myself. It was time to stop blaming my *demon*, as if my depression were something outside of me. It was part of me—a complicated nuance of my inner being. It would always be part of me. I had to live with that, be okay with that. It didn't mean I had to let it define me.

Circumstances don't create happiness. I know that better than anyone, based on the random times depression had overpowered me, sometimes even when everything seemed to have been coming up roses. Things can be as good as anything or as bad as anything and it doesn't affect a person's happiness. I could have been a Broadway star, making lots of money, or married to the most perfect man, and still been unhappy. After all, wasn't it so often the stars—the ones everyone envied—who ended up destroying themselves with drugs or alcohol, even with suicide? Why would I, with my demon, ever have wanted that kind of success and thought I could handle it?

No one really gets the life they want. We do the best we can with the life we have.

● ● ●

Friday was perfect for the art walk: sunny and pleasant. Summer's stifling heat had finally eased.

Andrea's paintings were to share one of the small indie galleries around Central Market with a local photographer. They would hang there for the full month of September, but today was the important day. It was a small gallery, with big windows facing the square, rough brick walls on two sides, and a small kitchen and bathroom opening from the back wall. Andrea had one wall, the photographer the other.

Our parents were there right at 4:00 as we completed set up. So was Peter Robinson, who still taught art at Lancaster High and had believed enough in Andrea's talent to let her turn his basement into a studio. He was incredibly pleased with her work. Our parents were proud too, but Mom couldn't help make a few comments about the abstract style. It reminded me of when she said she didn't understand my dance show. That was just her way. It didn't mean she wasn't proud of both of us. Dad took up position in a chair beside Andrea's exhibit with a big smile on his face.

When people started to get off work, the streets and galleries filled up. I could tell Andrea was nervous again. It was a new kind of personal exposure to stand in a room while strangers examined your creations. The very nature of her work meant not everyone would love it. But the overall reaction was positive.

When Andrea posted prices on the paintings, I made her stretch higher than she thought they were worth. She didn't want to sell the last one, and even offered to give it to me, but I insisted she put a price on it.

"Just price it higher than the rest, so you can't help but be happy if it sells."

She agreed and priced the first four between $300 and $400 depending on their size, while asking $600 for the fifth. She laughed at the price tags, thinking they were outlandish. I expected her to sell them all.

After the event was well underway, Mom and I took a walk to look at other galleries. We stopped at a wine bar, decorated with black and whites from another photographer.

"Thank you," my mother said over our glasses of rosé.

I smiled, understanding from her tone that she referred back to our conversation over breakfast at her hotel in June. Our mother may not have understood the abstract style of Andrea's paintings, or kitschy modern Broadway shows. But she saw what painting had done for her daughter, who now rose in the morning and worked her days with excitement and purpose. Perhaps she saw what dance did for me too, even though I hid my highs and lows better than my sister.

"Mom, remember my sophomore year of high school, when you talked me into taking zero period singing classes at the ungodly hour of 7:30 AM."

She nodded and sipped at her wine.

"I was remembering those mornings when you drove me to school."

"You were so grumpy."

"That's why you were so smart to talk me into the singing lessons. I didn't know at the time that Dad would never drive again. You didn't want to make it about him or make me feel like I was getting up early just so you could still get to work on time."

She looked away from me. It was uncomfortable for her to talk about these sorts of things, but I knew she needed to hear it.

"I liked hearing you tell stories about the guys you worked with... how every morning you'd point out those two trucks sitting outside the Shamrock."

This brought a smile to her face.

"Ron and Chubb. Had to have their morning shot and a beer to get them through a day's work."

I laughed.

"See Mom, we don't always say it, but everything I've done, what Andrea's doing today... none of it would have been possible if you hadn't been there for us all along. So thank *you*."

Walking back, the shadows of the buildings grew long against the brick square. We were surrounded by people I almost recognized but couldn't place. The buildings themselves, all around us, were intimately familiar to me. The people were the same. I had been around them all my life, even if I had never met them.

This was home. Saying that was neither good nor bad, it simply *was*. I couldn't escape it. I admitted to myself that I was staying here. I would go back to New York and visit... maybe soon. Perhaps I would even perform there again. I did know people now who were in that circuit. But I would not pack up my life again and stick myself there. The only way to do so now would be to plunge into credit card debt in the hopes of a big break. That sort of recklessness would be unfair to my family. That season of my life had passed. It made me sad, but it helped that the break and realization came gradually. It was time for me to build a career here. I would expand my teaching network. I would ask the jazz/modern group if I could choreograph a number for the spring show. I would try to embrace and enjoy that I *could* earn a living doing what I loved. Not everyone was so lucky.

I thought of Tom, whose life in the city I had so envied. Even he made sacrifices. Even he had regrets. What he'd always really wanted was to be a classical pianist, but what was he doing now? Making a living playing jazz, just as he had always feared. It wasn't so bad of a life. My life teaching dance wouldn't be so bad either.

Back at the gallery, Andrea grabbed my hands.

"I already sold two!"

"I told you. Which ones?"

"The first one... and the last one."

I smiled and looked up at the wall. A little *SOLD* sticker covered the price on those two. The buyers would have to wait a month to take home their purchases.

"How do you feel about it?"

"I don't know. I'll like getting the money. But it'll be hard to let them go."

"Think of your painting the way I have to think about dancing a show. There's no way for me to hang onto it. I create it and then it's gone. It can be the same for you. You have dozens more of these inside you. Once they're done, let them go."

"I like that."

My phone buzzed in my purse. I pulled it out and looked—a text from Percy in all caps.

"IT'S ON MY LOVELIES!!! REVIVAL PERFORMANCE!!! ONE NIGHT ONLY ON BROADWAY!!!"

I stepped outside the gallery, then hopped up and down and squealed with delight. Several people looked sideways at me. I didn't care.

I was about to text him back, but others beat me to it. He had sent a group text to the whole cast. I quickly absorbed the details as texts flew in. A Friday night in March at one of the big theatres on Broadway—right at the north end of Times Square! This was the real deal. Percy had been invited to take part in a week-long series showcasing indie works by New York directors. There would be an intensive week of rehearsals just prior to the show.

I finally threw my own short text into the dialogue. "So excited!!! Miss you guys."

I put my phone back in my purse and looked out across the square. I could catch up on the rest later. How perfect! one performance didn't mean moving back to the city, but it would keep me tied to that world a little longer. I already planned the trip in my mind, seeing Tom, seeing Heather and Elly, feeling the pace of the city again, if only for a short time.

The college wouldn't like me leaving for a week in the middle of the spring term, but they could hardly be surprised after my refusal to commit long term. The new dance group I had joined would be ecstatic for me. *Broadway!* This was the big time. And after this... who knows. But I didn't want to let myself go there. Not yet. Not now that I had finally come to terms with staying in Lancaster.

Chapter Seventeen

....

September 1986

his was it. Here he was at Carnegie Hall!

The walk out onto the mainstage took Tom's breath away. The auditorium shone in warm gold tones. The gallery seats curved gracefully above, under the ornate molding and circle of lights on the ceiling. He squinted, looking out into all those bright lights shining on him. He could tell that most of the plush red chairs of the main floor were filled, but there were some empty seats in the gallery.

When the applause died down, Tom sat at the piano as the singer, a baritone whom he'd only met a week before, prepared to start Shubert's song cycle, *Winterreise.* As Tom played the introduction, he imagined it was his own concert. He heard the repeated notes fill the room, followed by the first gentle chords. He reveled in his brief moment of glory. After only a few seconds the singer began, reminding Tom that nobody would remember the pianist tonight.

That was okay. Tom viewed this night as a taste of things to come—the beginning of a true career in classical music. He didn't see this as the fulfillment of that dream. It prefaced his future.

He had spent that day packing up his apartment. He cashed the check from the party in the Hamptons and used some of it to rent a pickup truck for the day. Whomever it was that ambushed them by the river knew where he lived. He hoped that was all they knew about him. He wasn't about to wait for them to come back and learn more. Vallia's unbreakable lease turned out to be a godsend. Tom wouldn't have been able to afford a new security deposit, but he did have money for rent each month, and her place was actually cheaper than his had been. September was just beginning, and his rent had been month to month, so the transition worked perfectly.

He didn't *want* to live in Queens. It was only a couple stops out by subway, but it didn't feel the same as being in Manhattan. On the other hand, it was better than returning to The Bronx and Momma. A minor setback. Tom wasn't ready to give up on the dream so soon—not now when he finally had his first tastes of success.

One song ended and another began. No audience members embarrassed themselves by clapping. Tom and the singer looked at each other briefly. A timed nod communicated their understanding of the rhythm and they were off again.

The exhaustion and emotion with which Tom had struggled through that day hadn't allowed him to savor the anticipation of this night. Maybe that had been a blessing, keeping him from getting nervous. Neither did he have a chance to consider how rare this opportunity might be. This had seemed so important to him, but now it paled compared to what the people he loved were going through. Soon he would be very alone. His brother was going to prison. Who would he play gigs with now? The girl who could have been his inspiration—his muse—was about to leave forever.

The song cycle was finished before he knew it, even though it lasted more than an hour. Tom had loved the feel and sound of the exquisite piano, the ring of its sound through the hall, and the silky tones of the baritone's voice mingling with the notes he played. He stood up to applause. The singer stood in front and took one bow, then reached back with a big smile, taking Tom's hand for them to bow together. Even though the audience focused on the vocalist, Tom appreciated his gesture acknowledging his contribution. This was different from when he disappeared into the background at ballet classes. Here he supported the soloist but also formed an intricate and vital part of the performance.

Tom looked out toward the audience, even though he couldn't see anyone because of the lights. Charles was out there. He had so much gratitude for his friend for believing in him and giving him this opportunity. He wished Vallia could have been here, but she had her own important performance that night. He wished his mother could have been here, too. He had told her about it but had not made much effort to bring her—he didn't know how to get comp tickets and didn't want to make problems. He would make sure she came the next time he played here. Ultimately it was probably for the best. Tomorrow he needed to go and tell her that he'd failed her. She had trusted him and now her oldest boy was going to jail. He forced himself not to think about who was *not* here and be glad Charles was.

Tom spent intermission in the plush, spacious green room backstage. So different from the cramped rooms behind the odd little theatres that dotted the city. This theatre had been built for the kings and queens of the music world. In this very room Duke Ellington, Glenn Miller, Benny Goodman, Frank Sinatra, Enrico Caruso, Maria Callas, Leonard Bernstein and so many others had prepared for the stage. Maybe even Pyotr Tchaikovsky who, Tom recently learned from Charles, graced Carnegie Hall for its opening performance in 1891. And now he, Tom Haley, was here in this magical place where musicians were born, made and even died.

The string players quietly fiddled with their instruments near him. He didn't understand why they so meticulously tuned their strings every few minutes. As soon as they walked out on stage they would have to tune to the A on his piano. Tom smiled. That felt good to say, even if only silently in his own head. *His* piano, on the mainstage of Carnegie Hall. He sat up straighter and puffed his chest in the tuxedo he had been wearing for way too much of the last forty-eight hours.

He had known these string players a little longer than the singer, but still only for about two weeks. They had worked on their quintet a few times. It amazed Tom how few rehearsals were required to play on one of the most famous stages in the world. If you were performing here, it was expected you knew what you were doing and could prepare quickly. Tom had made sure he had. Some practice time today would have been nice. But as things were, he was lucky to be here at all.

It was time. Tom and the four string players walked out, tuned, and began Shubert's quintet in A Major.

Now Tom was no accompanist. He unleashed all his pent-up expressiveness, through the elegant first movement, the plaintive second movement, the playful third, and into the strong fourth movement. In the finale, when the key turned minor, he struck the keys with drama, encouraging the strings to pull their bows with all the passion the music required. When the cello took over the melody, he gracefully arpeggiated up in support, then began to push the tempo, as they all looked toward him for rhythmic guidance, landing softly on the surprising ending chord.

There was a moment of perfect silence in the auditorium. The ending had been so subtle the audience was unsure for a second. The applause began timidly but quickly rose to an even louder pitch than after the first half of the concert. Tom stood with the others, beaming from ear to ear.

In later years he would try to recall that exact moment, standing on that stage, looking out on the famed room with the bright lights in his eyes, after playing the best piano he would ever touch. But whenever he recalled it, he saw the scene as if from a seat in the auditorium. He would have no recollection of his feelings as he stood there receiving the applause in the spot he had dreamed of. He would never be able to remember what it had really felt like at that moment. It all passed so quickly.

Before he knew it, he stepped out a side door onto 57th Street. As soon as he got outside, he breathed deeply, noticing a difference in the air. It wasn't summer anymore. The air had changed. The night air felt cool. The night when he lay on the beach with Vallia and swam in the warm ocean under the waning moon seemed long ago. So did the awful night when he stood sweating outside a warehouse, keeping watch with a gun in his hand.

The backstage door closed behind him, sharply expelling him back out onto the dirty city streets. It was dark between the shimmer of the Avenues. He looked back at the closed door. If he hadn't just stepped through it, he never would have guessed it was the back door of Carnegie Hall.

He walked across town to Lexington Avenue and up into the low sixties, hoping he would reach the bar before Vallia's show was over.

But she was finished and sitting at the bar with a beer. Tom ordered one, too, and sat beside her. They didn't need to ask each other how their shows had gone. Each understood that the other accomplished what they needed to.

Vallia looked incredible in a sleek black halter dress. Her curly hair floated loosely on top of her head. She had done her makeup the way he remembered from their first encounter at the upstairs audition studio. When she leaned in to kiss him, he smelled coconut and hibiscus, scents which for the rest of his life would remind him of their brief love.

"Did you get paid?" he asked.

She lifted her purse and nodded. "Cash."

"Still leaving tomorrow?"

"Please don't be sad. Meeting you has made it hard. But I have to go. Love me tonight, then let me go."

She paid for their beers with her new stack of cash, and they took the subway across the East River. Her apartment wasn't so empty now with Tom's stuff strewn about from his haphazard move. He had brought his table and chairs but left his shabby bed. Vallia's bed was better than his anyway.

Neither Tom nor Vallia wanted to sleep away their final hours together. But after the chaos of their last two days and nights, they were both exhausted. After making love they fell asleep in each other's arms. This was a luxury in itself—to share the tender intimacy of sleep. For this one night, they were the only people they had in the world.

Tom woke to the warmth of his lover's silky skin against his under the sheet. He wanted to savor every last moment with her. Having dated so little in the past, he had often tried to imagine what it would be like. These three nights with Vallia showed him a wonder he had dreamed about but never really believed possible. It wasn't the passion with which they made love that surprised him. It was the intensity with which their hearts had bonded in such a short period of time.

It had been the impossibility of staying together that made Vallia open herself up to him. Tom knew that. It was why she wouldn't go on a date with him in July but pulled him out to the beach for sex in September. She hadn't wanted the attachment, nor the pain of parting, and didn't want him to get attached either. How ironic that they fell in love anyway. It only took them two days. The parting would be as painful as if they had been together two years. Tom had had his first taste of love and would always remember how wonderful and how cruel it could be.

Too soon, Vallia was ready and her two suitcases were closed. Facing each other on the front stoop, Tom saw that she had tears hovering in her eyes. She dropped her keys into Tom's hand.

"It's your place now."

Tom walked with her to the subway station, three blocks from his new apartment. He walked down with her into the station. He kissed her deeply, wrapping his arms around her back, savoring the last feeling of her closeness. As they pulled apart, he saw a tear break free from under her eyelid and slide down her cheek. He gently traced its track with his finger. The eastbound train rumbled toward them. Soon the lights began to shoot toward the opening from deep in the tunnel. Vallia dropped in her token and slipped through the turn-style. Tom handed her both suitcases over the top of it. She kissed him again.

"Goodbye, *Caro*."

Tom watched until she boarded the E train and it disappeared down the track to the east. This was *his* subway stop now. The E would be his train He looked around for another minute before walking back up to the street. Then he looked around a bit more. This was his neighborhood. It was very different. The brick apartment buildings were lower, quieter. There were a few cafés and restaurants, a laundromat, a grocery and a corner bar; all the things he would need and become familiar with. It wouldn't have been his first choice, but he felt blessed to have it. He would feel safe here and could focus on his work.

He didn't linger long. He crossed the street and walked down to the other side of the subway platform, dropping in his own token for a Manhattan bound train. At Times Square he'd transfer north. It wouldn't be easy to tell his mother what had happened to Art, but it was his duty. He would have liked to take time to bask in the experiences of the concert and wonder at his first real taste of love. But the beauty of his night on the beach with Vallia and the glory of his performance at Carnegie Hall were clouded by the horror of the night in between.

He planned to visit Art at the hospital in the coming days. That would be a tough visit, too. He would only see Art this once. He determined not to visit him again after they locked him away. After today, his break needed to be clean. He loved his brother, but he had to protect himself and the new life he wanted to create. He had given Art a chance to start over, and he hadn't take it. He would give his mother his new phone number, but she didn't need to know his address. That would be for the best.

D may have been dead, and Tom may have slipped away from anyone who knew about the other night. But once you had a tie to those people and that world, they never really let you go.

The best Tom could hope for would be to keep them at arm's length. It might be the furthest away he could keep them for his whole life.

●　●　●

"Are you ready?" Tom asked.

"Of course not," Charles snapped. "Don't be stupid."

"I'm sorry. I know how tough it is."

"No, you don't."

"Come on, let's head down there. It won't be any easier tomorrow."

Walking south on Eighth Avenue, Charles put his hand on Tom's back.

"I'm sorry for snapping at you, guy."

Tom could feel through his shirt that Charles's hand was ice-cold. That said more than any words could. The weather had cooled from the blister of summer, but it was still a relatively warm day.

"You're an absolute prince for coming with me today. Here you just played the biggest concert of your life and all I can think about is myself."

They walked on in silence. Tom tried to imagine what Charles felt. Somehow like a defendant standing and awaiting the jury's verdict, knowing he never deserved any of it. At the end to walk out free, or forward to the chair. Even if he walked free, how could a man be the same after that?

Tom understood a little better than he did last week, when they came for the test. There had been a moment out by the warehouse when he thought his life was over. For a few moments, he had felt sure he would be dead or behind bars by morning. Even after it's over, how do you go back to the way you were, after emerging from those kinds of emotions?

How would any gay man who lived through this time come out unscathed? Even those who survived the warzone of AIDS would live with the guilt of having been spared, by a whimsical chance of fate. Tom would live with the guilt of walking free, while his brother would go to prison. There was no reason for him to feel guilty about what happened behind the warehouse on Riverside, just like there would be no reason for anyone to feel guilty for surviving a deadly scourge, but the guilt would be there either way.

Tom would never tell Charles about what happened that night, but he felt closer to his friend after it. He comprehended a little bit more of the terror and courage that made Charles's knees weak as he walked, and the terror that turned his hands to ice.

Was it only a week before that they made this same walk? It felt like an eternity had passed. Tom was a different man now. He had had both the best and worst weekend of his life, all wrapped up into those few days. He hardly knew who he was anymore.

It wasn't until they were walking through the doors of the clinic that Tom remembered he had his own results waiting. Illogical as it was, he started feeling nervous. It seemed impossible, but then didn't this entire AIDS epidemic seem impossible? Didn't everything that happened this past weekend—Vallia, D, Art, Carnegie Hall—seem impossible? He'd been around Charles a lot, and if Charles had it, couldn't it just be possible that the virus had touched him? Tom forced his mind back to Charles. He couldn't let his friend see the thoughts that were going through his mind.

The nurse came in with a smile on her face.

"I have good news. Both your tests came back negative."

Charles burst into tears. He laid his head on Tom's chest. Tom felt his own heartbeat slowing as he took deep breaths against Charles's head. It felt like a long time since he had taken deep, relaxed breaths. It would have been too much if it had gone the other way.

Once outside amidst the bustle of Eighth Avenue, Tom paused and looked Charles in the eyes. The older man had a look of relief, but it was far from a look of joy. He may have survived his own battle, but so many of his friends had fallen. Nor did surviving the battle mean he had survived the war.

"Are you ready to go see Julian?" Tom asked.

"*Ready* isn't the point, is it?"

"It took a lot of guts to do this." Tom inclined his head toward the clinic. "This was for you, so you can move forward living your life without that cloud over you. Now it's time to be strong for your friend."

Charles nodded.

It was a quick subway trip to St. Vincent's hospital. In the lobby, while Charles asked for Julian's room, Tom looked at the directory on the wall. It didn't take long for him to find the police ward. That's where Art would be, under guard. If Art was anything less than fully incapacitated, he would definitely be a flight risk.

Charles stood at his side. "Third floor. His sister Mary is with him."

They took the elevator and started down the hall in silence. A woman came out of the room as they neared. Tom could see that she and Charles knew each other. She looked warily at Tom.

After a nervous moment, she and Charles embraced.

"Thank you for coming. I was beginning to think you wouldn't."

"It took me some time."

She nodded without sympathy.

"You need to be ready for what you'll see in there," said Mary. "I don't want you to look shocked or disgusted, because Julian will see that on your face. He's sad enough as it is. He's wasting away. The disease moved slowly at first, but now it's moving fast, eating him up from inside. His skin is pale, his cheeks are sunken in. His hands are skeletal. He must have lost fifty pounds and you know he didn't have *five* pounds to give. I'm telling you this now so you can be ready and not be surprised. What he needs to see from you is love."

Charles nodded again, this time with a deep breath. He turned to Tom.

"Will you come in, too?"

"No." Tom remembered the insinuations at the clinic, as well as how Mary had looked at him just a minute ago. The last thing the dying man needed was to see his former lover walking in with a healthy younger man.

"You need to do this alone. Besides, I've got someone of my own I've got to see."

●　　●　　●

"*Demi, grand plié*, down," Charles called exuberantly. "Stretch, 4, 5, 6... Arms! Now *en bas. Tendu*. Repeat. *Demi plié*."

Tom played the rhythmic, expressionless music, but he had come to understand it; he appreciated its purpose. The studio was full of new girls and one boy. The fall season was in full swing.

"*Tendu à la seconde. Port de bras*, right arm. Turn, aaaaand hold." Charles was happy—in his element. The slow summer months were over and now he was immersed again in what he loved. "*Dégagé, piqué*, and side, and close."

When the class ended, Charles sat down on the floor while Tom noodled with one finger on the piano.

"It's good to be back in the rhythm," Charles said.

"You're glowing today, man."

"This is what I love. You get it."

"It's good to see you with that energy again."

"A part of me hates it."

"Why?"

"Because I love the feeling so much. Yet so many of my guys are dying. I'm an asshole for feeling this good."

Charles stretched and looked upward toward the ceiling. "I called my brother and my sister yesterday. It was the first time I've talked to any of them in years."

"Really?"

"I still didn't have it in me to call my parents. They think AIDS is God's judgement on the gays, so there would be no point in telling them I'm negative. At least my siblings were glad to hear I'm healthy, though both of them told me I'm working too hard, like I could catch it from dancing."

Tom laughed, though it hadn't been long since he'd had his own silly misconceptions.

"They both said almost the exact same thing: 'take some time for yourself,' or 'do something you've always wanted to do,' or something ridiculous like that. They still don't know me at all. This *is* what I want to do. It's the only thing. What would I do with myself if I stopped?"

Tom smiled.

"You'll do this till the day you die, or your knees give out 'cause you're so damn old. I would, too."

"Hmph," Charles snorted but he was grinning. "Dancing may be the very thing that keeps me alive."

Tom saw Charles looking into the mirror. He had often seen him look at his own reflection in that mirror with an expression of pride that he'd kept his body, his instrument so finely tuned. His expression was completely different today. His eyes were distant, and Tom knew he was thinking about all those friends and commiserates unknown, who had not been as lucky as himself. There was a hint of that guilt in Charles's eyes, but also strength, and Tom could only guess that the ballet master's days of facing life alone were over.

The sound of rushing feet, which Tom had learned to recognize from far off, came nearer until the room exploded with the chatter of girls. Outer layers of clothing were peeled off. The customary line of bags, sweaters and shoes lined the floor against the wall opposite the barre. Charles was up, full of vitality, scolding and barking out orders. In a moment, all the students were at the barre in a perfect line.

Tom began to play one of Mendelssohn's *Leider ohne Worte*.

"And five, six, seven, eight... and *demi plié, grand plié, tendu.*"

Act III

2020

. . . .

Chapter Eighteen

....

Winter 2020

ne night on Broadway! The final act. It felt like a dream. I could think of nothing else as the date drew closer.

The fall and winter months in Lancaster had been good for me. So different from the early days, because now I had something to look forward to. It makes all the difference in life to have something to look forward to.

March 13th. The date was etched in my mind. If I still kept a paper calendar like when I was a girl, it would have been circled with little stars drawn in crayon.

First, I had the debut show with the jazz/modern group, which was a blast, and then *Nutcracker*, the biggest role I'd ever had in a ballet show. I loved being the Snow Queen, in my silvery tutu and tiara, dancing under all that fake snow to the beautiful music for six shows over two weekends. Still, I made sure to complain about how sick I was of *Nutcracker* with all the other dancers because, well, that's just what ballet dancers do. Kate brought Celeste backstage to see me after one of the matinee performances while I was still in costume, which made me really happy.

I thought all the time about the first run of Percy's show, by far the best theatre experience I'd ever had. It was everything I could have wanted. How I loved the camaraderie and chaos of slapping together that low-budget affair! It made me look forward so much to one more curtain call with that strange and lovely group of performers. In preparing myself to appreciate my *dream come true* of dancing on Broadway, I realized that in many ways it already had.

I lined up a sub for my teaching job and planned to go up a week before the show for rehearsals. A few days before I was to leave, Dad started worrying about a virus that had spread from somewhere in China to other parts of the world. It was getting bad in Italy and now people had started dying from it at a nursing home in Washington state. I told Dad he worried too much and watched too much news. Then Mom started on it, too. New York was such a world hub, she said. There were already a handful of positive cases in the City and sure to be more. I said everyone was overreacting and there was no way I was going to miss this show. I'd been dreaming of it all my life and looking forward to it for six months. I'd get sick for it. Gladly.

I'd saved up enough from my teaching to get my own apartment in town in January. That was good. No one wanted to live with their parents in their mid-thirties. I had come over to say goodbye the morning I was going to leave, and Mom was just returning from the Giant with the trunk of her car stuffed to overflowing.

"You'll be glad I stocked up," she told me when I side-eyed her. "In case we're stuck at home."

"But really, Mom, six packages of toilet paper? There's 12 rolls in each?"

"You should have seen it in there. They'll be out by tomorrow."

"And it says right on there that 12 of those rolls are worth 36 of the other kind of rolls. I think you and Dad will make it till the store stocks up again."

I texted with Andrea from the train, and we joked about our mother's irrational panic buying. She started sending me toilet paper memes because apparently that was already a "thing." I was laughing hard until she texted, *What if they cancel your show?*

I frowned. Surely Andrea wasn't going to be hysterical about this, too. Canceling was impossible. Broadway never canceled. There was too much money on the line every night. It was as big an industry as a sports team. Were they going to cancel Yankee games? No! At worst we'd have a smaller crowd, and I really didn't even care. This wasn't about the size of the crowd. It was about me being on that stage.

I put the stupid coronavirus out of my mind, relaxed and let the excitement of New York start to fill me as I got ever closer to the city. It was nearly dark by the time the train plunged under the Hudson River. As the train slowed, nearing the deep underground hub of Penn Station, I caught the briefest glimpse upward, all the way to the street and above, where "New Yorker" shown in red lights on the hotel that bore that name, welcoming me back. Then it was dark again until the train reached the platform, far below the street.

Much as I wanted to leave Penn Station, walk up Seventh Avenue to Times Square and drink it all in, there would be time for that another day. I had been gone eight months, and I was already thinking like a tourist. That made me a little sad. Instead, I carried my suitcase up to the subway level and waited for a downtown 2 train. Heather and Elly were expecting me in Brooklyn.

I had plans to see Tom tomorrow, but it was better to be staying with other friends. I didn't want to make any assumptions. I couldn't even be sure what I would want from him until I saw him again. For a friendship like ours, eight months apart was a long time.

Heather, Elly and I stayed up late at their Boerum Hill apartment, laughing and reminiscing over wine.

I met Tom the next day for lunch. It was good to see him, but as I'd anticipated, it felt different. We had never met for a planned meal before. Our time together had always been completely organic. At first, the conversation felt forced. Even once it started to flow, there was a perceptible distance between us; I couldn't put my finger on why. Tom's expressions and manners were the same as always—kind, polite, secure. Maybe it was me who had changed.

I had rehearsals for the rest of the afternoon. Tom would play at the jazz club that night. At the end of our lunch, I said maybe I'd come see him play. I knew that if I went and then allowed myself to go back to his apartment afterwards, things would happen just like before. He had not waited for me while I was gone, but he was surely still open to that possibility.

Leaving lunch, I took the subway up to 72nd Street and stepped out of the station into the triangular intersection of Broadway, Amsterdam and 72nd. The moving throng on the sidewalk enveloped me amid the sounds of honking cabs and shouts in various languages. I walked the short distance to the rehearsal space Percy had reserved.

It *was* me who had changed, not Tom. I would not go see him play, and I would not take that walk back to his apartment for the night. I did miss Tom, but I was in another place now. On the surface it seemed like it would be a nice diversion to resume our affair for this week and then say goodbye at the end. As the trip neared I had even tried to talk myself into it. But once I was here with Tom my heart told me otherwise. I cared too much for him. What we had shared was too special. If I had spent a night with him this week it would have stirred things in my heart best left alone. I couldn't let myself fall back in love with him. It had been hard enough to leave New York the first time.

I arrived at the address and climbed to the fourth-floor studio. It was a multi-purpose art studio, with a ballet barre and mirror on one side, and the piano on the other. Bins of costumes and props had been shoved to one side, near the upright piano. A big fan rested in the corner, having collected a full winter's worth of dust. The windows on the far wall were opened a couple inches, cooling the studio enough for the hot exercise ahead. The windows looked straight across the narrow street to fourth floor apartments. Small decks dotted the building across at haphazard angles. The dance studio felt like it was inside five or six different living rooms. Two TVs shined obtrusively into the studio. An ancient woman sat in a rocking chair, watching us from one of the apartments, a dying cigarette balanced in her sagging lips.

The rehearsal was intense and wonderful. I had gotten myself into phenomenal shape, so I relished the work. Everyone was excited and focused. The choreography came back to us quickly. Percy was the only one who seemed nervous. That was understandable. For the rest of us this was a reward for the hard work we had already done. For him this was an audition for bigger things.

The rehearsal ended when Jonathan burst in with five bottles of good champagne and glassware that he had somehow managed to lug up all those stairs. We all rushed to hug and kiss him as Percy popped the first cork, in a better mood already.

Back at the subway station after the rehearsal, I suggested to Heather and Ellie that we take the local train only as far as 50th. I wanted to see the theatre where our show would be held the next weekend. They laughed at me but went along with it.

We emerged at the northern end of Times Square in twilight. I looked up at the blazing sign. It was a theatre I recognized but had never been inside. Tonight, the neon flashed the name of another show. Even for our night, it wouldn't have our names. It would only say *New Choreographers Showcase*, but it would do. I couldn't wait.

We walked on to 42nd, so we could get the express train south.

We rehearsed for two hours every afternoon. It was so much fun. Once the choreography got tight again, Percy relaxed. He had made a few changes to accommodate the bigger stage, but we picked them up immediately. Sometimes it was just the dancers, but usually the three musicians were there too. It grew sharper that way. They played to our movement and we moved to the energy of their music. Afterwards we'd sometimes go out together or I'd go back to Brooklyn and enjoy my time getting to know Heather and Ellie better. In some ways, those rehearsal afternoons and the evenings that followed were even better than the show last summer. We were all friends now, with shared history. The camaraderie was wonderful.

On the fifth day we had no rehearsals. I met Tom again, for coffee on the edge of Central Park. We sat at a table inside, but near an open window. This time it felt more natural, because I understood my feelings. Tom was exactly the same, but I think he sensed more than he let on. He was a gentleman and gave a girl space to privately process her emotions. But he had too deep of a wisdom about people *not* to understand.

As my big night neared, I asked him to tell me the story of his show at Carnegie Hall. He told it with a smile on his face. But he also had some advice.

"Savor every minute of this. When I played at Carnegie Hall, I didn't take the time to realize it was a dream come true. And then it was gone. It was the highlight of my career as a pianist, and I barely remember the experience."

"You expected to have another chance to play there?"

"Yes. Also, it came at a… complicated time to say the least. The two days leading up to the concert were easily the strangest days of my life."

A cool breeze through the open window of the coffee shop felt refreshing against the warmth from the ceiling heater and the hot cup of coffee between my hands.

"Tom, I've been thinking during our months apart, and I hope you don't mind my asking this. I realized that in the time I've known you, you haven't played a classical piano show. You've played for me. But in public I've only seen you play jazz. Why is that?"

"I got tired, I guess."

"How could you get tired of doing what you love?"

He smiled, but it was the kind of smile that told me right away there was a whole level of understanding I'd missed, and he was deciding whether he wanted to take the time to explain it to me. I quickly regretted my question.

"I got tired of the disappointment," he said. "I got tired of the rejection. I can't tell you how many times I lost parts to pianists I was just as good as, sometimes even a little better than. I only got the parts when I was noticeably better."

"Do you think it was racism?"

"Well, that's the thing. How can you ever really know? In all my playing career, I can only point to a couple times when it really felt that way. But over twenty years, after I lost classical parts to whites or Asians again and again and again, it sure starts to make you suspicious, doesn't it? At the same time, I could get practically any jazz part I wanted.

"You know what's ironic? Even back when I got my start in the Eighties, jazz wasn't black music. Black musicians were mostly doing other things by then. To other black musicians, me playing classical or me playing jazz was all the same—it was old-people music. But in the eyes of white musicians, and white audiences, I looked like what they thought a jazz pianist looked like. I still do. That's how a lot of racism manifests: in stereotypes that the white world perpetuates, long after they're no longer true."

I'd never thought of that before, and as soon as he said it, I realized how true it was. Worse, I realized that I had internalized many of those stereotypes myself, perhaps even helped perpetuate them.

"All the times I'd go backstage for my own recital and the white security guard would say 'you're not supposed to be back here, son.' Or the times I'd get up from the piano after my set, wearing a tux, and some white woman would try to order a drink from me, when I'd just been playing right in front of her. After so many years, it's easier just to go play some jazz with a smile on my face."

"I can't even imagine." I knew I couldn't possibly understand.

"It's worse than tiring, all those times. It can scare the hell of you too. When you're a black man, it can be really dangerous to choose your place. You don't want to turn up someplace you're not expected to be, whether that's backstage of a concert hall, on a lawn in the Hamptons, or just breaking up a fight on the street. Hell, or sitting on your own couch eating ice cream but you forgot to lock your door, like poor Bochum Jean. That's what Black Lives Matter is all about. We're scared, every day. Even me, though I don't like to talk about it. Scared for our lives, yes, but more subtly, scared to take risks."

He looked down at his coffee cup, where he slowly turned it between his hands on top of the table.

"I may have only played at Carnegie Hall that once, but I played some other pretty cool classical shows. For a while that made it all worth it. Eventually though, I got tired. To play classical music at the top level, it takes a ton of work, and you can never stop practicing that hard or you'll slip. You know how it is, it's the same for a dancer. I knew I had to work harder than everyone else, but after years and years of still not getting where I wanted, it became hard to stay that sharp. It's tough to work that hard when you're discouraged. So eventually, I stopped practicing as much. Gave more time to teaching lessons to kids, which is a lot more rewarding. So now, I probably don't deserve those classical gigs anymore."

"Do you have any regrets now, looking back?"

"I've made my peace with it. I've got a good life. I enjoy what I do. Sometimes the easy road's not such a bad road to take."

I looked out the window as people hurried by on the sidewalk.

"Did I tell you about what happened to my brother?" he asked after a moment.

"Bits and pieces."

"Art died of AIDS in '95. When he got out of prison, he said he'd quit his drug habit, but I never really believed him. Those needles of his were a thing of my nightmares. It was surely one of them, either in prison or afterwards, that did him in."

"I'm sorry. You hadn't told me that."

"AIDS was difficult for everyone here back in the '80s. It touched me in a very personal way, yet I was always somehow on the periphery of its effects. Mostly friends of friends who died. It wasn't my own people... until Art."

Another silence.

"That changed me. I realized just how close I could have come to going down a different road. I think for me, that was the start of becoming grateful. It took a few years more after that, but the gratitude helped me to become content."

"Let me guess, once you became content, that's when your playing started to slip."

He looked off out the window for a moment. When he looked back, he was smiling again. That beautiful smile that creased his half-gray goatee, but now I knew better than I ever had what pain hid behind that smile. "Enough about my past. This week is about you and *your* dream come true."

"Dancing on Broadway has been my dream for longer than I can remember. It's my Carnegie Hall. I'm going to take your advice and enjoy every minute of it. Maybe it's an advantage being older than you were. So I *know* this will be my last chance to do this."

"*There's still all the time in the world*, remember?"

I thought that, not so long ago. I sipped my coffee silently.

"I've had my run in this city," I said after a while. "It wasn't as long as I might have liked, but it was grand." I laid my hand on top of his across the table. "Now it's over and that's okay. This is a perfect final act."

He smiled. He understood. I looked in his eyes and think I saw that he would miss me too. I felt shy and pulled my hand away to fiddle with my hair.

Soon we stood on the sidewalk outside the café.

"You're coming to the show, yes?"

"It's still on?"

"Of course, it's still on."

"Then I wouldn't miss it."

He kissed me softly on the lips—not too quickly, yet not letting it linger. It was a *perfect* kiss—just enough, after everything between us, but not *too much.* Having not been kissed at all till sixteen onstage, I tended to overanalyze every kiss that followed. Tom was the best kisser I'd met. It wasn't close.

I walked into the park. Tom had been really good for me, but I was glad I hadn't tried to force our affair to continue longer than it was meant to last. As I walked away from him, the melody of Chopin's E Major Etude began to play in my mind. I smiled to myself. Ours had been a precious little love affair.

It was one of those magical, clear days in New York where the air was crisp, but you couldn't quite see your breath. With a scarf around my neck, I felt cozy instead of cold. The bare branches of the elm trees bunched together like wire brushes. The first bulbs were poking up from the grass crevices along the mall, but no flowers had yet broken out of the bright green stalks. I walked out of the shade until I could see the bridge over the lake and the two iconic towers of the San Remo on the west side.

I looked up as two airplanes criss-crossed in the sky—one flying out of La Guardia and the other flying approaching to land at JFK. When I had lived at that uptown apartment with Nikki, I would sometimes go and sit on our little balcony and watch the airplanes. The balcony was one of many over-looking an enclosed urban courtyard, surrounded by a network of individually shaped and colored apartments, fire-escape ladders and air-conditioning units sticking their butts out from grimy windows.

We tried to pretend you didn't notice the other people on their own decks, even though we could have talked to them without shouting. And we tried to pretend not to see through the windows into everyone else's apartments, just like later on we would pretend they couldn't see into our own. The only view from that little deck was up, so I would watch the planes, imagining where they were going to or coming from, and loving that I was here at the center of the world. It didn't take long before I no longer had to imagine as much, I learned the flightpaths to at least make an educated guess from which of the three major airports the plane came or went.

It felt good to be here again. Just enough time had passed. It would have been hard to come back any sooner. In the interim I began to feel established in Lancaster again and it was okay. No, it was more than okay. It was *good.* I had continued to spend most of my free time with Andrea. We were closer than we had ever been in our lives, even after what happened with Jason. I enjoyed the time with my parents too. I'd always had a special bond with Dad and as his health deteriorated, I knew it was important to spend as much time with him as I could. I was also developing a new closeness with Mom. What I had seen as her being critical was just her wanting the best for her family. She bore that responsibility for us all these years. I was old enough now to really admire and respect her for everything she had done to support and care for us. It was time for me to build a career and take some of that load off of her.

Being in Lancaster had forced me to come to terms with so many things inside myself. I couldn't have done that here, with all the distractions and ambitions. I hadn't fallen into depression again. A couple times I'd had to be careful—conscious of where my thoughts were starting to go—but I'd been able to stop myself in time. At first, I'd been motivated for the sake of Dad, Mom and Andrea. Now I was motivated for me. I wasn't ready to say I'd beaten my demon, because I would always face depression deep inside of myself. But I wasn't so afraid of it anymore. Maybe if it did, I'd even be brave enough to talk about it to someone.

Coming to New York had fulfilled a dream. It was a dream I'd needed to do something about after my rushed and ill-fated marriage sucked up the back half of my twenties—the best years of a dancer's life. I *did* wonder how things might have been different if not for that conversation in my mother's hotel room back in June. But that probably only hastened an inevitability. Even in the months here when I was teaching the most, I dipped into my meager savings. There was never a month when I made as much as I spent. It was *so* expensive to live in the city.

Maybe there would have been one or two more Percys who pulled me into their shows, but there was no guarantee. I was lucky to have found the connection to land *this* show. And all the while I grew older while the girls I auditioned against stayed the same age. Your technique and artistry could only take you so far in this business if you lost the tightness in your upper legs. I was in the best shape of my life, yet I was already fighting a losing battle against cellulite. It was time to stop pretending I would have a career as a Broadway Babe. I would have a night. I was grateful for it.

I pulled my arms close around myself as a breeze off the lake reminded me that it was technically still winter.

I had spent much of that time in Lancaster lamenting the opportunity I left too soon. Now I was finally looking forward to an unknown future. New York was good for that too. The city inspired me. Even if my future story would not be told here, I felt inspired by being here, and determined to keep coming, at least once a year, to renew my inspiration. I had a feeling New York City wasn't quite finished with me yet.

Chapter Nineteen

....

March 2020

Percy was glum when he arrived at the studio the next afternoon. He was late, which was unusual for him. Everyone except Cleopatro was already there and we had begun our stretches and warmups. We saw his worried expression, and all stopped and looked at him. Moments later, when Celopatro rushed in, he saw Percy's look and sat down quickly on the floor.

"Darlings, I don't want to alarm you, I think everything will still work out for Friday. But it's fair to tell you that the theatre management is worried about the coronavirus. They doubt it will be necessary but want us to be prepared to postpone."

"What?" It was Paula. "That would be a crime!"

"War, famine and pestilence, the show must go on, and I believe it will. I didn't want to tell you, but it's fair to let you know what's afoot. People are really getting freaked out about this thing."

I shifted uneasily from one foot to the next. I wasn't going to entertain the thought of the show getting canceled. It was impossible. Broadway didn't cancel. Especially not for some kind of flu.

Percy unpacked his dance bag, pulling out three bottles of hand sanitizer that he put on the piano.

"Might as well dance while we can, kids, and keep our immune systems strong. Picked these up on the way. They were only allowing three bottles per customer at Duane Reade, can you believe it? Rationing of hand sanitizer and toilet paper in New York City! Next they'll put a limit on dollar slices."

Maybe my mom had been onto something after all. I was going to look pretty silly when I ran out of toilet paper down the line and hadn't stocked up when I could. The thought made me laugh and that felt good. Percy was right, time to dance and I was determined to enjoy the rehearsal just as always.

It was Tuesday. Our show was scheduled for Friday. Andrea, my Mom and even my Dad were all planning to come up to see it.

Back in Brooklyn, eating Lebanese food delivered from their favorite spot on Smith Street, Heather, Ellie and I finally started paying attention to the news and it didn't look good. Governors across the country were talking about implementing social distancing requirements, to keep people from spreading the virus. In the few days I'd been here, the number of confirmed cases in the city had spiked. Still, the opera, the ballet, Carnegie Hall, Lincoln Center and all the Broadway companies were determined to stay open, stepping up their sanitary and safety precautions for the peace of mind of their guests.

Wednesday's rehearsal was lively and energetic. We all went out afterwards and the city was alive and buzzing just as always. People jokingly greeted each other with an elbow bump instead of a handshake or a kiss on the cheek, but that was all. New Yorkers weren't ones to worry about something until they had to.

By Thursday, they had to.

I posted on Facebook about the show—how excited I was and wishing all my friends could come. The comments ripped me to shreds. Apparently, I was a murderer for encouraging people to do something other than isolate.

We arrived at the big Broadway theatre late Thursday morning for our tech rehearsal and walk through. I began to sense that everything was wrong. The city was on edge. Its energy was sifting away into the cracks and gutters. On the subway, people had been quiet and edgy. Being in that theatre for the first time held none of the thrill that it should have.

The news came while we were there, bringing the tech rehearsal to a screeching halt. Governor Cuomo had called for a temporary shutdown of Broadway. A part of me must have known it was coming, but the news still struck me like a gut punch.

Percy tried to encourage us. It was only postponed, he said. Maybe two weeks, maybe a month. Did he really believe that? Percy, who was losing the most of any of us. Percy, for whom this could have been his big break.

They couldn't reschedule. I knew that. They had shows scheduled here next weekend and for every weekend a year out. The best we could hope for was a stupid mid-week matinee and even that would be a stretch. Once this theatre re-opened, they'd want to recoup their losses with shows sure to fill a house, not some artsy showcase. No, it was over. By the time something like this got scheduled again there would be newer choreographers and casts who knew next year's songs. There were a thousand Percys in New York waiting to get discovered and there were ten thousand of me.

I cried hard that night on Heather and Ellie's couch. It didn't seem to hit them as hard as it did me. I was devastated. Heartbroken. This was *everything* to me.

When I talked to Mom the next day she urged me to come home right away, but I couldn't do it. I knew it was over and that I had no legitimate reason for being in New York any longer, but I wasn't ready. I still couldn't quite believe this all wasn't just a bad dream.

"You can stay here as long as you want," Ellie told me as we made sandwiches for lunch.

"What about social distancing?"

"You don't count."

I smiled. "Love you two. I think I just need a couple days to come to terms with it." I turned to Heather. "What are you going to do?"

She made her living teaching dance and spin classes.

"Hard to say. I postponed a lot of my classes last week for rehearsals anyway. It looks like most of the studios will close up shop now for a while."

I was due to be back teaching my own classes on Tuesday. Surely the college wouldn't close. Would it?

"My office already suggested for everyone to work from home," said Ellie. "Next week they'll probably make it mandatory. At least I can work. We'll be okay if Heather can't work for a couple weeks."

I would probably still get paid too, even if the college canceled my classes. What about everyone else? I thought through our cast. Paula waitressed when she didn't dance. Darnell was a hairstylist. Cleopatro was a full-time performer, under various names and various personas. If things didn't get better soon, all three of them would be out of work within days. I wasn't sure what else Nick and Brian did.

Finally, Percy. He worked in theatre full-time, but most of what he did was more creatively rewarding than financially. At least he had Jonathan, who had a white-collar job that he could probably do at home. This would hit Percy hard, but at least he wouldn't lose his apartment.

Tom.

How had I not thought about Tom until now? I called him immediately, and he commiserated with me over my canceled show. He knew what it meant to me and how hard I'd take this. But when I asked about him, he assured me he'd be fine. He'd be playing tonight now that there was no Broadway show to go to, and he'd play again tomorrow, just like every weekend. I felt better after talking to him, but something kept nagging at me.

Heather, Ellie and I went out to the local Lebanese place again that night. We were the only ones there. The owner, a friend of theirs named Carim, came and sat at our table. He was anxious and depressed. All I could think was that at that very moment I should have been leaping around on a Broadway stage.

Lying on the couch that night I couldn't sleep. Things weren't right. The city didn't sound right. The seriousness of the situation was finally dawning on me. This was bigger than me and the Broadway show I didn't get to do. I wasn't all that concerned about the mysterious virus itself, but I worried about the collateral damage.

Looking at Facebook just made me angry. It was all I could do not to reply when I saw a post from Jason about the statistics of social distancing saving lives. Fine for him, with his computer job that he could do from his comfortable condo. What about the countless performers, trainers, servers and others whose livelihoods depended on social interaction? What would become of them, Jason? But I didn't comment. After being attacked earlier in the week just for posting about my show, I wasn't going to open myself up to that again. I was too fragile right now. I burned with rage, even while I knew deep down, that what he'd posted wasn't wrong.

The next night I went to see Tom play at the club in Hell's Kitchen. Whatever anyone said about social distancing, it was important to support a musician who still had a gig to play.

The uptown subway was sparse. Those who were on the train looked nervous. People sat far from each other. A young Asian couple wearing facemasks boarded at Chambers Street. The man across from me got up, looking aghast, and made his way quickly to the door between cars. He turned and shouted, "Stay home, fucking Chinese!" before slamming his way to the next car. The young couple didn't look up from their seats, but I could see that the woman was shaking. I was used to people acting badly on the subway, but they didn't usually look as middle class and sober as that man.

Tragedies and hardships were supposed to bring out the best in people. So far all I was seeing was their worst.

It was really sparse inside the club. Two couples were having dinner at tables and there were two men at the bar. I sat at the other end from them, on the stool where I always used to sit. Was this really a Saturday night in New York? The bartender came up to me with the prosecco bottle. I nodded and she poured.

"Good to see you, hon'," she said. "It's been a minute."

"Yeah."

She stayed at my end of the bar. There wasn't much else for her to do.

"Might be a minute or two more," she said. "We're closed after tonight."

"I'm sorry."

"Is what it is."

"You do anything else?"

"Only performing. I have a trapeze act in a burlesque show."

I smiled. I had suspected she did something like that.

"You're a dancer too, aren't you? Gonna be rough on a lot of us if they keep things shut down long."

"Yeah."

I didn't want to tell her that I'd be better off because of the college job. If I was still teaching uptown for cash and hustling for weekend gigs, then I'd be in the same boat. I had resisted it so hard, but it had worked out better for me than most.

Tom and the singer came out. It was the same young man who had been here the first night I came with Nikki, and again after opening night last summer. Tom smiled at me.

They only played one set. By then the two couples had finished dinner and left. Tom and the singer came and sat with me at the bar.

"It's been a good run," Tom said. "It's a tragedy, closing this place." He lifted his beer to touch my flute and the singer's martini glass. The bartender poured herself a half glass of prosecco and toasted us too.

"We'll be back here again in no time," said the singer.

"Maybe," said Tom. "Or maybe we'll never be back."

"They only said they'd be closing for a week or two. That's not so long."

"Isn't it?" Tom looked at the bartender. "Will you be here?" She shrugged and he looked at me. "Will you be here?" I shook my head. "I don't know if I will either."

"I will," said the singer.

Tom frowned, took a drink of beer, then went on.

"Maybe I can afford to ride it out without working, not sure yet, but this place might not ride it out. Do you know how much rent is on a joint like this? How they gonna pay that without customers?"

"Maybe the landlord will give them a break."

"Then who's gonna give the landlord a break? I've met the landlord. He's a good man. Owns this whole block. Folks usually assume the landlord's the bad guy, but take one look down this block at all these clubs and restaurants. He's had chance after chance to sell this block to a developer. You better believe that would be worth more, but it's not just about money to him. He's been in this neighborhood for a long time and he cares about it. If half these places can't pay next month and shut their doors, then he'll be forced to sell before the city wants its taxes and the bank wants its mortgage payment. You'll come back from your social distancing to hear some jazz and they'll have already broken ground for new condos."

The singer said, "We all have to make sacrifices. Otherwise we'll all suffer even more."

Tom bristled. "You should just stop talking now young man."

"What did I say?"

"You do realize, don't you, that social distancing is just another form of privilege? It's easy to say we all have to make sacrifices, when the sacrifice won't ruin you. How's a single mom with three different jobs supposed to work from home? Now her kids are going to be home from school too, so she's got to stay home and no free lunch for the kids. You know what else, maybe her parents live with them, too, and they're elderly, so they're at risk but now there's five or six people in a small apartment. And the same thing's true at each apartment on their floor, but the neighbors all help each other out because that's what poor folks do—sharing a can of soup here, a roll of toilet paper there. How's that social distancing going for them? It's going fine for the guy who can make six figures from his couch, watching his kids play. So you know where this virus is gonna spread? Amongst the poor folks, and those who don't get sick will lose everything because they can't work. And the media will say they should have been more careful and planned better. If, that is, the media even pays attention to how many black folks die in a jam-packed project in Queens."

I'd never heard Tom talk this way before. I liked it. I also sensed something worrying. This was more personal for him than he let on.

"Or how about the woman who's doing all she can to protect herself and her kids from the asshole she's stuck with, and now he's told to stay home from work with nothing to do but drink and brood and take it out on his family?"

The singer was silent. I think he got it.

"I'm sorry man," said Tom. "You know I love playing with you. I hope we can again soon." He reached his hand toward the young man, then thought better of it and offered his elbow instead.

The singer went home. A few more people had come in and ordered drinks, so Tom and I didn't feel bad about staying and ordering another round. The bartender was happy to have a little business. The earlier she closed, the less she'd get paid. I looked at all the little things around me, stamping my memories of this place, and of Tom. For the first time it really hit me how serious this thing was and how much damage it would cause.

It wouldn't be two weeks, like they were saying. They just didn't want to tell us yet. It would be at least a month. Maybe longer. Maybe a lot longer.

Even if this place survived, many like it would not. Once this ended, many of the restaurants, cafés, nightclubs, performance halls and dance studies that we loved would be gone. Some of us would be gone too.

I'd do my part. I'd lie low after tonight and participate in the social distancing. I'd become part of the solution, and in so doing, also be part of the problem.

"You gonna be okay, sitting around at home?" I asked Tom.

"Sure. I've got my piano."

I smiled.

We were sitting on bar stools next to each other. I leaned my head onto his shoulder and wrapped my arm around his other shoulder. He put his arm around my back.

"We're not supposed to touch each other you know."

"I don't care."

"Neither do I. I'm glad you're here, Cammie. I missed you."

That felt so good to hear.

With all the time we'd spent together, Tom and I had never talked about money, and while he carried himself like a man who had it, I saw the signs of an artist living a big, little life. He had always paid when we went out somewhere together and always in cash. I figured that was how his piano students paid him. But it meant it would be hard for him to get much in unemployment now. He had always known how to show a girl a good time without splurging. He ate out or ordered in for every meal, but usually from places where a ten-dollar bill was enough for a good meal and a good tip. He wore timeless clothes, so he didn't need to keep up with fashion, but some of his suits had gotten a little shiny in the elbow, and his crisp white shirts had been pressed a few too many times.

"What's going on with you Tom? Something's not right. I can feel it."

He was silent for a long time, sipping his beer with one hand, pulling me close with the other.

"In January I helped my mom pay off a debt. I shouldn't have let myself get sucked in, but she's my mom, you know. She's in her seventies, living alone. It's bad enough that I only go up to see her every couple months. And while she would never say it, I know there's still some blame on me for what happened to my brother."

"Have you been helping her all this time?"

"No. She'd ask, and I'd say no. She's got a pension and social. This time, and one other time about twelve years ago, I felt I had to cover her. I should have been tougher with her." He took a long drink from his beer. "I've never had extra. Always enough but never extra. I'm not worried about retiring because I can play and teach kids to play until I die. I kept a couple months' worth in the bank just in case something went really wrong. Now it's all going wrong, but I gave what I saved to Mama."

"What kind of debt was it, that you paid for her?"

"A neighborhood debt."

"Shit."

"Yeah." He shook his head. "More than thirty years since I walked away from that world and two times I let my heart get the better of my head. Because of those two times I'm still tied to all that bullshit."

"But your mom's debt's cleared now. They're already talking about waiving late fees on rent if this thing drags out. Even if this place closes you'll still have your students when things get back to normal."

"Maybe. Problem is they'll know I'm in trouble. If I don't pay my rent on time, maybe they'll pay it for me. As a 'favor.' You know what that means don't you?"

I nodded.

"Owe those guys one favor and next thing you know you're behind a warehouse with a gun in your hand. I've spent my whole life trying to get away from it all."

Never in my life had I wished so much to be the kind of person who could offer to just pay a friend's rent for a month. I offered the next best thing.

"If you need a place to stay, I have a couch, and my parents have a whole spare bedroom. It's not the city, but it's something."

He smiled. "You're so sweet. Thank you."

The way he said it made it clear he'd never take me up on it. I wouldn't have expected him to. He probably didn't want to 'owe' me any favors either. Well, at least I'd offered.

"A friend of mine once told me that there are four classes of people in New York City. Four levels, like stories on a house and you only see the people on your level. The top is the penthouse class, the celebrities, those too rich to work. They're up in the clouds and while we know they're there, we never see them. The class below is the car class, driving to high paying jobs, living fast but working their souls away. We may get a glimpse of them splashing by us on the sidewalk, but they don't interact with us. You and I are in the subway class and so are almost everyone we know. It's the best place to be. We gotta hustle, but live full lives while we do it. There's one more level though, and that's the gutter. All that crime and filth and despair is around us every day in the city, but we usually don't see it, and it doesn't really see us either. My friend told me that in New York City, you get to choose which class you're in. It's the only place in the world where that's true. Problem is, you have to put in the work it takes each and every day or you'll slip down to the level below. This pandemic will pull a lot of the subway class down into the gutter. I can already feel it snatching at my ankles."

He finished his beer and set it down away from him across the bar. He laid down three twenties. Even beer and sparkling wine were expensive in the city, but this was awfully generous of him.

"I'd die before I let the gutter take me again."

I understood. The gutter was his demon. I felt like I'd beaten mine, but I'd never be all the way in the clear. It snatched at my ankles every day. Tom must have sometimes thought, over these thirty years, that he was in the clear. Something like this reminded you what a prisoner you'd always be.

The bartender came back and tried to hand the money back to Tom as we stood up.

"Drinks are on the house tonight."

"Then it's all for you, hon'. You gotta eat too."

"Thanks Tom."

"Good luck."

"You, too."

She extended her elbow across the bar and touched Tom's, then she and I did the same.

Out on the sidewalk, Tom and I looked at each other. The night air felt like spring, fresh and beguiling, without a trace of the ugly pestilence lurking in the dark.

Here I was and a lot had changed since all those things I'd resolved about my life and my future that afternoon in Central Park a few days ago. There wasn't much future to be had for anyone. Only the here and now.

Tom tilted his head in the direction of his apartment.

"Once more, for old time's sake?"

I smiled and reached out for his hand.

Chapter Twenty

....

March 2020

Mom was really worried. I could tell as soon as I picked up my phone.

"I want you home, but I'm nervous about you taking the train. You're not still taking the subway, are you? It's so dirty even in the best of times."

"I'm staying in with my friends in Brooklyn." No need to tell her I had taken the subway again that very morning, coming back from Tom's. "I'll look into the train options. There's talk about closing the subways. If that happens, they'll probably close Penn Station and I'll have to stay."

"I can drive up and get you."

"No, Mom. I'll be fine. The college suspended my class. I found out this morning, so there's no rush. Let's just wait a day or two and see what happens."

The truth was, if there was a lockdown, I'd rather be in the City. If supplies started running low, they'd take longer to get out to the small towns, not that Lancaster was all *that* small. More importantly, here I was with friends. I didn't want to wait this out alone in my apartment.

"My main worry," Mom said, "is that if you get exposed there and come back... your dad could catch this. It would kill him."

I had thought of that, too. Dad was high risk. I hadn't thought that I might be the one to expose him though.

My phone buzzed, and I looked down to see that Percy was calling. When I didn't pick it up, he texted: *Call me when you can.*

"Are you still working, Mom?"

"Yes. None of the jobs have canceled yet. No one's tested positive for the virus here in town but that doesn't mean they don't have it. Work will probably get scarce, but the union will take care of us."

"Be careful out there, Mom."

There was a pause.

"I'm really sorry about your show."

"Thanks. It doesn't seem all that important anymore. Give my best to Dad. Stay safe and wash your hands."

Heather walked into the room.

"Did Percy call you too?" she asked.

"I was about to call him back. I was talking to my mom."

Heather sat down on the couch next to me.

"Jonathan tested positive for coronavirus."

I gasped.

Even after the canceled show and Tom's worries brought the crisis closer to home for me, the disease itself seemed far off and abstract. All anyone on the news had talked about was prevention and testing. Not what happened when someone you knew got sick.

Less than a week ago I threw my arms around Jonathan, hugging and kissing him when he came into the studio bearing champagne. We all had. Then we'd all danced and touched and hugged and kissed and sweated together.

I called Percy.

"Heather just told me about Jonathan. I'm so sorry. How is he?"

"Hi, Love. He's okay for now. Just tired mainly. We're trying to get him to the doctor, but they're stretched so thin. It might be a few days."

"How about you?"

"I have nothing to worry about. I'm strong as on ox. But Jonathan," he paused, "you probably didn't know this… Jonathan's HIV positive."

"Oh my god. What does that mean, with the coronavirus?"

"No one really knows yet. It's all so new. He's been healthy for years, but he is immuno-compromised, obviously."

I grabbed and squeezed Heather's hand across from me. I felt like I would cry. She squeezed my hand back.

"Percy, my heart just aches for you right now. First the show being canceled and now this. If there's anything I can do, let me know."

"You're a darling. You all are. Just stay home. Protect yourself. When this is all over, we'll get together for a big hug and a cry."

"How about a song and a dance. That's more our style."

"That's why I love you, Cammie!"

"Give my love to Jonathan."

Ending the call, Heather and I sat there on the couch with hands clasped for ten minutes or more. I was awash with thoughts I couldn't put into words. This thing had become very real.

Poor Jonathan. I imagined that the fear of the unknown was worse than anything. How could anyone know yet if HIV made you more at risk, or if he would come through okay? I couldn't even imagine what he would be feeling right now.

One thing was certain. I wouldn't be going home till all this was over. No way would I risk infecting Dad.

Days began to pass monotonously. It seemed every day there were fewer and fewer people out on the streets and in the stores. Heather and Ellie and I went for a daily walk, sometimes stopping at the supermarket. People looked at one another nervously, avoiding the close contact with which New Yorkers were so accustomed. It was weird. By the middle of the next week, I was getting scared. Not so much of the disease, but of the effects of the lockdown. I had already been worried about the livelihoods of the artists I held so dear, and restaurant and small business owners. Now my worry drilled deeper. What was this collective isolation doing to us that we looked suspiciously at strangers in the grocery aisles?

Social distancing was the phrase of the day, but it was a deeply troubling concept, no matter how necessary. If this was a week or two of our lives, we could do it, but if it lasted months, or longer, it would change us. How long before we forgot the feeling of another's touch? I was lucky to be spending my quarantine with friends. But there were a lot of single New Yorkers out there. We weren't used to going without physical touch. If this lasted too long, our collective spirits would begin to starve.

I called Tom. He said he was fine, but I had my doubts. He'd probably never spent a whole week without a human touch. I wanted to go to him, but there was a shelter-in-place order in the City now so I had to stay where I was. It would have been awfully irresponsible of me to hop on a subway when I knew I'd been in contact with someone who was infected.

Percy kept us informed about Jonathan. The first few days he hadn't been too bad, really just a sore throat and occasional nausea. Then the cough started, quickly moving into his lungs. They'd admitted him to the hospital now and were waiting to see if he needed to go to the ICU. Percy said he thought they were really waiting for a bed to open up in the ICU.

Percy himself had tested negative, so now they weren't letting him get too close to Jonathan, which made it all the worse. Percy claimed he'd rather catch it himself and get to be there to comfort his beloved. I would have felt the same way.

As devastated as I was to have our show canceled, I know it would have been ten times worse for Percy. For me it would have been a dream come true, but only for one night. For Percy, it could have been the night to launch his career. No assurance of that, but a chance is all you ask for in this business, in this city, and that chance was snatched away from him.

Yet now, only a week on from that crushing blow, this hit him—a real possibility of losing the man he loved to a mysterious disease. Percy had no time to grieve the show, certainly no time to feel sorry for himself. All of his heart and mind were with Jonathan. Deep inside the hurt would linger; someday, he'd have to make his peace with it.

And if all that weren't bad enough, Percy was now effectively unemployed.

The City congratulated itself for banning evictions during the crisis. Landlords were patting themselves on the back for waiving all late fees. So what, when all this was over they'd evict everyone anyway? Who could afford even one month of New York City rent without income? I couldn't have. Tom couldn't. Percy couldn't either.

Here in Brooklyn, Ellie still worked from home, but had lost her second income, while Heather started to navigate the complexities of claiming unemployment. I offered to help out, knowing the college would pay me through the end of the quarter no matter what. Would the virus be gone by then? If not, I'd be unemployed too.

I worried about overstaying my welcome for a couple days. Once the quarantine really set in I could tell Heather and Ellie were glad to have me there. And it wasn't all worry and stress. The three of us had some great conversations and I bonded with them even more than I did the night at the Lebanese night club. We made good food, drank wine late into the night, and swing-danced on the wood floor of their living room. But beneath it all rippled an undercurrent of anxiety—for ourselves, for our city and world, most of all for our friends.

It started getting to Heather. I had been trying to follow as little of the news as possible—only as much as I really needed to know. I barely looked at Facebook anymore. Heather, though, consumed as much of it as there was to consume. I know she was bored and edgy without work, and without much physical activity; I felt the same way. She followed every news story, every theory of a possible cure, every strategy the politicians bantered about, even some of the conspiracy theories. Ellie told her she needed to stop it, and Heather lashed out at her. I'd learned the night of the hot dogs that when Ellie told Heather not to do something, she only wanted it more. She became obsessive about Jonathan's case, constantly checking his and Percy's Facebook profiles for updates and texting Percy when we hadn't heard anything for a few days. Finally, I told her she should leave Percy alone. He'd tell us all news when he had it. She listened to me.

She bought three face masks for us and a package of rubber gloves, insisting that we wear them whenever we leave the house.

"Those masks must have been outlandishly expensive right now," said Ellie. "Haven't you heard that we're supposed to leave them for nurses and people who are actually infected?"

"They can't hurt," Heather snapped. "Besides, we could have all been infected by Jonathan. We just don't have symptoms. Wearing a mask is the least we can do."

Funny how a hardship brings out different things in all of us. I would have expected myself to be depressed. I had every reason to be. We all did. But I was fine. Well, *fine* might not be the word, but at least I had kept my demon at bay. I used to be the worst at letting my mind wander through all the *what if* scenarios until I tied myself up in knots and that's when the depression got me. I hadn't let my mind go there this time. All those other times were made-up crises of mine. This was a real crisis and I felt alert and ready. Meanwhile Heather, who had always seemed so self-assured and steady, was absolutely freaking out.

The way other people were handling the lockdown inspired me and helped me to get through it without falling into depression. A lot of people had this much tougher than me and were handling it like champions. The collective spirit of the arts community was amazing. It would have been easy for us all to say, *we're not at risk, why are we doing this?*

Some people were giving up their careers, some their life savings. They all did it with a smile because it wasn't their own life they were protecting. It was someone else's. Someone close to them—known or unknown—who was at higher risk. I started to change my mind about what I thought at the beginning of the pandemic—it was easy, in these times, to see humanity's worst— the suspicious looks on the street, the racists on the subway, the blustering politicians on the news—but over all that noise, humanity's best was on display in the silence itself. We were all quietly doing our part, with dogged, collective determination.

Tom had been right in all the things he said that last night at the club. But the singer had been right too. There was no good answer; only judgement calls on what was a lesser evil.

I did Facetime calls with Andrea. She was still going to the studio and had started some new paintings. She showed me, walking around with her phone. It sounded like things were mostly normal in Lancaster. A few precautionary measures had been taken, but the coronavirus seemed distant to her, something to talk about but not really to worry about. A part of me wanted to be back there, where life was safe and simple. But for the most part, I didn't want to be anywhere else but in the city I loved in the time of its crisis.

When Heather, Ellie and I didn't cook ourselves, we ordered takeout or delivery from all the small neighborhood restaurants, which were doing all they could to stay open. More than any, we patronized their friend Carim's restaurant. They were worried about him. It would be a tragedy if he lost his business. Every time Ellie called, he assured her that he was fine and that nothing would make him close. I also think we were often his only order of the night.

Two weeks after the city ordered restaurants to stop seating guests, Ellie called the restaurant and there was no answer. The next day we walked by and the restaurant was closed for good. Still Ellie called and called. When the police finally came, they found Carim on the floor of his kitchen, his debt books open on the counter, the gun he had shot himself with flung from his hand by his fall.

Chapter Twenty-One

....

March 2020

When all of this has ended, whether in weeks, months or even years, I hope we never again take for granted the joy of another's touch: of a loving hug, of a tender kiss, of a dance in another's arms, of laughing on a couch in a pile of friends, of brushing by a stranger on the sidewalk, of a handshake, of a high five. I hope we're better for having gone without these treasures for a while.

The city was swirling into chaos. Thousands of new cases a day, dozens of deaths. Scenes we'd seen on the news in China and Italy were now coming to us from Elmhurst and Fordham. Hearing about Jonathan had been such a shock. Two weeks later we all knew several people who had it. Ellie and Heather knew someone who had died. We all knew Carim. That creeping fear started to nag at me that our isolation would do us no good, that the disease was coming for us all and it was just a matter of time.

My initial concerns had been for performers like me who were out of work and for business owners like Carim. After a couple of weeks though, the full weight of what was happening hit me, and anyone who had spent as much time in New York as I had, could see instantly why an airborne virus was ripping through with such destruction. People packed like sardines on subway cars with stagnant air, their faces inches apart for an hour, pretending this kind of human intimacy was normal. It *was* normal here. Now all those same people were staying home in their crowded apartments, in old buildings with air that ventilated from one apartment to the other. Livelihoods didn't seem so important anymore. Shows were a memory of another life.

The gravity of the situation had become abundantly clear. This was about nothing less than survival—maybe not for me, who was young and healthy, but for those I loved like my dad and Jonathan. We all had vulnerable people in our lives. Only two weeks earlier I had said I'd be willing to catch the virus in order to have my Broadway show. But I wasn't willing for anybody to die for it. Two weeks ago, I couldn't even have imagined the world in which we now lived.

I was distressed about Tom. I talked to him by phone as often as I could, but to Tom, phones were for business and quick updates, not for connection and depth. Whenever I was on the phone with him, he was polite as could be, but it sounded like he couldn't get off the line fast enough. I didn't want him to be polite. I wanted him to tell me what was really going on. The phone was the only way for him to connect with the world right now, but it just wasn't natural for him. What would he do if he was in real trouble? Or if, God forbid, *he* got sick? He wouldn't call me. He wouldn't call anyone.

Tom probably hadn't had a real human connection since the night I stayed with him after his final night working at the club. What references would he have to make sense of what was going on, even to make sense of his own reality? As hard as I saw Heather taking quarantine, with two other people nearby her, I couldn't even imagine someone alone, especially someone as social and sensual as Tom.

Coming back to New York this time, I hadn't intended to rekindle romance with Tom. I thought it would have made it harder for me to let the past go. I'd said my goodbye and made my peace that day with him on the edge of Central Park. But that was before COVID. Now I'm glad I went home with him that night. I'm glad we made love in his apartment in the dark, and again in the streaming morning sunlight, before I took the subway back to Brooklyn. I'm glad for myself, to have savored the fresh taste of his lips, the press of his body against mine, the intensity of his passion and the gentleness of his care. More than that, I'm glad for him, that whatever this tragedy might do to him, I gave him a night of togetherness before he was forced to endure it alone.

Being alone would be bad enough for him. But it was worse. He had serious worries that went beyond loneliness. I couldn't forget what he'd told me the last night I saw him: *"I'd die before I let the gutter take me again."*

Carim's death didn't hit me as hard as it did Ellie and Heather—I'd only met him a handful of times. What felt most shocking to me about his suicide was how quickly it happened. A mere two weeks after New Yorkers stopped going out, not only were restaurants closing, but their owners foresaw complete financial ruin. He was the first, but there would be others. Small business owners yes, but people like me too, performers who were out of work. It wasn't just the financial strain. It was the loss of our identity. COVID would kill people who never caught the disease.

Was Tom the kind of man who would resort to such drastic measures? I didn't think so. The man had such a love for life. But how did I really know? Those words he'd spoken were upsetting.

So when he didn't answer my call, then didn't answer again the next day, and then on the third day when I called it said the number was invalid, I panicked.

We were under orders by the city to shelter in place. People were only supposed to leave their homes for critical items such as food or medicine. The grocery store and drug store in our neighborhood were being run like night clubs, with a line and bouncers. The subways were still running, but only for essential workers—those people who were keeping the city running on bare bones. Someone like me wasn't supposed to ride the subway. But someone like me was all Tom had. I decided to chance it.

I left early, leaving a note for Heather and Ellie, so they wouldn't try to stop me. I'd thrown on yoga pants, a tank top and baggy sweater, tied my hair back and wore the facemask and gloves Heather had gotten us. I stood alone on the subway platform, then sat alone in the train car. It was really strange, even surreal.

Deep in my heart I knew Tom wouldn't take his own life. Maybe we'd never talked with the same depth that some lovers talk, maybe we hadn't opened ourselves up to each other as completely as some lovers did, but still, we knew each other. It was one thing to know this in my heart, quite another to convince myself of it that morning, when times were desperate and everything we knew about each other, even about humanity itself, seemed to be coming apart.

I got off at the familiar 50th Street stop, although nothing looked like it should have. I recognized all the landmarks of course, but New York City was nothing without its people and the people were gone. No tourists milling about. No energetic youths peddling them tours. No gruff Greek man with his cart selling sausage, egg and cheese on a roll with coffee for three bucks. No friendly concierge in a ridiculous uniform standing outside the hotel wishing me good morning. No old lady in horn-rimmed yellow glasses and a pastel bathrobe walking her tiny dog. No hunk with coifed hair and a lime-green muscle-tee walking his even smaller dog.

Worst of all was the silence.

Everything was wrong about New York City with its people locked behind their doors.

I felt ridiculous in my mask and rubber gloves, like I was trying to survive on another planet, instead of in the place I had tried so hard to make my home. I took them off when I got to Tom's building.

A finch was singing in the honey locust tree in front of his stoop. The warble was obscenely loud in the unnatural silence. A man yelled at a woman in an apartment nearby, and I could make out every word. It was jarring. It was disturbing. Things that were always there which you didn't realize you had ignored amidst the city's cacophony.

Tom's building was quiet. I looked up at the fourth-floor window, out of which I had so often looked upon hopeful mornings after nights of indulgence. I didn't feel much hope this morning. There was still a lot of morning left.

I didn't really expect Tom to answer his buzzer but tried his intercom first anyway. Then I started trying random unit numbers until someone answered.

"Amazon Prime," I shouted as soon as I got a live person. The door buzzed open. I bounded up to the fourth-floor landing.

What did I expect? I couldn't knock. Tom was probably home and fine, with a reasonable explanation for not having answered his phone or his buzzer. I had humiliated myself by coming, and I would lower myself a peg in his mind and memory through my desperation.

Would he still be asleep? What time was it anyway; was it *that* early? What if he had another girl in there? Maybe someone he'd met during the months I was away. I couldn't even blame him, could I? Why should I even care? It would be awfully embarrassing to interrupt him with another woman.

No, I was supposed to be here right now, I felt it. Whether he needed me or not. Whether he was here or gone. Whether he was alive or dead. Somehow, *he* had called me here this morning.

I knocked.

I knocked again.

I leaned against the wall, deflated. He wasn't in there. I could feel it. I'd never been much for those kinds of sensations. Whenever other people talked like that, I'd laughed at them. But this time I really did feel that there was no *Tom Energy* across that door. Could that mean that he was dead? Maybe. I didn't really know what feeling the absence of someone's energy could possibly mean.

I knocked for a third time.

What could I do next? Find the landlord? How? And then what would I say? *I'm a friend of his. Well, no, I'm not exactly his girlfriend. We're sleeping together, or we were. Yes, of course he'd want to see me.* There was no way that conversation would go well.

I had been here in front of this door so many times. Usually, I had come upstairs following Tom, my hand tucked into his. The times I had come alone, as soon as I got to this landing, the door opened, and he ushered me in.

I looked down at the brass doorknob, in the heavy wood door with two unwelcoming brass bolts above it. Without really hoping it would turn, I tried the knob. It did turn. The door opened. I walked in.

The apartment was empty. Completely empty. Tom had lived here almost two decades, and there was no trace of him besides the furniture marks on the old wood floor. The keys had been left on the kitchen counter. I moved slowly through the apartment: first the kitchen, which was the first thing you came into, then the bedroom, in which I had so many beautiful memories. The bed was gone, and the closet was bare. A few loose wires and nails marked the walls. The bedroom still had his scent and it brought back all the memories of him.

I walked into the living room. In New York City apartments, the living room was where everything happened. The kitchen and the bathroom were tiny and purely functional and often the bedroom was too. Leaving one room where life happened. Such it had always been in Tom's apartment. I savored so many memories as I walked into that empty room. Where the couch had been were only four little circles stained into the old wood floor.

My eyes were drawn to the wall where the upright piano belonged. It was gone, too.

I've been involved in a few piano moving projects in my life and it's a traumatizing experience every time.

That missing piano, more than anything, told me that Tom was okay, even better than okay, wherever he had gone. Moving a piano out of a fourth-floor walk-up—during a pandemic no less—required ambition and strategy. It was what a man who had a plan for the next chapter in his life would do.

I'd probably never know whether Tom had escaped his past or made peace with it. Whether he had gone far away for a fresh start or gone back to his mother in The Bronx. Either way, it made me glad to know he had his piano.

New York City had finally beaten Tom. It took a lot longer than it took to beat me. But in the end, we both had to accept that our futures were elsewhere. It took more than hard work to make it here. It took a lot of lucky breaks. I didn't stick around long enough to get mine. Tom had his share of lucky breaks over the years. He'd needed one more. COVID was going to reverse a lot of lucky breaks for a lot of people.

There was something on the floor, between the browned lines that marked where the piano had been. I came closer and saw four pages of sheet-music lying on the floor. The only thing left in the empty apartment. I knelt down and touched the pages.

Chopin. Etude No. 3 in E Major.

My tears broke free and soaked the bare wood floor.

The sheet-music was a love letter. I understood now why the apartment had been unlocked. Tom knew I'd be the first to wonder about his disappearance. He knew I'd be the first to worry, the first to come. He must have known, too, that eventually I'd try the door.

I was smiling as my tears fell. My heart was far from happy, but it was warm and full. I knew I'd never see Tom again, and that was for the best. In time, this crisis would end, and my future was in Lancaster. I'd already made my peace with that and the coronavirus didn't change it. My heart ached for Tom. I missed him so much. I don't think I'd ever felt more in love with him than now, holding those pages of music, humming the tune that had brought us together.

I lingered awhile, sitting on the empty floor. Finally, I took the sheet-music and left. I didn't bother to put on my mask or gloves. The day had started to warm. The sun was out, and the air felt the freshest I could ever remember it in the city. No wonder; there were no cars on the streets. Reaching Broadway, I didn't feel like getting back on the subway just yet. I walked down through Times Square. It was surreal to see it so empty. One solitary taxi prowled by. One police car was parked about a block off. Weirdly, all the advertisements on the buildings and most of the theatres were still lit up. Gigantic faces and bodies, lighting whole sides of buildings, rotated away, selling their products to no one. I walked as far as the red TKTS steps and stopped.

Once the people returned and Broadway was back in business, people would forget that it was once silenced. It would go on, with new singers and new dancers to replace the old. We were all replaceable and had been for a hundred years. It would seem impossible that there had been days when no one danced on Broadway.

This didn't have to be one of those days.

Walking out to the middle of the square in front of the steps, I laid the sheet music open on the concrete. I took off my sweater and set it down along with my mask and gloves. Like always, I had a pair of dance slippers folded up in my purse. I slipped my feet out of my street shoes and into the slippers, setting my purse and shoes beside my other things. I did a couple quick stretches.

Looking down at the sheet music, I struck a pose. I sang the first few notes of the familiar tune out loud, then let it play on in my head as I danced. Every note was perfectly remembered, perfectly clear in my head.

How wonderful it was to dance! I felt light as air. For a few minutes the world was good again and I was alive to enjoy it.

I don't know how similar my dance may have been to the time I danced to this same song alone on that forgotten stage, somewhere in the bowels of Lincoln Center, but it felt the same, and the music was as clear to me now as if Tom was there playing it beside me. I danced for as long as the song played in my head. With the final notes, I folded my body down toward the ground and waited.

When I stood up, I saw someone walking toward me from where I'd seen the police car parked. When she got close, I timidly waved.

"You really should be at home, Miss," said the officer.

"I know. I'll go back now."

"That dance was lovely though."

"Thank you."

I put on my shoes, sweater, mask, and gloves. Before descending to the 42nd Street subway station, I took one last look around me. Well, now I *had* danced on Broadway, even if there was no one but a lonely policewoman there to see it.

I should have known better. Didn't I learn a long time ago, that in New York City, you were never *really* alone?

Another solitary subway trip. It was so strange. So wrong.

As soon as I stepped back above ground at Bergen Street, my phone was buzzing with texts. I didn't want to bother with taking off my gloves to check them. It was probably Heather or Ellie and I'd be back to their apartment in five minutes anyway. They were waiting for me when I walked in.

"What is it?"

"First," said Ellie, "Percy called. Jonathan turned a corner. It looks like he'll make it."

"Oh, thank God!"

"Aaaand," Heather drew out the word, "you're all over the internet."

"If you're going to break quarantine, you might as well make it worth it," added Ellie.

"What do you mean?"

"Check your phone. I texted you the link."

I tore off my gloves and looked. Her text linked to YouTube. So did texts from several other friends. The video was titled: *Solo*

232

Ballet Dancer on Broadway #nycquarantine #newyorkstrong. It was my whole dance, filmed from an upper window. I didn't know whether to feel proud or ashamed of myself.

"You look amazing in it," said Heather.

"The strangest thing is the silence," said Ellie.

Funny, I hadn't even noticed. It wasn't silent for me. The music that played so loudly in my head while I watched the clip was for me alone. The silent song was Tom's gift to me. The silent dance, alone, on the busiest street in the world, was my gift back to New York City. Perhaps it would give those who saw it a spark of hope.

"It already has almost ten thousand views," Heather said. "You're going viral, babe."

GREGORY ERICH PHILLIPS

rom a prolific literary family, Gregory Erich Phillips tells aspirational stories through strong, relatable characters that transcend time and place. His debut novel, *Love of Finished Years*, won the grand prize in the prestigious Chanticleer Reviews International Writing Competition. His second novel, *The Exile*, won first prize in the Pacific Northwest Writers Association Literary Contest. Gregory is also an accomplished dancer and musician who has performed on stages in New York City, San Francisco and in Seattle, Washington, where he lives.

Made in the USA
Columbia, SC
14 December 2021